TOMORROWVILLE

TOMORROWVILLE

THE ISAAK COLLECTION

DAVID T. ISAAK

Dedicated to David's dear friend and longtime colleague,

Dr. Fereidun Fesharaki

Quam minimum credula postero.

*("Put no faith in tomorrow;" the oft-ignored line that
follows his famous admonition to Carpe diem.)*

—Horace, Odes

Arbeit macht frei.
("Work will set you free")
—Inscription over the gates of Auschwitz

INTRODUCTION TO *THE ISAAK COLLECTION*

My husband, David Isaak, and I first met in January of 1969, in ninth grade world history class. When I saw him walk into class, I immediately decided we needed to be the best of friends. He had similar feelings. Our first date was to an Iron Butterfly concert in February of that same year.

David and I were together for over fifty years, ever since that first concert, and I thought we'd have lots more time together. That was not to be. He was only sixty-seven when he died—he turned sixty-seven laying in a hospital bed after a massive stroke. He died three weeks later, and did not come home to me. However, he left behind a treasure: five glorious novels. I won't judge you if you feel like I may be biased. I am. His novels *are* great, though. Here is what a fellow author, Rufi Thorpe, says about the first of the novels, ***Tomorrowville***:

> "Funny, unexpected and frighteningly insightful, Isaak's *Tomorrowville* takes the problems of today and stretches them to their logical and disturbing conclusions, presenting the reader with a vision of Christmas Future Dickens-style. Isaak has deep things to say about America, debt, the future of technology and the value of life, but his most valuable contribution may just be his profound mirth. Isaak finds delight in human beings, despite or perhaps because of, our smallness and imperfection. It takes a lot of heart to look at a future for America so dark and find what is funny in it, but that is what makes Isaak a visionary."
>
> —Rufi Thorpe, author of *The Knockout Queen*, a finalist for the PEN/FAULKNER award

My mission in life now is to ensure that this literary treasure is David's legacy. We did not have children, but David encapsulated some of his fine mind in the form of these thought-provoking, amusing, diverse, passionate stories.

These five books form **The Isaak Collection**. In addition to the cyberpunk future-fiction of **Tomorrowville**, the collection includes: **A Map of the Edge** (a coming-of-age story with some dark elements), **Things Unseen** (a murder mystery with metaphysical underpinnings), **Earthly Vessels** (magical realism, with the forces of light and dark battling on Earth), and **Smite the Waters** (a political thriller with a twist).

Here, in David's writing, you can hear the voice of a man who is now silent, but whose words will live on—reaching across time. Words that speak loudly of David's passions, of his sense of social justice, and of his appreciation for other humans and the complex relationships we have with one another. Please join him—and me—as he continues his journey.

Thank you.

David's wife, Pamela Blake
Huntington Beach, CA
July 2022

Four Million Nine Hundred Ninety-Three Thousand Six Hundred Eighty-Four Dollars and Eighteen Cents

In the dream, he fell through the air until he hit the asphalt with bone-shattering impact. A moment of blindness, a glimpse of a shiny black shoe, and then he died.

That's ridiculous, part of him insisted. You don't die in dreams, you always wake up first. *So wake up…*

…and then he'd be off again, tumbling from the balcony, slamming into the asphalt…

Finally, a light, a blurry focus, a face leaning over his. "Blink slowly if you can hear me."

Toby blinked, long and slow.

The—Nurse? Counselor?—whatever she was, beamed. "*Ex*cellent. I'm Karen Carruthers, and I'm here to get you *ori*ented." Her hair was parted just above one ear and combed sideways over her head in a huge swoop. It was a style he had seen before only on balding men, but her hair was full and puffed up. It must be a look.

Toby realized he had a huge tube down his throat, taped in place around his lips, and he started to panic. He was on a ventilator. That could only mean full-body paralysis. He tried to talk around the tube and found his lips would barely move.

"Now you just stay calm. I know things are strange. We gave you some mood enhancers a bit ago, but I'm afraid *you* went and surprised us all, and woke up just a *little* early!" She talked like the host of a children's show.

He was definitely in some kind of hospital bed, but the place was awesomely high-tech. The bed frame was surmounted by a huge panel of readouts and displays, like a canopy bed designed by Intel.

Ms. Carruthers said, "Now, if we feel up to it, I'd like to teach you a way of talking to us for the next couple of days. It'll only be just a couple of days, and then we'll be *all* better again."

She reached up and tapped a button on the canopy above, and a flat screen descended on a long arm and positioned itself before his face. The screen brightened, and big bright letters showed the alphabet and the numbers zero through nine.

My God, he thought, I've died and gone to first grade.

"Now what I want you to do is spell something. Let's spell the word 'yes.' Now what you do is look at the letter, focus real hard, just squinch up your eyes, and then relax and go to the next letter..."

Toby saw the glittery red of twin ruby lasers at the top of the panel and stared. *I don't believe it.* It had to be Eye-Convergence Monitoring, the focusing device they'd been working on for RatBot. *Somebody beat us to it, and we didn't even hear about it...*

He moved his eyes. *Y*—squinch—*E*—squinch—*S*—squinch.

She glanced at a smaller screen by her elbow. "Why, you just figured that out right away, didn't you?"

He kept going. I—I-N-V-E-N-T-E-D—T-H-I-S.

"Did you! Well, isn't that *nice*." She brushed back her hair. Her eye shadow was bizarre, orange to the right fading to blue on the left, but identical on both eyes rather than symmetrical. "Are we feeling any better yet?"

He was. In fact, he was beginning to feel positively cheery. Y-E-S.

"Good. Now, we don't have a huge amount of experience with this, but what research we have shows that the clients always do best if we just get right to the point. You had an accident. Do you remember it?"

M-A-Y-B-E.

"Oh good. Often the trauma... Well, I have some *very* good news for you. The injuries you suffered were extensive at the time, but they can *all* be repaired! Isn't that wonderful?" She studied him. "I can see you don't believe me. But in just one moment you will, because the other big surprise is that it's now the year twenty-eighty-eight!"

Toby would have laughed if he had control of any motor functions. He felt fine, just fine. He spelled, W-H-H-A-T.

"You do remember that you had an account with South Coast Cryogenics, don't you?"

That? It was more of a joke than anything, a voluntary matched deduction from his paycheck at a firm where the owner was a confirmed loony. If this was a practical joke, it was just too funny. If it was the truth…well, that was too funny, too. Y-E-S.

"You were lucky. You were declared dead, but your bracelet got you rushed to South Coast. Now most people who were frozen back then were…well, they're frozen. But a few lucky ones happened to have consumed cryopreservatives. Do you remember what you ate and drank that day?"

He thought. E-G-G-S—T-O-A-S-T—O-J. He considered a little longer. G-I-N—T-O-N-I-C.

She actually clapped her hands. "There it is, then: juniper berries. What a lucky young man you are! We can't bring many back, you know. But with the advances in medicine since your day, we can not only bring you back, but restore your spinal cord. In fact, that's what's happening right now—and the reason you're being kept on artificial respiration for a while is so you don't start moving around while the nerves regenerate."

G-R-E-A-T.

Her attitude cranked down a notch or two. "Now, I'm afraid there is a minor formality. I'm going to certify you as mentally stable and sane. But as soon as you are certified mentally stable, federal regulations require that you be notified of certain things. It's really *your* rights that are being protected." She stood. "Mr. Metcalf! Mr. Simmons can see you now." She gave Toby a smile, and said, "I'll be back to check on you after you've had your meeting with Mr. Metcalf."

Mr. Metcalf took the nurse's place at the bedside. He wore a green jacket with huge lapels. His hair was cut very short and seemed to be greased down, but his little Hitler-style mustache was unruly, like the tobacco from a cigarette butt disintegrating in the sink. Metcalf squared his shoulders and cleared his throat, not looking at Toby. "At present you are uninsured and indigent. With no current source of income, the United States of America has paid for your hospitalization." He cleared his throat again. "The people of this country have undertaken a significant financial burden on your behalf. This will have to be repaid. The amount of your debt and accrued hospital expenses as of your official revival time of"—he consulted his clipboard—"11:26 a.m. this morning, is four million nine hundred ninety-three thousand six hundred eighty-four dollars and eighteen cents. Of course, this is simply an estimate, and additional charges are likely to accrue during your period of recovery, and neither the government of the United States of America nor this hospital warrant the accuracy of this information, nor does a discrepancy between this information and any actual accrual owed to any party diminish your debt obligation."

Toby was high, cruising on whatever they had given him. Mood enhancers. Whoa. Mood orgasms, more like. Four million something-or-another indeed. He spelled, I-N-L-A—N-O—I-N-F-L-A-T-I-O-M—N.

Metcalf read it off the screen at his elbow and said, "On the contrary. You died in, what, 2003? Net inflation since your day has been essentially nil. You missed The Great Deflation. No, this is a substantial debt, Mr. Simmons, a very substantial debt. Normally, when a debt of this size is due from an unemployed person, the only remedy is a work-prison; but in exceptional cases such as yours, certain allowances can be made by the court. You should understand that your continued freedom is a privilege, not a right, and is revocable at the pleasure of the court."

Inside, Toby swelled with laughter, but all he could do was spell, N-O—D-E-B-T-O-R-S—P-R-I-S-O-M-S—I-N—U-S-A.

Metcalf stood. "There, my friend, you are wrong. There are no penalties for owing monies to private parties, more's the pity, but that isn't the case here. Keep in mind that it is the US Treasury that has paid for your revival."

He held a sheaf of papers in front of Toby's face, and Toby scanned the top of the page stupidly. "No," Metcalf said, "down here." He tapped his finger at the bottom edge:

Due and Payable in Full Upon Receipt
Internal Revenue Service
United States Department of the Treasury.

2 | Déjà Vu Was Not Going to Be a Problem

"In the case of serious brain trauma, you can lose whole days, even weeks of memory," Dr. Pankhurst said, "and they may or may not be recoverable." The doctor leaned and made a final adjustment to a drip tube in Toby's arm. "In your case, the damage was largely spinal, so I think we have a good chance of retrieving almost everything…though it may not come in sequence."

W-H-A-T—D-R-U-G-S? Toby spelled.

"Hmm? Oh. Big dose of mood elevators, since trauma can be, well, traumatic, and a memory enhancer. Nicotine-based."

N-N-I-C-A-T-I-N-E?

"Of course. Even back in your day, all the scientific evidence showed that nicotine expanded recall and enhanced performance of intellectual tasks. The fact that so many of you abused it by inhaling tobacco set development of these drugs back about twenty years, but…" He frowned at the reading on a console. "You should just shut your eyes and relax now."

H-O-W—L-O-N-G?

"Pardon? Oh, this procedure? Not long." He patted Toby's arm, a practiced, reassuring touch he'd probably learned in Bedside Manner 101. "You'll know when you're done."

His apartment. His computer.

He scanned the list of parties logged in, found Dad's address, double-clicked.

A flicker, a pause, and his father appeared on the screen, wearing a headset. "I see you," Dad said. "Can you see me?"

Toby grinned. "Sure can. We should have thought of this years ago. Of course, you guys didn't even have cable out there until recently, so we couldn't do broadband. Does Mom know yet?"

"She knows we have a surprise, but she has no idea what."

"Well, what are we waiting for? Bring her in."

"I'd like to talk to you about a few things first, before we get her all excited about this new gadget…"

He didn't really need video for what followed—a long discussion of problems Mom and Dad were having with their HMOs, plans for turning the garage into a woodworking shop, their vacation ideas…

"I'm sure it'll work out," Toby said to his father. It seemed like a safe statement, though he had no idea what Dad was talking about. He'd been sipping at his drink while his father talked, and was feeling loose enough to interrupt the old guy. "Why don't we bring Mom in now?"

Mom's mouth fell open with astonishment when she saw Toby on the screen. Toby crossed his hands over his chest—*I love you*—and Mom broke into a torrent of American Sign Language, the words coming so fast that Dad clearly had trouble following them; Toby, versed in it from birth, stayed with her as easily as if she'd been talking. He smiled, broader and broader, and realized his eyes were wet. Thirty-two years old, and this was the first time he had ever phoned his mother.

After a long time she calmed down, and even ran out of anything to say, other than, *It's so wonderful!* Hands up, palms out, pushing way up and down, rah-rah. *I love it!* Point at the monitor and cam, then hug palms to chest.

Toby went alphabetic, spelling out, *Welcome to the 21ˢᵗ century*, and his mother laughed. He couldn't hear her through the headset, but his mind recreated that weird, sawing sound she made. It had embarrassed him so much when he was a kid; now he thought it was adorable.

Mom and Dad said goodbye, each in their own way, and Toby signed and mouthed farewell simultaneously. Mom stopped Dad from logging off, and frantically signed, *Call Again, Soon.*

Kneeling on the living room rug. Pushing the EPROM chip he'd just programmed into the slot in RatBot's anodized aluminum back.

That's right, he remembered now. He'd brought the HIMIRIMU module—unofficially dubbed RatBot—home from OSMOCORP for the weekend because the optical-control unit was behind schedule.

Slapping mags onto wrists and ankles, pulling on mag-gloves. Donning the VR goggles and powering up.

Moving around the room, seeing things from RatBot's perspective. Playing with the ratio controls, adjusting the number of steps RatBot took for every one of his own.

Finally, looking around through RatBot's electronic eyes, and letting the tiny lasers in the goggles read the degree of pupil convergence. Look far away, focus; look close, focus.

It worked. It wasn't perfect, but it worked; Eye-Convergence Technology was a solution to the remote-vision problem.

Finishing his second drink, sprawled in his desk chair.

Across the balcony, the drapes in Monica's apartment moved. Hard to see through the glare on the glass at first, but then she stepped into view. Talking on a cordless phone, wearing nothing but a long t-shirt and stockings. Black fishnets.

And then she disappeared from view.

Hey, she wouldn't notice, would she? And if she did, well, he could laugh it off, fascinate her with the gadget...

He grabbed RatBot and pushed open the sliding-glass door to the balcony.

The railing was a broad wall of stucco, about knee-high. Atop it ran a wood balustrade on steel posts. The balustrade was too narrow, but the stucco wall below it... He sat RatBot down next to one of the posts. Just enough room to get by, if he was really careful. He looked over the edge at the street three stories below. *Don't fall, little buddy.*

A short walk for a man, a long journey for a minibot, but at last he could see into her apartment…

Suddenly the sound of a siren from the street below, louder and louder, and, all glory be to god on high, Monica came bursting out of the bedroom, naked but for thigh-high fishnets, trailing a silk robe, trying to pull it on as she ran—

Toby ran in parallel with Monica to make Rat follow, RatBot's head turned to the side to watch her as it scuttled along the footwall of her balcony—

Toby felt the tiles under his feet and realized he had charged out onto his own balcony—that's right, he'd turned when Rat started along Monica's balcony wall—and he skidded as he tried to stop. His knees hit the stucco footwall and his side hit the wooden railing, hard. He just had time to understand it all and say, "Oh shit," before the rail gave way.

And then he was back in that recurring dream: falling from the third-story balcony. The impact of hitting the ground made everything go black for a moment, and then painfully bright.

Then a black shoe and white pants, right in front of his face. Excuse me. Above the shoe, nothing but white up as far as you can see.

Well, if you're going to fall, try to do it next to an ambulance…

He tried to make his voice work. It didn't.

As his vision dimmed, he wondered what had happened to Rat.

Great. A thirtysomething guy kills himself trying to get a peep at the girl next door. He would have laughed, but he didn't have the motor skills, so what came out was a gurgling sound around his ventilator tube.

Dr. Pankhurst looked at him in alarm, and bent down to examine the intubation. "Is there discomfort?"

O-N-L-Y—M-E-N-T-A-L.

"The mood elevators I administered ought to be more than enough…"

I-M—O-K. What he wanted was a good long belly laugh, but nothing worked from the neck down.

"Oh. Good, then. Were you successful in recovering any memory content?"

Y-E-S.

"Excellent." The doctor flipped open a gadget on his wrist and poked at it. "This is something we're studying here. Did you lose any time, or did the memories come right up to the moment of death? That is, do you remember how you died?"

Toby figured he would have died of embarrassment if the fall hadn't killed him, but contented himself with, Y-E-S.

"Good, good." That reassuring pat again. "The nurse will be in to disengage you from the micropump." He was already on his way out the door when he added, "Any additional memories popping up unexpectedly, or any strange déjà vu feelings, let someone know… We might have to schedule a bit of follow-on work."

Toby wasn't sure about unexpected memories, but he was fairly certain that, in 2088, déjà vu was not going to be a problem.

A man's head peeked around the doorframe, eyes darting, and then the head swung into the room, followed by the rest of the man. Clearly not a hospital employee, the guy was dressed as if he'd stepped right out of a mid-70s disco, and his body language matched the look, nervous and twitchy as if he'd snorted one line too many.

"Toby Simmons? No, don't bother to answer. Look, I don't have much time, I just want to say that you shouldn't sign on with anybody before you talk to TGB Industries. We know you were some kind of engineer, and our benefits—and our time to parole—are better than anybody else in the business, especially for technical skills. Some of these other places—they're no better than workfarms—dump you in the CORE when you've outlived your usefulness, but TGB has really got the goods. If I could just take a minute—"

Ms. Carruthers cleared her throat from the doorway.

The man held his palms up as if surrendering. "Just letting Mr. Simmons here know about some of the options that—"

"Out." She stepped into the room. "The patient is not to be disturbed. And furthermore, whoever you are, nothing that Mr.

Simmons agrees to when he's intubated and on mood enhancers will be legally binding anyway."

"Just letting him know about the possible benefits before someone who doesn't have his best interests at heart—"

"Out."

The man slid around her and out the door in a writhing move that would have done Travolta proud.

Carruthers undid the drip tube from Toby's elbow. "Damn vultures," she said.

3 | Fifteen Hundred Is Because I Like You

Lexington Colter hated his job.

That wasn't true, really. He loved his job. But he hated some of the things his job made him do.

He'd risen in the Bureau because of his computer skills, his fine-tuned ability to find the plumpest pigeons and balance the costs and benefits of bringing them down. He liked the hunt, and he liked the trophies, but…

Lex played the part of scary black guy as well as he could—it really helped in breaking down resistance—but he always felt like a fraud. He wasn't from ComptonCore, he wasn't even a COFfer. His dad had been a surveillance engineer in Reno and his mom was a boundary controller. He'd gone to prep school, and then on to the University of California at Riverside, an expensive private college.

He looked at the video monitor. Ottmar was still crying, strapped into the interrogation chair alone in that room. Sometimes Lex thought about delegating this part—*come get me when the guy's all cried out, I'll be in the coffee room*—but that seemed a little cowardly. You make it happen, you keep it in your own lap.

But that doesn't mean you have to stare at it.

He turned and studied the view. Corner office, the perk of being Agent-in-Charge. The Anti-Terror squad had great offices—28th floor of the OSMOCORP building, right out on the tip of the Huntington

Peninsula. Just in front of the building, the remains of the Pacific Coast Highway ran down the slope and into Sunset Bay. Moving water, surge and chop, a big shallow bay all the way up to the skyscrapers of Signal Hill in New Long Beach. Here and there, the white flash of breakers over the remnants of a building; only boats with minimal draft could sail there, but the fishing was tremendous.

Wenner came into the office without knocking. "Whatcha got today?"

"Entertainment lawyer. Major contributor to a scheduled organization. Guy named Ottmar Hernandez-O'Brien, if you can believe it." Lex jerked his thumb over his shoulder at the screen, but didn't turn to look.

"Jesus, the guy is crying like his family died." He could hear Wenner's intake of breath; the man always swelled up before he got pompous. "I don't recall signing any physical coercion releases. I will not have any of my direct reports—"

"Didn't touch him. Didn't so much as slap him."

Wenner paused. "Well, I'd like a complete explanation of exactly what you did to him."

Lex made a point of clasping his hands behind his back and strolling to another window and looking down the coast. Fancy residential area once, they said. Only skyscrapers out here now, massive foundations to withstand the pounding of the surf. Sea level creeping up about two inches a year.

Used to be faster. Who said things only get worse?

Wenner sniffed. "I'd like that explanation now."

Lex kept a polite tone, but didn't turn to face him. "I just told him the situation. He's been giving money to a terrorist org."

"Which one?"

"Committee to Preserve Old-Growth Forests."

"Never heard of 'em."

"Homeland Security just scheduled them last week. A member of their organization dumped sand into the rollers of a Cascade Zellerhauser papermill up in Salem, Oregon."

"Sand? Sounds like vandalism, not terrorism. I can't imagine this is what the lawmakers had in mind."

Wenner—who had acquired the obvious nickname by the end of his first afternoon at IFBI—had been a senior accountant at GAO, transferred to the Bureau as temporary supervisor to give the joint more "fiscal discipline." What the hell did GAO know about fiscal discipline? Congress gave GAO one hundred percent of their budget every year. Like most guys who came in from agencies on soft money, he just didn't get it. Lex took a deep breath. "I don't make the rules, Mr. Wenner. Rollers are expensive. Damage was in the millions. Well over the threshold. The guy in that room gave money to the organization that caused that damage."

"Has the organization claimed responsibility?"

"Did RMP claim responsibility for Miami? When the Yankee Point reactor blew, did you hear the Carson League claim responsibility? Claims don't enter into it."

"But can't he fight it? I mean, he can say he didn't know, that the organization didn't know—"

"Knowledge doesn't matter. How would you catch anybody if you had to prove foreknowledge?"

The intercom on the desk dinged twice, a crystalline tone. Lex stepped back from the window, slapped the circuit pad, and said, "Colter."

"Elijah out front. The UNICOR guys are here, want to know if they can start processing him."

"Tell 'em to pump down their auggies, Eli. The guy hasn't even signed yet."

There was a soft humming pause while Elijah leaned on *mute*, and then said, "Sean wants to know if they should go get coffee?"

Lex sighed. "I'd rather they didn't. Tell 'em to hang fifteen, maybe twenty minutes. If it's longer than that, we've got a problem." He slapped the circuit closed.

Behind him, Wenner said, "So it's not certain that we've got him. He can still contest our arrest and seizure."

Lex went back to the window. There was something big moving under the surface just offshore—Gray whale? Orca? "Sure. He can fight it. And maybe somebody from his firm will talk a criminal lawyer into taking his case *pro bono*, 'cause as of today, *he* doesn't have a dime.

We RICOed him. That's civil, not criminal, so we don't have to prove guilt: he has to prove innocence. And until he does, he hasn't got the money to hire a babysitter, much less a defense lawyer."

He heard Wenner take a deep breath and swell up again. "Agent Colter... Lexington. I want you to turn around. I want you to look me straight in the eye and tell me that you haven't physically...coerced that man. Because the display of grief that I'm watching here seems out of proportion for a man who has simply had his assets frozen."

Lex looked out the other corner of his office, southwest across the Huntington Shallows towards vanished Balboa, where you could just see the surf crashing against the skyscraper-reinforced cliffs of Costa Mesa and Upper Newport. He took his time, and when he turned he had on his patented scary black guy look—eyes focused three inches beyond what they were supposed to be looking at, head tilted forward so eyes stared from under the brows. He'd learned it from a guy who used it to pick up women in college bars.

Lex allowed the look to settle in, and then said, "I told him his money was gone, that we were going to pursue criminal charges as well—against him and against his wife too. Community property."

"And?" Wenner seemed to be getting nervous. Good.

"And I did my job. His wife doesn't work—used to be a schoolteacher, ages ago. Head money for her will be maybe six hundred dollars. Head money for him, more like twenty thousand, I'm guessing. So I told him he could risk a trial—with a public defender—and both of them probably go to prison, his kids end up COFfed. Or he could sign a full confession and waive the trial, and we'd let the wife go. No home, no money, but at least the kids'll have a mom."

Wenner seemed a little distressed by this news. "And what happened? What's he going to do?"

Jesus, get with the program. "And he's deciding. Or he thinks he's deciding. We checked him out before we arrested them. No major problems in the marriage. Loves her, loves the kids." Lex had to turn his head and look out the window again. Thirty, forty brown pelicans, sailing along, then folding their wings to lance straight down into the churning surface of Sunset Bay. Lex knew he shouldn't, but he added, "What the hell d'you *think* he's gonna do?"

It seemed like a long time before Wenner said, "So what are his assets?"

It was going to be a pretty good week. The guy's estate was worth probably five million, twenty-five percent of that to the Treasury Department, the other seventy-five percent kept at the Bureau. That should get the whole team some incentive pay, plus the head money from UNICOR. Most of the people who gave money to the Committee to Preserve Old-Growth Forests were too small to bother with, but there were a few within the local jurisdiction who could be popped for a million or more...

Lex never gave money to anything, not even the Girl Scouts. You could never tell.

On the screen the guy looked all cried out, though you could never know for sure. Lex took one last glance at Sunset Bay, white foam in the distance flinging high as the ocean hammered Boeing Reef, and stepped out into the hallway.

Outside the interrogation room his project team waited on the benches that flanked the door: three women, two men, everybody in slacks, their hair cut neither too short nor too long nor too stylish. They were a good bunch. All of them had coffee except McKinnon, who was drinking from a carton of buttermilk.

He gave a little wave, rolled his shoulders a few times, put on his face, and entered the room.

Ottmar Hernandez-O'Brien wore his hair parted in the center and sported a waxed, pointy mustache—typical trendy law guy, pandering to the 1890s look popular in Hollywood this year. His face was still wet and his eyes were red, but he sat upright in the chair.

Without waiting for Lex to start, Ottmar asked, "Would she—is, is there any way she could keep the house?" Lex said nothing. "Or, or at least the cabin at Arrowhead?"

Lex waved this away as frivolous. "Just forget it. The assets are gone. She'll have to move way downscale, get an honest job." He waited. "But at least there'll be a mother for your children. Make me send you both to trial, and..."

Ottmar nodded, accepting it. The guy was tougher than he looked.

"There's some papers here for you to sign and thumbprint." Lex flipped open the folder on the desk, set down a scribing stylus. He undid the straps on the guy's right arm, wheeled the chair to the table.

Ottmar picked up the stylus, fit his thumb to the channel, and signed his name.

Lex put his hand on Ottmar's shoulder. "You're a good guy. This is the right thing to do."

Lex was back in the room after the confession and waiver had been entered in the registry. Technically the guy was property of UNICOR now—*Factories With Fences*—but he wanted to find out the head-money total without waiting for the paperwork, so he decided to hang around while the two induction officers finished their appraisal.

Sean, the senior UNICOR guy, got toward the bottom of his interview sheet. "Ongoing medications?"

Ottmar swallowed, but kept his face under control. "Sedarex, Millageron, Thrustex, rotation for Type II diabetes."

"Guess we won't be needing the erection enhancers for a while. The rest are mandies, I imagine?"

Ottmar just nodded.

"Make a note of the diabetes cycle," Sean said to his coworker. "Fine. Last of all, skills or professions?"

"I'm a lawyer. Entertainment law."

"Anything else?"

"Not really."

Sean turned to his partner. "Write *no skills*. Manual labor."

Ottmar opened his mouth to protest, but Lex was already on his feet, yelling. "What kind of shit is this? Fucking guy's one of the highest-priced lawyers in the county."

Sean refused to get ruffled. "We got lots of lawyers. And we've been downgrading their assessed value every month, they aren't worth shit inside. Plus, he's been convicted of a felony, so he ain't a lawyer anymore."

"Bullshit. TGB paid me thirty-six grand for a lawyer last year."

"What kind of lawyer?"

Lex thought. "Patent attorney."

Sean shook his head. "They weren't paying for a lawyer, they were paying for the guy's engineering background… I can give you fifteen hundred for this guy, as a favor."

"Fifteen—! Shit. I've got half a mind to turn this fucker loose."

"Right." Sean was already standing, gathering up his paperwork. "The Bureau's gonna let five or six million in assets walk away 'cause you're miffed." He stuffed papers into his soft briefcase while his partner packed up the palm unit and recorder. "Fifteen hundred is because I like you. Our new guidelines suggest about nine hundred as a baseline, and on top of it, the guy's a medical liability—full diabetes cycle every year. You know what that costs to treat?"

"I'm about to conclude that bringing our business to you is a big fucking mistake. Maybe we should go back to TGB, or that new USPS subsidiary—"

"Yeah, well you just check into that. When you calm down you'll see that we've been cutting you the best deal you'll get anywhere— even when you bring us the same kind of labor force we can get from ComptonCore for half the price."

"Sonofa*bitch*." Lex stomped out and slammed the door behind him. His whole team still waited on the benches, eager to find out what their extra pocket money would be this week. "Sonofabitch," he said to the upturned faces, "there's no goddamned justice."

4 | Even If He'd Been One for Naughty Nurse Fantasies, Lyra Wouldn't Have Been One of the Guest Stars

Toby had first met the Sensory Homunculus in a Physiological Psych class. The Homunculus is a distorted drawing of a human—usually a male so that the breasts don't dwarf the trunk—with the body parts drawn so their relative size is proportional to sensory nerve density. Of course, everybody's eyes go to the genitals first, and the poor deformed guy does have an impressive whang, about the same length and girth as his shrunken chest. Still, it isn't even in the top five of his big body parts. Spindly, fragile little torso, thighs, and calves; but enormous hands, feet, and head—and on that colossal, low-browed face sit massive, swollen lips, a giant tongue that flops out like a waterbed, protruding eyes like basketballs, and a huge, fat nose that fights to breathe between the crowding eyes and lips.

Toby was learning exactly how accurate that picture had been.

At first it wasn't too bad. Little electrodes all over one side of the body made the muscles twitch, and made all the sensory nerves jump up and ask, *Hello, who's there?* But after ten minutes it was as if he'd been lifting weights, and something had allowed, no, *forced* him to keep going, on past the burn, on past exhaustion, on into the land of cramps and clenchings.

Even with the painkillers, after ten minutes it was nearly intolerable. And still it went on. Then another round of injections into his spine, and then endless electrostim, electrodes on one side of the body for an hour, then on the other.

The doctor had explained that every nerve ending and muscle bundle in his body needed to be set off, over and over again, as the severed nerves in his cervical vertebrae searched out their mates, and the motor patterns reprogrammed themselves where the wrong connections were made.

If he could have talked, he would have asked why the hell they were doing all the electrostim on his face, too—weren't the facial nerves *above* any spinal injury he suffered? But after a few hours, he was beyond any desire to argue. He would gladly have let someone knee him repeatedly in the groin in exchange for leaving his fingers and lips alone.

And his toes. Why do we have that many nerve endings in our toes?

By the end of the day he was a limp wreck. He could barely turn his head to look when a female technician opened a kit on his bedside and began poking at the inside of his forearm, just below the wrist.

She gave him a quick jab with a needle, palpated his forearm, then pressed something that looked like a giant staple gun about three inches below his wrist. There was a sucking sensation, like some undersea creature had given him a humongous smooch.

She held up some kind of small device, studied the display, then flipped it off. She began packing up her kit without so much as making eye contact.

Toby glanced down. Under the skin, a little below where you'd cut to slash your wrists, there was something the size and shape of a peanut. "*Wha?*" he managed.

"Oh." It was as if she had only now realized he was animate. She still didn't look at his face. "Oh, just a little ID tag, so we can keep track of you."

He noticed that her left wrist wore the same sort of double bulge.

After that he started checking whenever he got the chance. So far, everybody had them.

Hmm.

The next day was different. Maybe it was the mood enhancers. Maybe it was the endorphins from so much acute pain. In any case, by the second day the electrostim started to feel kind of good. Not the kind of good you'd pay for, but a kind of good that at least headed in the right direction, the kind that had you saying, yeah, uh-huh, like that, there—no, no, just a little bit lower…

After his final session of the second day, Mr. Metcalf dropped through just to remind him that the US Government was continuing to pay the hospital expenses of one Tobias Simmons, indigent and uninsured, and that the outlay on behalf of the Treasury Department had increased by more than one hundred thousand dollars each day, *ka-ching*, and that Toby should really be considering his options for reducing that debt rather than allowing it to just rise unchecked in an irresponsible, fiscally unsound fashion…

Metcalf had one of those little peanut gadgets, too.

Toby would have liked to ask just exactly what the hell he ought to be doing about his hospital bill, but he still couldn't talk. He contented himself with trying to give a big smile. He had no idea what it might have looked like, but it made Metcalf go away.

A terrible noise summoned him back to consciousness, and he awoke in tears.

He'd been dreaming that everyone he knew had died, all of his friends, all of his family, all gone without even saying goodbye…

And when his eyes opened, he realized the dream was true. He'd been frozen for about eighty years. Everyone he knew was gone.

The horrible sound was his own sobbing, an ugly, flabby howl working its way past his flaccid tongue and lips.

There were voices around him, but his moaning drowned them out; there were figures leaning over the bed, but they were blurs through the wetness of his eyes. Quick injections in his shoulder, motions in the room.

As sleep embraced him again, he was aware of someone at his bedside, murmuring, stroking his arm, but with the lightest of touches, as if he might break.

Pretty much everybody accepts the premise that we have a hefty supply of creepy stuff inside us, stuff we don't let out. Maybe it was having a deaf-mute for a mother, but Toby always saw the flip side of that, too: a lot of the best in us doesn't get out, either.

Back in third grade, there had been a genuine spazz, Greg Lawson—one of those kids in a motorized wheelchair, with sideboards on the headrest because they can't even hold their heads up for long. Quite a few of the kids made fun of Greg, but always in secret and with a certain degree of shame; what they mostly did was avoid him, so that whatever powerful curse had fallen on him would have no chance of rubbing off. But Toby had been fascinated by the guy—first as a puzzle, trying to understand what Greg was saying—and then as a strange kind of private treasure, someone with a truly cockeyed perspective and no one to share it with.

And, to tell the truth, he'd desperately wanted to ride in Greg's spin-on-a-dime wheelchair; but Greg was always in it, and couldn't get out. Toby had been pretty sure that, in the future, everybody would have one of those instead of walking. One that could get up to, say, fifty miles an hour.

But as his mother often said—hand out, index finger up for caution—*Be careful*—palms together over to side, dreamy expression—*what you wish for.*

After two days of thrashing, quivering electrostim, eight hours each day, a surgeon who looked like a TV doctor had examined him and pronounced him nearly done. The doctor showed his gleaming white teeth in a smile that didn't extend to his eyes, and told Toby that he was proud of him, as if Toby'd had something to do with it.

"A couple of short 'top-up' sessions of electrostim, and then our job will be done. After that, it's up to you. No reason you shouldn't get back full coordination and speech control. Quicker than you'd expect—a week or so." The doctor paused, made a couple of notations in his palm unit, and said, "Congratulations. You're the first cryonaut where we've repaired such traumatic injuries." He reached out toward

Toby and then paused, as if unsure where to touch him. He settled for a soft pat on the shoulder.

The doctor didn't have a peanut under his skin. He did have a translucent, hot-pink plastic bracelet, though, as if Barbie had advised him on how to accessorize.

Hmm.

Then two orderlies loaded him into a wheelchair and taught him how to use the controls, and he understood he'd gotten his wish at last: should have listened to Mom. As he heard himself say *thah goo* when he meant thank you, he realized he didn't just have Greg's chair; for the time being, he *was* Greg Lawson.

That section of the hospital had little traffic, and seemed to be more of a research facility than a treatment center. The orderlies paced along beside him as he learned to work the joystick, but when they were satisfied that he could handle himself in the hallway, they retreated to the nurse's station to chat with folks behind the desk.

Okay. Let's see what this baby can do—

Not much, as it turned out. It could spin round and round, it could corner and swerve better than any sportscar; but the top speed was a fast walk.

He let his body hang over the side and tried to see underneath. Electric motors didn't seem to have changed much, but the battery pack or whatever it was had evolved whole generations from the blocky car batteries of the past—black and tapered up like a shark's fin, green and red LEDs winking on the sides… Toby's palms twitched with the desire to reach down and touch it, study it, open it up and learn its secrets.

He heard running feet come down the hall but didn't bother to look up. Despite his incoherent protests, the orderlies sat him upright in the chair. They gave him the *and-don't-do-that-again* look and headed back to the desk. They were probably right: he wasn't entirely sure he could have made it back up unassisted.

He guessed that the red anodized housing he'd seen on the motor probably hid a governor. So if you could unclip that and pop the governor… Now, at some speed the motor would give, but he knew engineers—it had to be designed for at least four or five times the actual spec speed of about five miles an hour. So fifty mph? No way. But maybe twenty, even twenty-five—

He had his eyes closed, trying to chew thoughtfully on his lip without drooling, when he heard footsteps approach.

Time for another electrostim session. Just to "top up."

Even if he'd been one for naughty nurse fantasies, Lyra wouldn't have been one of the guest stars. A Hispanic woman with a strong face and stronger build, she was attractive enough. In fact, so far people in the future were all better-looking than at the turn of the twenty-first century. But she attached electrodes to his bare skin, including some very intimate bits of anatomy, with the kind of attitude someone might apply to hanging out laundry, and the effect was the opposite of erotic.

She pulled the rails of his bed high on both sides, flipped a switch on the overhead console, and dialed up the voltage. When she had him jerking and quivering all over the right side of his body, she fiddled with some electronic device strapped to her arm like an oversized wristwatch, then went off to do something at a desk in the corner.

With the combination of electrostim and his limited motor skills, it took some time to work his twitching right hand down to the side of his right buttock. It took even more time, and finer adjustments, to get to where he could make his wrist electrode and hip electrode touch. When he did, however, the result was astounding—a huge jolt of sensation that made him suck in a sharp breath.

He rolled his arm away from his body just as Lyra jumped up and ran to the bedside. "Are you all right?"

He made a feeble *OK* sign with his left hand, his whole right side still juddering. She peered up and down his body with suspicion, then nodded. Good to know that they still recognized the *OK* signal. Maybe next he should try flipping someone off.

She went back to her desk. Toby lifted his shaky right forearm, pivoting it on the elbow, and laid it against the side of his stomach. He pulled in a silent breath, held it, and touched his wrist electrode to the one pasted right at the juncture of his belly and his thigh.

Whoa. It was a serious, thrown-through-the-windshield-of-your-car sort of rush. He wasn't sure if he liked it or not. But it was something to do.

He exhaled carefully, pulled in another breath and held it, and readjusted his arm closer to his midsection, searching for another electrode.

Hmm. The future. You had to admit, the place was just fraught with possibilities.

5 | Nice for the Plants, Sticky For Us.

It took only a week for Toby's basic motor skills to return, but a painful, boring week: putting pegs into holes of corresponding shapes, walking a treadmill while immersed in a pool of water, pushing buttons to navigate a video maze. Worst were the sessions with ASTRID, the Automated Speech Therapist. "'*Thuh—thuh—thuh,' said the silly goose!*"

"C'n I habb the adult versiona this soffware?" Toby asked ASTRID. "And whassa 'R—I—D' inyer name stand for, anyway?"

"That's a nice try, but let's work on it just a bit more. One more time: 'Thuh—thuh—thuh,' said the silly goose!"

They'd moved him down one story, to a room with a less elaborate bed. Still too weak to walk, but he was free to roam the floor in his wheelchair. The first day he'd wanted to peek at the wider world, and spent a fruitless hour searching for a window.

It made him wonder what it was like outdoors.

Nobody would answer questions about anything. His family? What's it like outside? Can I please watch a television? Always the same answer: *Got to get your health back before we worry about anything else, okay?*

There was something in what they said. He woke up every morning planning to explore the building, but by the end of the day's physical therapy he was content to sit in the hallway and watch people pass.

Toby'd never bought into the pointy-shouldered-polyester-jumpsuit, blaster-strapped-on-hip portrayal of the future, but he'd expected that clothing would be more, well, *futuristic*. Instead, it seemed fashion had been in a fatal car crash, and its past was flashing before its eyes. Beneath the smocks and lab coats in the halls were miniskirts and muumuus, tight slacks and baggy shorts, suits and sundresses. Every conceivable hairstyle was on display, from tonsures to dreadlocks.

He searched for a pattern. Was style related to age? Ethnicity? He gave up when he saw an orderly in droopy shorts held up by paisley suspenders, athletic socks pulled up high from his oxblood wingtips, topped off by a white dress shirt with a lavender cravat.

Toby had turned to steer his wheelchair back into his room when it struck him, and he spun round, Greg-Lawson style.

People were better-looking. Everyone's teeth were perfect, brilliant white. No glasses, with the exception of a pair so ridiculous that they had to be for show.

And something else, something vague nagged at him until at last he saw it.

No one was overweight. No one.

After a few more days with ASTRID, they'd decided his speech therapy could be discontinued.

He'd dozed off after breakfast. "Toby?" He opened his eyes and tried to focus. The speaker was a black woman with thin, elegant features. Her head was shaved. "Toby? I'm Odelia, your re-entry counselor. They've decided that your fine-muscle control is adequate now, so you'll be spending a few mornings with me, and afternoons building strength."

"Fine with me," he said, pronouncing every word with precision. "Another morning with that arsenal of PlaySkool toys and I'm afraid I'd lose it."

She pulled a chair to his bedside. "I have a lot of experience easing people back into society after serious accidents, but your case is a little more complicated—"

"Because I've been an ice cube for most of the century."

"If you like. I've worked with half a dozen people who've been revived, but no one born in the 1900s. The longest revival I've dealt with was about thirty years."

"How many people from my time are there? How many have they brought back?"

Odelia chewed her lower lip with even teeth. "They've tried to bring back a hundred or so—but nobody understood cryoprotectives back in your day, so it seldom—well, it usually doesn't work." She ran a hand across her bald scalp as if brushing hair back. "We can talk about that more another time. We've discovered that, in the process of re-entry, it's best if we get you acclimatized to the present in a certain order."

Toby shrugged. "Fine. But I would like to know if anybody I knew is still alive—if any of my—my family or friends…"

"I understand. And we're in the process of doing a thorough check. But—"

"But after eighty-some years…"

"Yes." She put her hand on his. "I can see you've already been thinking about this."

Toby nodded.

Odelia took a deep breath. "That's something else we'll come back to again… Now, I'm sure you're probably in debt to the US Treasury for the medical treatments, and you've got to be concerned about that."

"Oh, what's five million dollars or so?"

She blinked a few times. "Could you tell me a little about your profession and background?"

"I was an electronics engineer." Something about this statement made her stiffen, and Toby asked, "Did I say something wrong?" She shook her head, and he continued. "Specialized in writing software interfaces for hardware control. Worked for a company called OSMOCORP—are they still around?"

"Oh, yes. They're huge."

"Well, maybe they'll give me my old job back."

She studied him, then gave a slow smile. "I'm not used to irony so early in the day. For a minute there I was wondering if I needed to explain that it was unlikely that your job still existed…but the idea isn't completely out of the question. OSMOCORP is still one of the biggest high-tech employers. Tell me about your educational background."

Toby chuckled. "There I'm in a little bit of trouble. I was an electronics geek in high school, and a pretty hotshot programmer. Started college, but in my sophomore year I got busted for hacking into a bunch of systems."

Odelia sat straight up in the chair. "You were a *hacker?*" she asked in a harsh whisper.

"Sure. No big deal, just fooling around. Anyhow, OSMOCORP was one of the places I busted into. It was 1990, still the dawn of networking computers together. Instead of pressing charges, they offered me a job."

"And why did you want to break in to their system?"

"To see if I could, I guess."

"Well," she said. "That's nice." She rolled her head on that long, slim neck, as if trying to loosen tight muscles, but Toby had the impression she was studying the ceiling and walls as she did so. "Tell you what: would you like to take a break, maybe go outside for a bit?"

They rode the elevator down three floors to a lobby, Toby steering his chair expertly through the pedestrian traffic. He tried to calm himself—stay open, don't anticipate—but sci-fi images of the future kept rising in his mind. Would it be the dark, industrial world of *Blade Runner?* A glossy, sterile world like *Star Trek?* Elevated roadways and flying cars like *Metropolis?*

The heat and humidity slapped into him like a sopping towel as soon as they went through the automatic glass doors. But it was beautiful outside—clear blue sky, concrete walkways winding their way through a profusion of tropical foliage. They motored over to a bench by a tree whose trunk was completely hidden by clinging philodendrons. She indicated he should back the chair next to the bench, and then she sat beside him.

Toby swallowed. "Where am I?"

"Where are you?" Odelia seemed puzzled. "At the hospital, on the Goversity campus…"

"City?"

"Umm—you wouldn't recognize the name. We're right by Fountain Valley Bay…really part of Los Angeles."

"But the *air*. And it's *wet*."

"Oh, my. History and technology aren't really my strong points. I guess there has been some climate change globally since your day, but LA—well, I guess things have changed a *lot* here. I've seen pictures of what the city looked like back in the twentieth. Amazing you didn't all die of emphysema."

"Yeah. But wet?"

"But wet? You said it. All the cars, all the buildings, everything runs on fuel cells now. Only waste product is water—but you get this much energy demand in one place, it's going to get damp. Nice for the plants. Sticky for us."

Toby looked across the grounds to a wide street, empty of traffic. Beyond it was an expanse of grass and trees, seemingly wild. "Big park for the middle of LA."

Odelia glanced over her shoulder. "Oh. Greenbelt. It's along a boundary fence."

"Boundary fence?"

"Between districts. There's an electric fence inside to keep people from crossing from one district to another without going through a checkpoint. But that's not important right now—"

"Where do you get all the fuel?"

"Huh?"

"For all the fuel cells?"

"You're asking the wrong person." She lowered her voice, though there was no one around. "Look, Toby: You're in trouble. 'Hacker' is a dirty word nowadays. You owe the government a fortune. I don't know enough about programming or electronics to know if your skills are anything like up-to-date, or even updateable—they probably aren't— but if you've got that kind of tech background, the government will want to put you in prison and let you work off your debt while coding from inside a cell."

"But I—" Toby began, then just shut his mouth. There was too much to understand. His body wasn't working right yet. Maybe his mind wasn't, either.

"Look, we don't have much time before we should go back inside." She lowered her shoulder bag to the ground and squatted to open it.

Toby considered the curve of her panty line under the taut fabric of her charcoal jumpsuit and decided his body was going to be okay after all. "What's the rush?"

She stood, put an inhaler to her mouth, and sucked a deep breath. "Asthma?" Toby asked.

She shook her head, then exhaled a fine mist. "No. Meds they don't have implants for yet. Okay. There's nothing illegal about us being out here talking, but it looks kind of funny. I just thought you'd like to hear a few things without being recorded. The—"

"Recorded? What do you mean, recorded?"

"Pretty much everything inside public buildings is recorded—audio at the minimum, video lots of places."

"Why?"

"Insurance liability, sexual harassment suits, theft control—million reasons, I suppose. But what I'm trying to say is this: I don't know much about the twentieth, really, but I can tell you that things are a whole lot different now. And there are just legions of folks who'd like to lock you up and work you until you're seventy or so."

"But my skills have to be stale by now—I mean, we're talking *computers* here, electronics… Even Twinkies don't have an eighty-year shelf life. Say, do you still *have* Twinkies?"

"Six flavors. Stop changing the subject. They'd be happy to lock you up and train you inside. It sounds like you have a track record. And the Fed has got a clear excuse to either lock you up themselves, or sell you at a felon skills auction."

"That's ridiculous! I didn't consent to all this money being spent—and, I'm not a slave. I just wouldn't work. They can lock me up, but they can't make me work."

"Oh yes they can. This is exactly why I wanted to come outside—you have any idea how seditious you sound?" Toby started to argue, but she cut him off with an upraised palm. "Just listen, Toby. You've got to trust me here. Nobody can do anything with you until I certify you as mentally competent to leave the hospital. I can hold off on that for two, maybe three weeks—any longer, they'll transfer you to a mental ward, and you don't want that. So just take it easy, follow my lead, and I'll see if we can't come up with some way of finding you an employer that will—I don't know, guarantee your debt or something. We need to go inside."

"And what are we going to do inside?"

"Start your aptitude tests." She turned and headed back to the hospital entry, and Toby pulled up alongside her. At the bottom of the ramp, she paused. "Just stay calm, go along with the program like you're still a little dazed. And Toby?"

"Yeah?"

"Don't have opinions about anything for a while. Okay?"

<h1>6 | Never, Ever Go Inside</h1>

The Los Angeles-Orange-Ventura Unified Police Department—LOVUPD, usually pronounced *Love-You PD*—provided the law-enforcement services for upwards of sixteen million people, distributed over twenty different Boundary Districts. The most populous district was ComptonCORE, the Compton Consolidated-Overhead Residential Environment. There were perhaps four million people in the CORE, maybe five million, maybe more. Nobody was really sure.

No one planned on checking.

Some cops liked working the COREs—the chaos, the wild-west level of justice, the lack of supervision.

Until three days ago, Jace Roper had never been in ComptonCORE. Never had the slightest desire to visit. In fact, up at Westwood Central, he'd been happy behind a desk.

He'd also, on many lunch hours, been happy in the bedroom of the captain's wife. Hence the transfer to patrol; hence the transfer out of BeverlyWood.

His new partner, Puntip Sulakorn, sat behind the wheel of their Light Armored Cruiser, her seat jacked up and forward to the maximum. Tip was so small that Jace first assumed she was more of a department mascot than a patrol officer, but on their second day out he'd seen her handle a fight at a Baptist Federal Food Distribution Center: a shouted order to break it up; a pause; sudden, explosive violence. She booted one of the fighters in the groin and then flew into the struggling knot of men, lashing right and left with her StunFists turned up so high you could smell the ozone every time she landed a punch. Thirty seconds and it was all over—seven men on the floor of the center, most of them unconscious. Jace hadn't been sure if all were still breathing.

He also wasn't sure that all of the people on the floor had been involved in the fight.

No arrests, no report other than an e-filed "Dispersed Violent Crowd, Unknown Individuals, 10:43 a.m." Welcome to the CORE.

The CORE was about eighty square miles of concrete towers in various states of disrepair. The buildings weren't all identical, but they were similar enough that Jace had to read the GIS display to have any idea where their LAC was driving.

"Watch the people," Tip said.

"Huh?"

"Don't watch the screen—sure, it'll tell you street co-ords, but they don't matter in here. Get to know where you are by the folks on the sidewalk."

Jace studied the street. Poor people, mostly young. Blacks, whites, Latinos. No particular clothing style other than worn-down. "Looks mixed to me."

"Uh-huh. Watch the body language."

He stared. Against a wall, a black man with his head tilted back, eyes closed, body bouncing slightly in rhythm with whatever audioplug was in his ear. A white kid, strolling along, snapping his fingers. A young Latino woman, strutting her stuff in six-inch heels, her hips rolling side to side as if she were dancing.

He saw more and more people moving to the music being piped into their skulls, and his brain seized the pattern. The majority of the people in his view seemed to fade out, leaving only those who were all swaying, tapping, bopping, as if they shared a single dance floor...

"New Havana?"

"Close." Tip gave him a sly smile. "The beat is Latino, but further south. Little Rio." She pointed. "See how many poi dogs?"

"Poi dogs?"

"Mutts. Persons of mixed racial ancestry. Not that I mean anything by it—I know you EuroAmerican types tend to be kinda mixed. Anyhow, that's Rio. New Havana, you got the same ethnic groups, but they don't have each other's babies."

"I didn't know California had so many Brazilian immigrants."

"We don't. It's more like a social choice: A small community with specific external characteristics tends to accrete to itself persons of like social tendencies, no matter what the ethnic origin of the community." Jace stared at her, astonished. She glanced at him, her smooth Thai face smug. "Hey, I been to college. Didn't you pay attention in Social Control Theory?"

"Didn't take it. Look, if you have those kind of smarts, what the hell are you doing on street patrol in ComptonCORE?"

"Want to be chief of LOV-U someday. No way you get to the top slots without street cred, and the tougher the street, the less anybody can knock you. Plus it's a laugh a minute down here."

"Oh, yeah. Pretty funny so far." Jace had no desire to be chief. He didn't even care if he made captain. His main goal was to do something notable enough to get him out of this district, and back behind a desk somewhere.

Tip leaned over and turned off the GIS display. "Okay. No peeking. This next one's easy." She rattled off some instructions through her mag-glove, and the cruiser controls steered the car through a left turn without a pause. Other than pedestrians, there wasn't much traffic in the CORE: cop cruisers, morgue wagons, delivery trucks, autopilot buses. Anybody who drove a personal vehicle in the CORE was just begging to get the three Rs—robbed, raped, and rubbed out.

ComptonCORE was dark most everywhere, since streets were about the only break in the acres of concrete cubes, but now the cruiser zigzagged down some narrow alleyways that hadn't seen sunlight since the place was built. Jace rolled his shoulders, trying to offload some tension. There weren't many people in the alleys, but the few faces that stared out from doorways looked either demented or demonic.

The cruiser turned out onto a main street, and the dim light seemed bright by contrast. "Okay, Roper," Tip said, "this one's easy. Where are we now?"

He looked for a body rhythm, didn't see one. People were rigid, arthritic. Well they should be: white, black, Asian, Hispanic, the bulk of them were old. "GrayTown. It's gotta be."

"See? It's easy if you keep your eyes on the street instead of the screen."

Every block had at least one man or woman with a gun slung over the shoulder—mostly rifles and shotguns, but here and there he spotted automatic weapons with imposing mags. Jace wondered about the protocol of the whole thing; a dozen years earlier the Supreme Court had affirmed that Americans had the right to carry guns, but decided the Constitution hadn't guaranteed any right to ammunition. "You ever check these folks out? I mean, why all the guns if they aren't carrying ammo too?"

"You bet they're carrying ammo, and more power to 'em. People get shot over here, at least sometimes it's the bad guys. Listen, Jace: you ever end up on foot, by yourself, in the CORE, you head for GrayTown. You get wounded, you head for GrayTown. You ever lose me on the street, you better head for GrayTown, 'cause that's where I'll be. These are the only folks on our side. Shit, I'd *buy* 'em ammo if I could."

Tip disengaged the autopilot and seized the steering wheel, turned a hard right.

"What are you doing?" Jace asked, his voice thin.

"Driving." She made a left, steered down an alley. "Gotta go manual to get over to SouthSide; most of the subsurface grid has been ripped out. Anyhow, I *like* driving."

Jace knew how to drive; it was part of basic training. And he even had a few friends who took their cars out to the desert on the weekends, where you had no choice but to go manual. Driving made him nervous. It was like a big VirtGame—split-second decisions, but with real-life consequences. In school they'd emphasized that back in the 20th, most adults could drive, and did so every day, tens of millions of them hurtling down the roads, no grids, no controls, the tiniest loss of concentration an event that could maim or kill dozens.

Jace didn't buy it. Descriptions of life in the 20th always seemed like myth—no mandatory meds, no district boundaries, no ID implants, almost every adult eligible to vote. Just go wherever you want, do whatever you want to do, in whatever sort of mental state you happen to arrive at… Nah.

Tip drove fast, and seemed to like it. Jace saw that she'd told the truth—down the middle of the alleys, the asphalt had been ripped up so that someone could pull out the magnets that ran the steering grid. More in hopes of slowing her down than because he cared, he asked, "Why the hell would anybody rip out a street grid?"

Tip, of course, didn't slow. "Metal. Sell it to the recyclers. Hell, half the illegal ammo factories in the CORE are probably melting down grid-mags to make rounds. Grid-mags and whatever plumbing can be ripped out of the walls."

"Well, why do we need to go this way anyhow?"

"We're a patrol cruiser. We're patrolling. Plus, there's this great noodle shop over in Edge City—can't hardly get there without driving manual."

She left him in the cruiser—"Don't let 'em spray paint the car"—while she fetched an order of pad thai to go. He resisted all her offers to buy him lunch—Pad thai with shrimp? Pork? Beef? *Tofu*? Hey, they could make it extra-mild, Europussy style…

The noodle shop sat in the base of a large residence building, adjacent to the First Lutheran Federal Food Distribution Center. The locals swarmed the wide sidewalk, carrying in their scrip, carrying out sacks of staples; bargaining to trade their food for tokens, sex, booze, drugs…

At first a few people stared at the cruiser, and some of the transactions became more furtive. Jace had learned in school that some animals—was it frogs?—could see only motion, and were blind to stationary objects. The folks on the sidewalk must have had frog blood in their families, because when he showed no signs of getting out of the car, the street scene ignored him as thoroughly as if the cruiser had vanished.

There were dozens of crimes happening in front of him. Little drug sales, mostly ampers from what he could see. A pickpocket worked the crowd, slow and steady, but without much apparent luck. Plenty of prostitutes of both sexes. Hell, trading government-supplied food was itself a crime. But there was no collar to be made here that would earn him any praise or notice.

Near the front wall of the noodle shop, a white woman held a food sack to her chest and argued with a thin black man. The man looked down his nose, his head back so far it seemed like his purple beret would fall off. There was already one food sack on the sidewalk, wedged against the wall by his legs.

The man briefly displayed something in the palm of his hand, then tugged open the top of her food sack. After more heated negotiation, she put the sack down at his feet, and he handed her a glassine envelope. Jace just caught a flash of green.

DTMA. Rock sugar. Newest thing on the DEA's hit parade.

Now that might be worth something.

Jace checked that his ear unit was on, that the tracker on his belt was flickering. He flipped up the safety cover on the cruiser console and flicked the X1P switch—going eXternal to cruiser, solo, hot Pursuit— and there was a blink from the console as it queried the ID peanut in his wrist. He wiggled his mag-gloved fingers through the combination that armed his StunFists, and felt the hum across the knuckles of both hands.

He waited until the man was occupied with hoisting his two armloads of groceries, then hit the *Auto* rocker on the passenger door.

The armored door rolled onto the cruiser roof like a hundred-pound Venetian blind, and Jace vaulted out and ran toward the noodle shop. He heard the peep-peep as the cruiser registered his exit and rolled down the door behind him.

The man in the beret was only about twenty feet away, but before Jace had made half the distance, the man spotted him. He threw the groceries toward Jace and took off at a run down the sidewalk.

The crowd pounced on the spilling food sacks. Jace jacked up the voltage on his 'Fists and slapped right and left, forehand and backhand, and heard shrieks of pain. He jumped over someone as they fell.

The man in the beret was a half-block away, sprinting, shooting glances over his shoulder. He looked back a little too long: he slammed into a pair of teenage girls and all three of them crashed to the sidewalk.

Lucky. Now Jace was sure he'd be able to bring the guy down. A twitch of the mag-glove activated his ear unit; he wanted Tip behind him, but he wanted to collar the guy on his own. "Tip," he panted. "Rock salesman. West on sidewalk."

Her voice was loud in his ear unit. "Roper, what the fuck?"

"Can't talk." Another twitch of the fingers sent the volume of his receiver to nil.

Jace was only a dozen feet away when the man regained his feet. One of the girls clutched her elbow, crying; the other grabbed the man's ankle. He stumbled, kicked her hand away, and made a dash into the nearest doorway.

Jace followed. No door. A wide, dim hallway, almost black after the daylight outside. But Jace could see well enough to make out his quarry, and he closed the distance, their footfalls clattering hollowly. About thirty yards into the hall he was almost within reach, close enough that he could hear the man sucking in air. Jace wanted to yell for the man to stop but couldn't spare the breath. At last, both of them still in full sprint, Jace poured himself into one last effort, raised his 'Fist, and smacked the man in the back of the head, a crackle of blue electricity sharp against the gloom.

The man pitched forward onto the floor and skidded along, limp. Jace stumbled up next to him and fell on all fours, breathless and nauseated.

When his gasps had subsided to a steady pant, he jacked down the voltage on his 'Fists and VelCuffed the man's hands behind his back. He rolled him over, dug through pockets, came up with six little envelopes of powder—black powder in the murk of the hallway, but he was sure they would glow green once he was outside.

Jace powered up his ID wand, waved it over the guy's wrists. Nothing. He knelt closer, made out a white scar against the black skin. Crazy fuck had cut the peanut right out of his arm.

Noises in the hallway behind him. He turned, expecting Tip.

A crowd filled the wide hallway. Ten people? Twenty? They were silhouettes against the light from the open doorway, the doorway that now seemed miles away.

A huge figure stepped forward—white guy, Jace thought, but wasn't sure. "What you doin' in here? Somebody invite you in?"

Jace stood, jacked his 'Fists to full power, the hum audible. "Just back away. My business is with this clown on the floor."

The figure stepped closer. Big, fat, bald, like a pro wrestler gone to flab. He had a length of pipe in one hand, smacking it lightly against an upturned palm. "Anything happens in here is *my* business. This is *our* place." There was a murmur of agreement from behind him.

Jace reached for his sidearm. The fat man swung the pipe. It connected, hard, with Jace's right hand, and the voltage from the StunFist arced up the pipe. Both of them shrieked at once, Jace clutching at his bruised knuckles, the big man toppling backward.

There was an era-shattering boom, and, for one crazed moment, Jace thought it was the sound of the fat man hitting the floor. A gun. Someone had fired a gun. In his ringing ears, he heard Tip's voice: "Thirty seconds. Clear the hallway. Thirty seconds, and then I shoot somebody. *Thirty…twenty-nine…twenty-eight…*"

By fifteen there was only Jace, Tip, and the two men unconscious on the floor.

Jace had jacked down his 'Fists and sucked his knuckles through his glove.

Tip stood next to him. "You stupid, stupid, sonofabitch. Let 'em go, ignore 'em, shoot 'em—do whatever you want in the CORE. Just one rule: never, *ever* go inside."

A Person's Greatest Virtue is Often the Thing That Squeezes Them

Toby's mom had been fond of making broad moral and metaphysical pronouncements. Once, when he'd been fifteen minutes late coming downstairs for dinner, she crept into his room and stood over her seven-year-old son, watching for several minutes as he intently glued parts of a model rocket together. When she kicked him lightly with her toe, he jumped so hard that he nearly lost his grip on the model. Nearly, but not quite.

"Your concentration is wonderful," she signed. Then she went alphabetic, as she often did when she wanted so say something she felt was profound. She spelled out, "A person's greatest virtue is often their greatest vice." Back to sign. "Come to dinner now."

At the time, Toby had been puzzled. *Virtue* was a word he understood, but the only thing like *vice* that he knew was *vise*, and it sounded like his mother had made a weird poetic connection: *A person's greatest virtue is often the thing that*—squeezes them? Holds them in place? It made a crazy kind of sense, and *vice* had never quite lost its *vise* association for him; it was only reinforced even when he learned about *Vice Squads*, who always seemed to be entrapping people or putting pressure on them.

At the moment, his concentration—his focus, his *vise*—had his butt pinned to the floor of his hospital room, sitting crosslegged next to his motorized wheelchair. Using a tray of sterilized surgical instruments, over the previous ninety minutes he'd managed to undo the housing on the motor of the chair and locate the governor that kept the speed in check. The matter had become more urgent since his physical therapist had informed him that, two days hence, he would have to begin walking full time—with a cane, of course.

A hex wrench and socket set would have solved the problem in a minute, but all he had was some kind of surgical clamp. The governor was a pole that fit across the coils of the dynamo the way the needle arm of old-fashioned record players reached across the spinning platter. The pole turned in an *L*, wrapping down the outside of the dynamo housing, and a trio of hex bolts clamped it down at the terminus. So far, he had loosened one of the bolts.

He'd left the door an inch ajar so he could hear any approaching footsteps, a measure that might have worked if he'd remembered to pay any attention. As it was, Odelia opened the door and said, "Oh, reckdross!" before Toby looked up from his work, guilty as a dog caught in the pantry.

She shook her head. "I'm going to come back in ten minutes, after you get…dressed and cleaned up." Weird. He was already dressed. Oh. Recorders in the walls. "Then maybe we can take a little walk outside."

She shut the door, hard.

Sometimes all it takes is a break in concentration to see the problem in a new way. Toby knew this, intellectually, but always had trouble putting it into practice.

When he looked back, he saw the solution immediately. You didn't *need* to undo the hex bolts. He thrust the tip of a scalpel into the crevice at the corner of the *L*, twisted, then pried. The governor pole popped off and clinked onto the floor.

What an idiot. He could have done the whole thing in maybe five minutes; hell, thirty seconds, if he didn't mind scratching up the outer housing. Typical. As a kid, he'd figured out that everything took a thousand times longer when you were learning, and that it was a lot harder to put things back together than to take them apart. In fact—

In fact, he needed to put it back together, now; in his gloating over solving the problem, he'd forgotten about Odelia.

He clamped the outer housing down over the motor, tossed the governor pole and the instruments he'd been using—the tip of the scalpel now bent to forty-five degrees—onto the surgical tray, and piled his tray of breakfast dishes on top. He hoisted himself to his feet by pulling on the edge of the bed. His legs were still weak, and the pins and needles told him they'd gone to sleep while sitting on the hard floor.

He motored out of the room with the trays on his lap, found a service cart and stuffed them in amongst the rest of the breakfast detritus, and was sitting in front of his room by the time Odelia returned.

She gave him a narrow-eyed look. He assumed it was intended to express disapproval, but it just added to her glamour. "Shall we go out for a bit before we start some more aptitude tests?" She started down the hall toward the elevators.

"Sure." Toby pulled the chair up next to her and matched her pace. "What's *reckdross*?"

"Gunk. The stuff in garbage that can't be recycled, usually can't even be identified. The part you have to dump in a landfill somewhere." She frowned at him, cutting off further conversation.

Outside, at the bottom of the ramp, she hissed, "What the hell is wrong with you? I don't know what you were doing down there on the floor—I don't even *want* to know what you were doing—but it doesn't qualify as staying out of trouble. What were you thinking?"

Toby headed his chair for the bench under the trees where they usually sat when they came outdoors. "I wanted to see how it worked. I'm getting bored in there."

Odelia exhaled loudly. "God, you're such a kid."

Toby laughed. "I've been told that a few times. What's the matter, don't you like kids?"

"Not all that much, to tell the truth. I assume you realize everything you were doing in there was captured on video and stored on wafer…"

"Nope, don't think so. I've located all the cameras. They can't see down on the floor on that side of the bed."

"Don't you think somebody's going to wonder what you're doing, disappearing down beside the bed like that?"

He shrugged. "Probably assume I'm masturbating. I mean, they don't expect you to jerk off for the cameras, do they?"

She led them down to the street. "I don't think they monitor them that closely. In fact, I'm not sure they monitor them at all unless some question is raised."

What looked like an aluminum tube on wheels passed by, and Toby stared before asking, "Then what's the big worry?"

"Hey, you aren't worried, then I'm not worried… I'm trying to keep you out of prison, and you treat everything like you're at—at summer camp." Odelia stepped down the pedestrian ramp into the street and Toby followed. On the other side he drove up the ramp and they passed onto an asphalt walkway that led into the overgrown greenbelt.

A hundred yards through a tunnel of trees and clinging vines the path ended in a signpost bearing a cautioning hand and a cartoonish lightning bolt. "Come on just a little further," she said.

Toby motored carefully off the path onto the uneven duff that littered the ground. After a moment, Odelia stopped and pointed.

At first he saw nothing, but then he made out two wires crossing in front of them, the lowest at knee height, the other at shoulder level. Both of them seemed to shimmer blue. "See that? Boundary fence. Cross it and it zaps you. The whole country is cut up into districts now, surrounded by these wires. If we could get past these, you'd find yourself in another part of LA, one that's not quite as nice as the Goversity campus." She crossed her arms. "I don't know that much about the twentieth, but I can tell you one thing for sure: This isn't your world. Things are different now. You're already inside a fence. You step out of line, you're going to end up behind bars."

"I'm… I'm sorry. I know I'm not taking this as seriously as I should. But if I did, I'd probably just, I don't know, give up…"

She squatted next to him and put her hand atop the armrest of the wheelchair. "I know. I know. And I understand a lot of what you're going through. Just try not to be so…impulsive. Learn the lay of the land first."

"I'll try."

"Good." She looked back at the wires. "Wanted you to see that."

She turned and led him back to the Goversity campus. She didn't speak until they were back at the bench outside the main entrance. Toby spun the chair around, and backed up beside the bench with more force than he'd intended; removing the governor from the motor had resulted in some real torque.

Odelia sat down on the bench, tapped her index finger against her lips. "I've been thinking that maybe we should take a closer look at OSMOCORP. I've been out on their digisite the last couple of days, studying the place. Maybe we can get someone from the company to sort of adopt you; they have a huge legal department, and, hey, it's OSMOCORP's cryo program that got you here in the first place…"

She held up her left arm and consulted what looked like a large wristwatch. When she tapped, it unfolded into an equilateral cross. There was no screen apparent, but as she powered it up he saw the twin red lights of Eye-Convergence Tracking lasers. He'd always believed ECT was the wave of the future. It must be everywhere by now.

If only he hadn't died, he'd be wealthy. Hey, maybe he *was* wealthy…

Sure. The wages of death are zip.

Odelia was pulling on a mag-glove when she looked back toward the hospital and froze, fingers just inside the cuff.

A man stood at the top of the ramp leading to the hospital doors, scanning the grounds until he saw Toby and Odelia. He headed straight toward them.

Odelia stopped making conversation and waited. The man looked to be in his mid-fifties, his silver hair whipped up into a high poof that made Toby think of televangelists. His creamy linen suit jacket had impossibly wide lapels.

"Toby Simmons?" he asked as soon as he got to the bench.

"Professor Spengler?" Odelia said. "I'm sure you don't recognize me, but…"

Spengler peered at her narrowly, then said, "On the contrary. Odelia, Odelia…Jackman. Odelia Jackman, am I right? It must be five years."

"Six. I'm amazed you remember me. Toby, this is Dr. Garrett Spengler, one of the leading social-control theorists in the country. And my former Civics prof."

Spengler nodded at Toby, but continued to address Odelia. "I hardly recognized you without any hair. You seem to have done well for yourself…"

"I'm a counselor at the hospital now, and I have a place in town. And I applied for divorcement from my family status, and it got approved—so I'll be able to vote. Not bad for a COFfer."

"Not bad for anyone, Odelia. But I always knew you'd go far… Now, Mr. Simmons…" Spengler smiled, a practiced, fatherly smile. "I'm sure this is all a little bit much for you to take in, strange new world and all that, but you'll have to make some decisions soon. I've checked up on your status, and, as I'm sure you can compute, at three percent annually, the interest on your debt to the US Treasury is in the order of a hundred and twenty thousand per year."

Toby groaned.

Spengler continued. "I think you'll find that the average salary of a free citizen is about fifty thousand a year these days, so this does pose a problem for you. But I think I may have a proposition that could at least delay, if not remove, some of the consequences of your debt." He leaned in a little. "I don't need any commitments right away. But I do need to know if this is worth pursuing. Are you interested?"

Toby glanced at Odelia. She gave him a slow but definite nod of the head. He looked back at Spengler. "Sure. Definitely."

"Fine then. Just fine. I'll have one of my grad students drop by your room later and outline the details of our little proposition." He held out a hand to shake, and Toby saw a bright-pink bracelet around Spengler's wrist.

8 | As in, Shining Armor?

They made their way back up the ramp into the hospital. "What's a COFfer?" Toby asked. "And why's it a big deal?"

"It's from C-O-F, Children Of Felons. Commit a felony, you lose custody of your kids and the State takes over. The kids also lose a lot of their civil rights, like the right to vote."

"*What?*" Toby stopped his chair. "How's that possible? I mean, everybody is entitled to vote. It's in the Constitution."

She stopped in front of the hospital doors. "Oh? Seems to me I read there was a time when only white men could vote. And people have always lost the right to vote when they got convicted of a serious crime. Back early in this century, they decided to get tough—commit a felony, and your kids lose their rights, too. It's not that weird. I mean, back in your day, felons couldn't vote, could they? People in prison couldn't vote…"

"Sure they could…" he began, and then realized he wasn't sure. "Anyway, what kind of system lets children suffer for the actions of their parents? It's—"

"Children suffer for what their parents do under any system. Parents don't earn money, the children suffer. Parents are sick all the time, the children suffer. Parents are crazy, the children suffer. It how life works, Simmons. It's how life's always worked." Odelia looked down at him from her full height. "If it weren't for the government, I'd probably be dead or worse. And I *can* vote. 'Cause I earned it."

Toby waited a few beats before he said, "Sorry. It's just a little hard to take it all in."

Her face softened. "No. I'm the one who's sorry." She moved her hands in front of her as if waving away invisible dust. "That was completely unprofessional of me… I grew up in the CORE. I still have some sensitive spots. Isn't your fault."

They passed through the automatic doors. "What's the CORE?" he asked. They angled their path toward the elevators.

"Another time. I'd rather not get into it right now."

"Okay. What's the deal with the pink bracelets, then?"

"That's an ID bracelet you wear if you're Exempt."

"Exempt from what?"

"Just about everything." The elevator doors opened. "I'm not going to try to explain the whole world to you, because I don't understand it myself. Let's take it a little bit at a time, all right?"

»»❯ ❮«««

Odelia contacted reception through the intercom in Toby's rooms and made them promise to page her when anyone checked in to visit Toby. "Don't agree to anything until I'm here, okay?" she asked Toby.

He nodded.

She started through the doorway, paused, and turned back. "If you'd like, I think maybe you're ready for a little television. It's something we keep tightly restricted at first—it can be kind of jarring."

"That'd be great—I can't imagine a quicker way to get in touch with what life's like these days."

She chewed her lip. "But no dramas, no news shows, no documentaries, no cartoons. Not yet…and I'm going to have the content chip set to block all of those. No honor system here."

The digicaster television was fascinating. It consisted of twin metal poles about four feet high, set on circular footings. Thin, glass-filled slots ran vertically all around the shiny metal of the posts. The techie who lugged them in positioned both on the floor, about ten feet apart. He clicked a control on a tiny remote and the set crackled to life.

A rectangular holographic projection came alive between the two poles. "*Help me, Obi-Wan Kenobi!*" Toby said in his best female voice.

The technician looked at Toby like he belonged over in Psych, passed him the control, and left without explaining how to operate it.

It wasn't full 3-D holography. If you leaned to the side, you could see a little around the side of the figures, but if you leaned too far you saw a static-laden edge behind anything in the foreground.

If you stayed there for more than a few seconds, the picture adjusted as if the screen had been tilted to follow your head. Toby peered at the poles. Ah. Little winking red lights; Eye Convergence Technology, yet again.

The control wasn't hard to work. It changed channels; put innumerable picture-in-picture windows in the screen, so you could watch dozens of programs simultaneously. You could zoom in or out, within limits. You could toss up windows that held banners streaming the weather, sports scores, or available programming. Many of the channels, and most of the banners, were blank—probably Odelia's content controls.

The technology was fascinating, but the same could not be said for the content. When he ticked off Odelia's list of restricted content, Toby realized that it left only SitComs available for him.

After watching for half an hour, Toby concluded that the most amazing thing about the future was the way they had taken an insipid medium and made it even stupider: a seemingly impossible feat. Actors received giant canned laughs merely for appearing on the stage; delivery of a line like, "Oh *yeah?*"—with immense attitude and posturing—stopped the whole show for lengthy canned applause.

At least Toby *hoped* the audience responses were canned.

He'd found it hard to pay attention to television back in the 20th, and this was even worse. The technology was intriguing, though…

He crossed to one of the poles, still a little unsteady on his feet. He spun it around. The picture—which seemed to stand right next to him, so close he could have touched the actors if they hadn't been made of light-wave interference—flickered and settled back. Apparently the poles could broadcast in any direction; the lasers must be tracking the focal angle of his eyes. How did it handle multiple viewers?

"Yeah? So what you gonna *do* about it?" a man in baggy shorts demanded, right next to Toby. Gales of laughter. Toby squatted, hanging on to the top of the pole for support, and looked at the pedestal. No apparent electronics there. He rolled the pole a little more, watched the flicker.

Behind the man in shorts, a woman, her blonde hair pulled back in a tight bun. "Am I interrupting you?" Remarkably lifelike.

Toby tapped at the slots incised in the pole. Glass? Some sort of plastic?

"Are you Toby Simmons?" the woman asked.

He almost lost his balance.

He hoisted himself out of the squat, legs wobbly. "Are you really there?"

She frowned. "Well, yes…"

Another burst of laughter and applause.

He stepped back to the bed and poked the power button on the remote. There was a fuzzy, receding sound, as if photons were being sucked back into the poles.

The woman remained. "I'm sorry, are you Mr. Simmons?"

"Toby. Yeah, that's me. Sorry. I was trying to figure out how this thing works, and then you were sort of in the scene…" He sat on the side of the bed.

"I see. Dr. Spengler asked me to come by and talk with you, if this isn't a bad time…" She sat her briefcase on the floor, held out a hand. "I'm Night Enderhew."

"Toby." He shook her hand. "*Knight*? As in, shining armor?"

"*Night*, with an *N*, as in *Nightingale*. More memorable than *Gale*."

Odelia came into the room, apologizing for being late, and made sure that Night didn't mind if she sat in on the discussion.

Odelia sat down in the wheelchair; Night pulled a plastic chair from the corner. With her tan suit and dark-rooted blonde hair, she could have been a young businesswoman circa 1995.

Toby didn't understand some of what was said, but the gist seemed to be that they were offering him a $30,000-per-year stipend, the chance to take free classes at the Goversity, and an indefinite deferral of the money he owed to the IRS, with no interest charges accruing.

In exchange, he had to agree to occasional interviews with scholars; to ongoing observation by a member of Spengler's staff; and to provide, if requested, his input on certain matters.

"My input on certain matters?"

Night nodded. "For example, we might, say, present you with a problem, and say, 'What would your solution be?' We want to see how your perspective might differ from the perspective of someone born recently."

"And I don't have to be right? It doesn't need to be useful?"

"No, not at all. That's not the point." She shook her head, very intent. Toby decided she was beautiful; that kind of beautiful where they dress a stunning actress in a boring suit and prim hair and pretend that no one sees she's attractive until she finally undoes her bun. All that was missing were the glasses.

"And who would be observing me?"

"Well, actually, I would." Her eyes were large and blue, but seemed somehow shadowed.

Toby was ready to say, fine, sign me up right now, but Odelia interrupted. "And what exactly would you be observing him *for*?"

Night turned to Odelia. "I'm doing my dissertation in Comparative Temporal Psychology, and I'm a specialist in the late twentieth. This is what people from the twentieth would call a 'godsend.' Most people have to speculate on differences between the past and the present. This is like a…" She trailed off.

"A coelacanth?" Toby asked. "A living fossil?"

"Well"—Night frowned—"I don't really mean something like that…"

"It's okay, it's fine, it's great. Beats being Ruffo, the Dog-Headed Boy."

Both of the women stared at him for a moment and then turned back to one another.

"So how would his time be structured?" Odelia asked. "What specifically would he have to do?"

"We're flexible. We need to have some access to him, but basically his days are his own—we can work with him. As far as what line of business he wants to pursue…that's up to him. With a little bit of luck, maybe he'll be able to make enough money—a patent, or his own company, or something—to clear his IRS debt. Better than—"

"Better than working for nothing in prison," Odelia said.

"Well, that's a little blunt," Night said.

"Sorry, chiquita, sometimes my manners go astray. I'm a COFfer, you know."

Night took a deep breath and locked eyes with her. "So," she said, "am I."

They stared at each other, and Odelia started to nod. "Okay, then. So you know the story."

"I know the story and then some." Night leaned closer to Odelia, and lowered her voice. "We're on the same side here."

Toby said, "I'm hoping that the same side you're both on is *my* side."

"I think," Odelia said, "that maybe it is."

"Great," Toby said. "When do I start?"

"What Toby means is," Odelia said, staring straight at him, "*I'd like a few days to think this over…*"

"I can tell you for sure tomorrow," Toby said.

"Awesome," Night said.

Awesome? Toby asked, "Is there anything else I should know?"

She leaned toward him. Her face was flawless, childlike, but her eyes looked ancient. "There is. I need to be completely honest with you. You're going to be valuable. Other universities will approach you with offers, and some of the big, rich private schools—Harvard, CalState Fresno, Chemeketa College—will come through with much, much bigger salaries and stipends. Fifty thousand. Maybe even a hundred thousand or more. But I can tell you that none of them—*none of them*—can guarantee that your, uh, *loan* from the IRS will be deferred. So nobody else can guarantee your safety."

"Hey, this sounds like whaleshit," Odelia declared. "Does this just maybe have something to do with the fact that you want him here for your own little dissertation?"

Night's face stayed serene, and Toby wanted to kiss her as she looked over at Odelia. "I can see you're protective," she said, slow and careful, "and that's excellent. I honor you for it. But the fact is, I'm as good as it gets in late-twentieth psych; and if he goes somewhere else, they'll want to hire me there. I'm with Spengler because he's really got clout. Washington loves the guy. If you'd met him—"

"I have. He was my prof."

"Then you know. He's good. Plus he can protect Toby. Oh!" She put her hand to her mouth. "I almost forgot. You're entitled to student housing, but Dr. Spengler has a guest cottage behind his house; he asked me to tell you that you could stay there, rent-free. If you want to, of course—no pressure at all."

"Where's Spengler live?" Odelia asked.

"Slater Park."

Odelia whistled. "Nice real estate."

There was a long silence. Finally Toby said, "Sounds pretty good to me. Unless Odelia says something to talk me out of it by tomorrow, consider me signed up."

"Groovy," Night said. "That's so fine. Trust me, this is going to be *bad*, this is going to be totally *tubular*."

Toby and Odelia stared at Night with blank faces.

"Isn't that the word? Tubular?"

"Umm, yeah, sure…" Toby said. "*Totally* tubular."

"Great." Night stood, picked up her briefcase. "I'll be back tomorrow, late afternoon. This is *so* sick."

Odelia stared at him, long after Night had left the room. "Sick?" she asked at last. "*Bad?*"

He held out his hands, palms up.

Tubular. Hmmm.

The FCC Has Their Trousers Around Their Ankles

Lexington had no idea why the meeting had been called, but Wenner wanted it: a hint that it would probably be long, tedious, and useless. He arrived at the executive conference room before anyone else and positioned himself so that he could look out the window at Catalina. He pulled his SaveMe pager out.

Julie McFadden, the redheaded AIC for Surveillance, was next to arrive, trailed by the AIC for Computer Ops, Raymundo Delgado. Lex rose and greeted them both, wondering what the hell was going on—was Wenner calling in all his division heads?

Wenner marched in, sat down, and waved the three of them into their seats. "Since we're all here, let's get started."

We're all here? No Accounting folks? No Support? Julie and Lex exchanged looks; Delgado arched an eyebrow.

Wenner rubbed his hands together. "This is about Boots DeVore."

Lex felt like groaning. Delgado rolled his eyes.

Wenner stopped his washing motions, held his hands up as if demonstrating the number *ten*. "I know, I know. Hear me out. The latest reports suggest that DeVore is likely to be operating out of the SoCal area—probably the LOV counties, in fact."

Delgado leaned forward. "I've seen some of those reports, and I find them completely unconvincing. More packet traffic in this area means nothing, absolutely nothing; if it were that simple, they would have traced him down long ago."

Wenner moved his head as if dislodging something Delgado had tossed into his hair. "Perhaps. I'm not a technical man myself." Lex, Julie, and Delgado all avoided each other's eyes. "But the government is increasingly concerned about this man. In the last six months—the last six months alone—Boots has taken over the television systems twelve times, once for nearly eight minutes. Not to mention the number of times he has taken over whole computer nets. It's becoming an embarrassment."

Delgado said, "It is. And it should be the FCC's embarrassment, not ours. Back when it was all analog, this couldn't have happened. You want to digicast everything, then anybody who is smart enough to grab control of a hub can pump whatever they want through their computers and out through the nation's televisions. They should just go back to broadcasting. Or catch the guy."

"Or we could catch him."

"Everybody knows his face," Lex said, "but nobody knows who he is. We don't know if he's worth a dime."

Wenner nodded. "Asset forfeiture isn't the only criterion we should use in deciding what criminals to pursue, but—"

"If we chase down people on government money and don't bring in anyone with cash value, the GAO will ride our asses out of town."

Wenner exhaled heavily. "If you'd let me finish, Agent Colter? The circumstances around Boots DeVore have changed. Washington wants him brought down without respect to property values, and Washington fully agrees with Raymundo that the FCC has their trousers around their ankles on this. The reward for the capture of DeVore has been increased to ten million dollars."

Julie shrugged. "All that does is make me want to quit my job and go find him. We're not eligible for reward money. Incentive pay, yes; head money, yes. All we'd probably get for DeVore is whatever the clowns at UNICOR decided to pay for him."

"*That* situation has changed as well. The Bureau and Congress have decided that, in this particular case—this case only, mind you—the reward can be paid to staffers directly. In fact, I have a written guarantee that, if we bring him in, the reward gets paid to this office according to my distribution instructions."

Lex chewed on his lip. Ten million dollars. How many people worked here, sixty-five? Of course, it probably wouldn't be split up into equal shares…

"Now," Wenner said, leaning onto his elbows, "the reason the three of you are here is that your teams are the guts of our investigative arm. I'm drawing up papers that will, if you are successful in finding DeVore, transfer the whole of the reward to you and the members of your teams. Not to the support staff, not to management. Not to me. Straight to the people who do the work."

That was different. Agents in Surveillance, Computer Ops, and Lex's Field Ops: probably eighteen, all told. More than half a million apiece.

"Now, I know you aren't crazy about me. The new broom, the GAO guy. But I have nothing but respect for all of you. And I'm pitching this to you because I've seen you in action, and I think that if anyone in the country can do it, it's you folks, the people right in this room."

"Can we use IFBI staff and facilities for something like this?" Julie asked. "It seems like there'd be problems from the accounting side."

"It can be handled. Trust me on that. I may not know law enforcement, but I know accounting."

Lex pushed the button on his SaveMe pager, pushed it again. This sent a signal to Ruben, his second-in-command. One buzz, page me out of this meeting; two buzzes, page Wenner out of the meeting and keep him busy.

Wenner's pager went off. He glanced down. "Sorry. It looks like a call I'll need to take ASAP. I'll be back as quick as I can…"

As soon as the door shut behind him, Julie asked, "Which one of you…?"

Lex smiled.

Delgado said, "Me too. So he's going to get two urgent calls right in a row."

"Is this for real?" Lex asked.

Julie nodded. "I think so."

"How do we know it isn't some kind of a setup?"

"What good would that do him?"

"I don't think he likes me much." Lex looked back and forth between them. "Maybe he doesn't like any of us."

Delgado shook his head. "I'd be happier if he was offering to split the money with us, or something. This is weird. Why's he suddenly Mr. If-Anyone-In-This-Country-Can-Do-This-It's-You-Folks?"

"You guys still don't get him, do you?" she asked. "Things are heating up around Boots. If Wenner's division can bring the guy in, Wenner will be praised, promoted, probably moved back to head GAO audit division."

"*Blech*," Lex said.

"Oh, I agree, but it's an accountant's idea of glamour. Plus, you can bet that if it pans out, he'll be wearing a little pink bracelet afterwards."

They all thought about this. Delgado asked, "What do we tell him?"

Lex stared at Catalina. Most of the town of Avalon was gone, but there were new developments up on Wrigley Heights, and one of those houses now had his name on it. "We tell him yes, hell yes. And then we drop everything else."

Delgado nodded. "It's going to be happy days for the rest of the terrorist community until we finish, then."

"Fuck 'em," Julie said. "You have to set priorities."

"Who cares anyway?" Lex asked. "I can't remember the last time I arrested someone actually dangerous. How about you guys?"

They thought about it, but no one said anything.

10 | I Like Myself Because I Can Speak Sign

Toby rode down the elevator unaccompanied—nobody had explicitly told him he shouldn't—and took a wheelchair tour of the Goversity campus. Away from the hospital, it looked much like a university from the late 20th, except for the tropical vines that draped so many of the trees. The University of Hawaii, he thought, must look like this.

Even in his hospital robe, he didn't merit a second glance from most of the students. The students, too, could have been from the 20th, though the styles suggested that several time periods had merged. The people here were nowhere near as soap-opera good-looking as the employees of the hospital, but they all seemed trim and healthy.

When he found a deserted straightaway down by the stadium, he paused, steadied himself, and leaned on the joystick. The chair took off slowly, but the whine of the motor increased and the chair accelerated, the wind starting to whip his hair side to side, and there was a growing sensation that his center of gravity was too high for the speed, a premonition that he might lose control and tumble everything to the ground…

He slowed and stopped. It was hard to estimate. The feeling had been one of tremendous speed. Faster than a person could run, certainly: maybe bicycle speed? Thirty-five mph or so? He contemplated ways of rigging a speedometer.

It was not to be. The next day his physical therapist took away the chair and replaced it with a cane. Two days later, he moved to Spengler's cottage.

Night had volunteered to help him move. Toby accepted the offer, but pointed out that, other than a toothbrush, he had no possessions. Not even clothes.

So it was that Toby found himself in front of the side doors of the hospital, dressed in striped bellbottoms, a silky, wide-collared disco shirt, and sandals, with a fringed buckskin jacket tossed over one shoulder "just in case."

"It'll do until we can order you something you want," Night said, "but my friend says there's no rush getting them back to him. He's into the forties look now." She noted that Toby leaned heavily on his cane. "Do you need to sit down?"

"I'm fine. I need the practice."

"Okay. *Epiglottis*," she said, in a very different tone. "Taxi. Check ID. For two, forty-eight thirty-three Springdale…*Epiglottis*."

Toby blinked. "What was that?"

"Calling a pubcab."

"'Epiglottis?'"

"Oh. Guess you don't know…" She pushed her index finger into her left ear as if digging for wax, and brought out a small, flesh-colored thimble. "An ear unit. What was it you called portable telephonics back in the twentieth—spell phones?"

"Cell phones."

"Whatever. Anyway, you need a code word to turn the phone on, and it ought to be something you don't say much in casual conversation."

"Where's the mouthpiece?"

"Uses conduction through the Eustachian tube. Have to spend a lot of time—at least an hour—training it so it recognizes your voice and then modulates it so it doesn't sound like you're talking into a trash can…"

A driverless car pulled up in front of them—low to the ground, shaped something like a sunflower seed with a glass dome on top, but clearly a car. Night waved her wrist at it. The dome opened like a lid, and a gap slid open on either side, like two-foot-high elevator doors.

She helped him lower himself into the car, walked to the other side, and swung her hips neatly into what should have been the driver's seat. There was no steering wheel, no controls except for two buttons: *Open/Close* and *Emergency Exit*. She hit *Close*.

"It drives itself?" Toby asked. The pubcab pulled out into a horseshoe driveway.

"Well, it's illegal to drive yourself inside the city…" She stared at him with a look of amazement. "Whoa, *lock-down*! *You* must know how to drive."

"Sure. And?"

"What was it like? Wasn't it dangerous? Tell me about it."

Driving on the Harbor Freeway had always seemed tedious rather than an act of daredeviltry, but he knew enough to accept admiration when it was offered. And, come to think of it, it really *had* been dangerous: tens of thousands of traffic deaths a year, and who knew how many people crippled or disfigured. He settled back into his seat and adopted a storytelling voice. "Driving was easy," he began. "The real problem was the other drivers…"

The district where Spengler lived was, as Odelia had remarked, nice real estate: towering trees along either side of the street; big houses ranging in idiom from faux-Colonial to glass-block modern.

Spengler's own house was a massive Spanish-style affair, the red-tile roof mossy beneath the shadow of the trees. The backyard was a small park, shaded by a half-dozen jacarandas. The guest cottage sat far to the rear, bougainvillea vines clambering across its roof, searching for the sun.

Night pointed to a numeric keypad by the door. "Your wrist…"

Toby waved the peanut in his left wrist at the pad and the deadbolt thunked open. Cool. When in doubt, wave your wrist at the problem.

It was a small cottage, a queen bed sharing the main room with a pair of armchairs and a desk; a convenience kitchen; a tiny, old-fashioned bath. It was sheltered, shaded, and quiet; everything about it could have been from the mid-20th.

Everything except the twin slotted poles on the desk. These stood atop a flattish metal box, about the size of the thinnest of attaché cases. "Television?" Toby asked.

"Computer. You can watch digicasts on it too, of course."

"Huh." He stepped over to it. "Keyboard? Mouse?"

Night laughed. "Most people would have no idea what you're talking about. You either train it to respond to your voice commands— or, if you work on them a lot, you glove it."

"Glove it?"

"Mag-gloves. Sign language. You form the letters with your fingers; that changes the position of the magnets in the glove. The computer recognizes the hand positions, changes them into letters of the alphabet. It's kind of a pain at first, but you'll have to learn it if you want to go professional."

It was Toby's turn to laugh. "No problem." He signed, expansively, *I like myself because I can speak Sign.*

She stared at him. "What was that?"

"Sign language—American Sign Language, ASL."

"Oh. Well, I didn't mean gestures, or whatever that was. I meant spelling, with your fingers."

He went alphabetic: *You mean like this?*

She blinked, and asked, "What are you doing?"

"I was spelling. You spell something."

She frowned and held out her hand. Even palm down, Toby could read it as she spelled, *My name is Night Enderhew.*

"'My name is Night Enderhew,'" Toby said. "It's exactly the same thing I was doing."

"Well, I can't *read* it."

Toby sat down on the corner of the bed, frowning. He rattled off, *How about you and me get naked?* and she just continued to stare. "I don't get it. You know how to speak sign but you don't know how to read it?" The idea had never occurred to him before.

"Why would anybody read it? We only use it to talk to computers, or to take notes in palm units… People don't use it to talk to people."

"Except for deaf people."

"We don't have deaf people anymore, Toby… Toby? Is something wrong?"

The first sob came from nowhere, and once it started he couldn't control it. He bent forward and held his face in his hands, unable to stop crying, unable to explain, and he rolled sideways onto the bed. The tears just kept coming, still rolling down his face long after Night lay down beside him, talking to him, holding him, rocking him slowly, to and fro.

11 | It'd Be Fun to Go Around Changing Everything's Color By Waving A Wand

"Right arm straight out," Cara ordered. "Now wiggle your fingers."

Toby did as the Avatar Tech asked, and waited.

The woman scanned the results on a small monitor. "Looks pretty good." She glanced over at where Toby stood, his arm still sprouting wiggling fingers, and said, "Oh, sorry. You can cut it out now."

She stepped over and removed the large plastic collar from Toby's neck. "Let's give this a try. Sit down in the chair and lean forward."

The chair looked like a sleek version of a barber's chair, with a lever for reclining and a U-shaped headrest. When Toby was seated she placed a small clamp on his neck, like a miniature pair of brass earmuffs, right at the base of his skull.

"What's this for?" Toby asked.

"PonsClamp," Cara said, seating it a little more securely. "You don't know how this works?"

"No idea."

"Hmph. Well, we scanned an image of your body and stored it. Then we had you go through that repertoire of body movements, and neuromapped your brainstem. You know about the Jouvet area? No? Ever wonder why your body doesn't do things when you're dreaming, like why it doesn't run when you dream you're running? In your pons, there's an area called the Jouvet area, after some scientist from way back. The Jouvet area activates when you're asleep. It inhibits the voluntary spinal nerves so that your body doesn't do what your brain is commanding."

"So why are we doing this?"

"Lay back and I'll show you." Toby leaned back, and the chair reclined. "Look up at the monitor… Okay, now I'm going to energize the clamp. Your eyes and mouth should still work, but the rest of your body will be paralyzed."

True enough. Toby tried to lift his arms, shift his hips… "It's a little scary," he said.

"Got to put up with it if you want to work in the computer business. Relax. And look up at the monitor."

A 3-D model of his body appeared, floating facedown a few feet from the ceiling, the trunk bent slightly to mimic the way Toby sat in the chair. "Lift your arm," Cara ordered.

He raised his right arm—or, rather, he *tried* to raise his right arm, but it remained limp at his side.

Above him, the model raised its arm.

Toby tried to wiggle his fingers, then wave at himself. His body remained inert, but his doppelgänger above wiggled fingers and waved at him. He grinned, and his avatar grinned back. "It mimics what I do with my face, too?"

"With great precision. The clamp reads signals to the facial nerves, mouth, and larynx, but it doesn't inhibit them. Otherwise you couldn't talk." She fiddled with the clamp, and suddenly Toby could move his body again. "Everything looks good, so let's go virtual. This is a full headset." The device she dangled in front of him looked like a flimsy gas mask minus the tubes: goggles, an earpiece, a mask shaped to fit over nose and mouth, and a PonsClamp hanging from the rear.

"Why the mask?"

"Microphone. Picks up what you say and relays it to anyone you're talking to in VR space. Also keeps the real world from having to listen to everything you're saying. In the grad student lab, there can be forty people in VR at once. Imagine having to hear all of that." She slid a mag-glove onto his right hand and helped him pull on the headset.

The goggles displayed a light-blue background, nothing more. From far away, he heard Cara say, "When you turn your right hand palm up and flap it twice, sort of like *bye-bye*, it activates the PonsClamp and turns your body off. That's physical, but you can think of it as a toggle—if your avatar does the same thing inside VR space, the interface software will read the avatar's motion, and it will shut off the PonsClamp so your body can move again."

"Suppose there's a computer crash, or the software gets corrupted, or something gets deleted—am I stuck in VR forever, with my body paralyzed out here?"

Cara laughed. "Everybody always asks something like that before their first time. First of all, the problem isn't likely. Second, if the computer goes down and stays down more than five minutes, if the Clamp isn't getting feed from the system, it shuts itself off. Third, even if your particular piece of exit code got corrupted or destroyed, the worst that would happen is you'd sit at your desk until somebody noticed and just pulled your Clamp off. So, it's not exactly all that risky—but if you do it at home, by yourself, you should set the timer on the headset." She blew out a breath, rubbed her hands. "So. Ready?"

Toby turned his palm up and waved bye-bye.

1971, the year that Intel gave birth to the 4004, the first "computer on a chip," was also the year that Toby was born. By the time the IBM PC reached the market in the early 80s, Toby had already learned the rudiments of assembler on garage-built, breadboarded computers that he and his friends had soldered together. After working with instructions like *fork / cmp ax, 0 / jne DOChildProcess*—sometimes coded directly in hexadecimal—high-level languages like FORTAN, Pascal, Basic, or C seemed like straightforward English. He learned to patch through university computers to get onto BITNET and USENET, and wander around the nascent Internet. Object-Oriented Programming, which sent many first- and second-generation programmers into retirement, was to Toby just a logical extension of subroutines and procedures.

But his first week at the Goversity Computer Lab scared him.

Night had arranged for an assigned cubicle and computer, a privilege usually reserved for grad students. By the end of the third day, his desk and the floor around it were hidden by books and manuals—a librarian's nightmare, most of the volumes open and stacked atop other open volumes. So much for the bookless, paperless world of tomorrow.

The future was out there for him to see, but the limits of his world were his cottage, the Lab, and the pubcabs that shuttled him back and forth. Clothes, groceries, sundries—all could be ordered via computer, billed against your ID peanut, delivered to your house by an automated truck. By his second day at the cottage, he was back in uniform—Dockers, running shoes, polo shirt.

He spent most of every waking hour at the desk in Lab, trying to catch up, trying to understand. His mag-glove was now like a permanent skin on his right hand; even after he'd trained the computer to his voice, he found rattling off alphabetics just as fast, and less distractingly public. Night spent at least an hour beside him each day, sometimes asking questions, often just watching. After a few days, she expressed concern—shouldn't he take some time off? Perhaps she could show him around?

"Not yet." Not until I Get It. If I can Get It. Maybe I've just been away too long…

If he couldn't get on top of it, if he couldn't get to the cutting edge of how code was written in the late 21st, then his chances of ever paying off his IRS debt were about nil.

And he didn't know how long Spengler's deferment would apply.

A lot of the programming was done in VR space, connecting up block-like objects by constructing code pipes between them. It was an allegorical approach: A program was a cathedral, and programmers were the stonemasons, the plumbers, the bricklayers, making sure that it all fit into the larger design. It was fun, floating through space and connecting huge blocks into gaps in the walls. But who came up with the blueprint? And who made the bricks?

The Spenglers were out of town, so, aside from Night, Toby's only contact was with grad students in adjacent cubicles. None of them knew where he came from, and none inquired. They were pleasant enough, though they could hardly disguise their puzzlement that someone who asked such rudimentary questions merited a cubicle.

The grad students were the most alienating feature of the Lab. Toby was used to a particular programmer type—talkative, opinionated, obsessive, eclectic, and usually just the least bit immature. People who leaned on your partition and held forth about Libertarianism or which *Star Trek* season was the best or what Hitler should have done to make his invasion of Russia a success or why Jerry Pournelle was a better writer than George Orwell…passionate, misinformed misfits, for the most part. The programmers of 2088 weren't like that. They were calm, friendly, given to shrugs and smiles in response to questions. Few of them worked in the evenings. No one seemed to work all night.

The cube on his left was inhabited by Baxter: squarish, olive-skinned, orange-bearded, an oversized Mediterranean leprechaun. Bax was more inclined than most to try to answer Toby's questions.

"Bax? These Architectural Objects—where do they come from?"

Bax dug into a bag of Maca Crisps. "Lower-level Objects. Factory Objects, somewhere." He delivered a fistful of chips to his mouth and crunched away.

"And who codes those?"

He paused to swallow. "I don't know. Low-level object programmers. You're at the wrong school for that stuff. CalState Fresno, or one of the other private schools."

"CalState Fresno is a private school?"

"*Hey Toby, incoming data… Yay*-yuss! Only one of the most expensive schools in the country…" Bax offered the bag to Toby, who declined with an impatient shake of the head. "I know, I know, I shouldn't either." He slapped his middle, which was bulky but by no means fat. "I have a tendency to gain weight, even with appetite meds; five more pounds and they'll probably fine me, and who can afford that?"

Toby nodded perfunctorily, then stopped. "Fine you?"

"For going outside my FDA weight range."

"Am I understanding this? Are you saying that the government can assess fines if you get fat?"

"Well of course. I mean, the public health costs of obesity used to be huge, and…" Bax yawned, shook his head, then leaned forward in his chair. Suspicion crept across his face. "I get it," he whispered, "you're not from this country. Right?"

Toby looked over Baxter's head. On the wall over the entrance to cubeland, a small camera continuously pivoted, a relentless thirty-second scan of the room. "Sort of. But I'm not supposed to talk about it."

"I knew it." He pushed his hand back into the Maca Crisps. "Hey, don't worry," he said around a mouthful of chips, "your secret's safe with me."

Once he'd managed to find some sample Factory Objects out on the 'Net, it was fairly easy to find their Properties, Methods, Avatars, and Morphs, and then climb the seemingly endless ChildOf-ChildOf-ChildOf inheritance ladder back to some primitive public domain code written in something that was recognizably a supercharged version of C++.

In another week, he had at least the outlines, if not the details, and he called Baxter over and installed him in a chair to show off what he had learned.

Toby started with the GRIP methods and properties, the VR tool that allowed a user's virtual hands to grab onto an Architectural Object and drag it around in cyberspace. He ran back up the inheritance ladder, cracked open an ancient ancestor, and let the code spill out onto the screen.

Baxter gave a loud snore, started, and looked sheepish. "Oh, I'm sorry, Toby…they've got me on new meds, trying to get me balanced, and they just keep wiping me out." He peered at the screen. "So, what's this?"

"That's the underlying code. C, pretty much. That's how you start building the inheritance sequence that leads to GRIP."

"Huh. C, huh? We learned about that in a history class once. Never thought I'd *see* C, though. Hey, *see* C…"

Night was more enthusiastic, though it was clear she didn't follow the details. She rattled off alphabetics into her palm unit as he talked, and Toby had to make himself stop staring at her hand; even though it was aimed down, he could read what she was writing. It wasn't quite as hard as tuning out a conversation, but it was difficult—the familiar patterns of her finger movements drew his gaze as surely as if he were a cat and some small creature kept scuttling across the room.

Four days later, he'd completed his first Architectural Object, MagicWand. He made Night, Baxter, and Rosslyn, the programmer from an adjacent cube, put on VR glasses and follow him into a large sample program he was building.

The program was structured like a maze, the walls made of gray-green blocks an arm's-length wide. "What's the program do?" Rosslyn asked.

He saw her avatar to his right, floating in space. Like most of the students at the Lab, she had customized her avatar; Rosslyn had chosen to represent herself as a kind of Tinkerbell creature, with two pairs of wings.

"It's nothing interesting; manipulates a lot of data, receives it, ships it out; big data warehouse."

"It's huge," Baxter said. He was wearing an avatar reminiscent of Conan the Barbarian. "Were you working on this before you came to the Lab?" Beyond him Night sat crosslegged in the air, wearing, like Toby, a scan of her own body.

"Nope. If I were more experienced, it wouldn't be so damn big. I was just learning, so I threw in an example of anything I was curious about. And the architecture's pretty sloppy, too—I probably have double the number of instructions I need." He drifted closer to the outer wall of the maze. "Now, suppose you're working here, and you need to see what's on the other side—read the specs off a block on the next wall."

"I'd note the coordinates," Rosslyn said, "teleport along the Y-axis about three units, quickblink open and read the specs on whatever was in front of me, and teleport back."

"Manifest the handle, pull the block out of the wall, quickblink through the hole, read the specs through the hole, stuff the block back in," Baxter said.

"Those were fun at first," Toby said, "but there's a lot of walls in a maze. So I made this little guy." He held up a wand that glimmered with multicolored pixelations. "Check this out." He waved the wand at the block in front of him and it went glassy—transparent, but still visible from its shimmer. He waved the wand a second time and the block vanished with a loud *whoosh*.

"Ouch," Night said.

"Sorry. Guess I should set down the volume gain a little." He aimed the wand through the hole at a block on the opposite wall of the maze corridor and jabbed. The block glowed red. He flicked the wand straight up and then pulled it steadily back toward his body. The red block eased out of the wall, floated across the corridor, and slid neatly into the gap just in front of him. He quickblinked and the spec panel on the face of the red block opened. "I'll make a couple of changes, just for fun…" He punched a couple of buttons on the spec panel, changed the block's appearance to a crystalline, faceted surface, gestured away with the wand. The crystal block, still glowing red, sailed back across the corridor, locked into its place, and lost its crimson fire. Toby tapped the empty space in the wall in front of him, and the missing block reappeared with a *pop*.

"Whoa," Baxter said. "That was so *pinpoint*."

"Pinpoint?"

"Excellent," Night clarified. "Boss. Groovy."

"Do you want a copy?"

"Sure. You got an instruction manual?"

"Quickblink the specs and it'll roll out of the handle." Toby gestured, and two more wands appeared in his hand. "Rosslyn?"

She buzzed upward on her translucent wings, settled back down. "Why not? I'm best at coord teleporting, but it'd be fun to go around changing everything's color by waving a wand."

Toby tossed a wand to Baxter. Bax gestured, and a little dragon appeared and swallowed the wand, smoke curling from its jaws. He threw another in Rosslyn's direction, and she flicked her tiny Tinkerbell fingers. An old rural-delivery mailbox popped up, daffodils around its base; the front creaked open to accept the gliding wand.

After they left cyberspace they sat around Toby's cubicle. Everyone offered congratulations, and Baxter drew Toby off into a discussion of VR games that might be designed based on similar objects.

A few minutes later, Baxter nodded off into one of his frequent naps, and Toby heard Night questioning Rosslyn: "So how hard is it to write a program like that? Could you do it?"

Rosslyn laughed. "Once upon a time I wrote my own Objects from scratch, yeah. But that was before they put me on Daviril for my obsessive-compulsive tendencies."

"Was that a mandie, or your own decision? If that isn't too personal… I only ask because they've got me trying it out, pills only."

"My own decision, at first—was getting to where I took hour-long showers. But it's a mandie now… Any rate, there was a time when I wrote Objects—but no way I could have written that Wand in a few days. More like six months."

Toby yawned and stretched to remind them of his presence. This woke Baxter, apologetic as always. Baxter and Rosslyn congratulated Toby once more and retired to their respective cubes.

Night scooted her chair closer to Toby's. "You seem happier."

Toby let out a long breath. "Relieved is more like it. Man, for a while there I was afraid I was just going to stay lost, that I'd never catch up…but the same principles are still behind all this stuff, its just harder to track them down at first." He paused. "In fact… In fact, it's kind of surprising, when I think about it, that more hasn't changed. It seems like there would have been huge leaps, things I really wouldn't be able to understand."

He watched as Night signed, *Progress of industry slower than expected* into her palm unit. She noticed his gaze, gave him a beautiful, embarrassed smile. "Does it bother you," she asked, "my taking notes?"

"Not at all. It's just that I can't help reading them sometimes."

"You *read* that?"

"Uh-huh." He quoted it back at her.

"Hmm. Guess I shouldn't write anything too personal in front of you. But we should have a frank talk about that topic sometime."

"About me reading your notes?"

"No, about your perceptions of the rate of societal progress. Oh, by the way, we have your first pre-interviews setup for tomorrow morning."

"Pre-interviews?"

"People from the Goversity who are interested in aspects of the late twentieth. They get fifteen minutes to chat with you, see if you're knowledgeable on any of the topics they want to pursue. If you are, then they can approach us with a proposal to do a more formal series of detailed interviews…with your consent, of course."

"Sure. And speaking of acclimatizing, about a week ago you offered to show me around town. Would that offer still hold?"

She nodded her head slowly, and something moved in her eyes. "That'd be *heavy*…"

I think she likes me.

"…but it can't be tonight."

Toby'd hoped to celebrate completion of his first major VR Object, but he tried not to let his disappointment show. "Oh. Prior engagement."

"Actually, it's you who has the prior engagement. I checked my messages just after we came out of cyberspace, and Spengler and his wife and daughter all came home this morning. They'd like you to have dinner with them tonight."

"Oh." Great. "Are you coming?"

"Wasn't invited."

"Where at?"

"The house in front of your cottage, of course." She tilted his chin up a little. "Hey, buck up. I've had dinner there, it isn't that bad."

Toby twitched his shoulders forward like a horse dispelling flies. "Oh well. I haven't had a good home-cooked meal in—in about ninety years, I guess."

12 | Who Cares? Most Of 'Em Are Completely Swiss Already

"What's your *real* name?" Jace asked again. "May as well tell us. We're running your prints already."

The man VelCuffed into the interrogation chair said, "I want my beret back."

Tip and Jace had dragged the man out of the hallway, thrown him in the Pen in the back of the LAC, and brought him into the station, cuffed. Only when they had him sitting up with the parameds checking him over did they notice that his beret was still on his head.

Tip had yanked it off. It was attached to the top of the man's gleaming black skull with a cross of double-sided tape.

"You'll get your beret back on parole day, bullethead," she said. "What's your name?"

"I'd told you. It's Rufus T. Firefly."

Tip looked at Jace with a flat expression. Jace exhaled. "That's bullshit. I've never heard of such a name."

The man looked back and forth between them. "Thought you types had to go to college to get your jobs."

"So?"

"You never heard of Rufus T. Firefly? They don't teach you much about culture."

Jace figured that was true enough. "Where'd you get the rock sugar? If you can give us somebody upstream, we can probably cut some kind of a deal."

"I already told you—wasn't rock sugar. Just some buzzer I cooked up myself."

"Buzzer is white," Tip said.

"Yeah?" Rufus sounded interested. "Mine always comes out kinda gray. But color it green and you can get a lot more for it."

"Sounds like a good way to get killed—a sugar addict who thinks they've got rock and then doesn't get any sizzle."

"Yeah, it's risky, but I need a lotta income to support all my contributions to the Philharmonic. What is it with you two, anyway? Nothin' better to do than pop some guy dealing doses for groceries? Never heard of such shit."

Tip walked past Jace and he heard her murmur, "Me either." She tossed herself down into a chair. Jace searched for something to say, thought better of it, and sat down himself.

Captain Bolker came through the door and shut it behind him very carefully. "So," he asked Tip, "is there a story behind this fuck-up?"

"I was out of the car, sir, and Officer Roper was already X-1-P by the time I heard anything."

"Roper? Care to fill me in?"

Jace rubbed his eyes. What had seemed like a master career move at the time was looking less brilliant by the minute. "I saw the suspect conducting a street deal for DTMA in exchange for government-supplied food staples. Since I had read the DEA circular a week ago, alerting us to the fact that interdiction of DTMA had been moved to top priority, I attempted to restrain the suspect. He fled, I pursued, and I found him in possession of several street doses of DTMA."

"Yeah, or so you thought," Bolker said. "The lab tells us it's buzz-powder of some sort, with green food coloring added."

"Told you so!" Rufus said.

"*You* shut up," Bolker said without looking in his direction.

"It was an honest mistake," Jace said, "and he was representing the material as DTMA, and, in any case, buzzer is illegal too. Plus he's removed his ID implant."

"If we're going to pick people up for buzzer or slicing their IDs, we're going to have to arrest the whole CORE."

"No shit," Rufus said.

"You won't be so amused in a little while, buzzboy," Bolker said. "Roper, you don't get the picture here. Sure, the DEA cares if your precious little private schoolkids up in BeverlyWood are snarfing rock sugar. But nobody, I mean nobody, gives a shit if a bunch of morons in the CORE are eating holes in their brains. Who cares? Most of 'em are completely Swiss already. You pop this clown and drag him in here—if he had anything worth forfeiting, he wouldn't be in ComptonCORE, now would he? So we'll get billed for the expense of a trial, the head money won't amount to diddly, and it'd look way better on our budget if we just cut him loose."

"I'm all for that," Rufus said.

"Well, too bad, because desk-jockey here is a stickler for paperwork, and he e-filed everything on your arrest before they even got back to the shop. Prosecution is automatic for drug offenses."

"What!" Rufus's voice moved up an octave. "Are you telling me you're gonna take me to court for this? That's total whaleshit, man. I mean, there's a dozen murders in the CORE every day, and—"

Bolker finally glanced in his direction. "Tell me about it. But thanks to Captain Terrific here, you're on your way to Montana."

"No way! Hey, you gotta—"

"*Shut…up.* We've already got you on felonious tampering with federal ID, sales of a controlled substance, illegal receipt of government stores and staples, and whatever else Roper jammed into his little report. If you don't keep your mouth shut, I mean completely shut, until I leave this room, I guarantee you I'll find another half-dozen charges to add to those. Got it?"

There was a silence as Bolker dared Rufus to add anything.

Bolker sighed. "You know, the best folks in LOVE-YOU earned their stripes in ComptonCORE. This could have been a real chance for you, Roper. You wash out of here, your chances of climbing very high are narrow as a snake's ass. But you're on your way out of my shop, and down to the Big Orange."

Jace couldn't hide his smile. "Yes sir."

"Yeah, you think this is what you really wanted, but you wait ten years, when you find yourself stuck in the same pay grade, and you'll wish you'd toughed it out."

Tip stood. "Well, Jace, guess I'll see you round."

"You will indeed," Bolker said. "You're going with him."

She looked like he'd slapped her across the face. "But—"

Bolker held up his hand. "Decision's already made, Tip. You're one of the best street officers I've ever had, but there's more to rising in the Force than kicking butt. There's leadership. Diplomacy. If you can't bring a junior partner up to speed without him porking the poodle in his first week, then you've got some things to learn—things you aren't going to pick up down in the CORE."

To his amazement, Jace saw that Tip's eyes were wet. "Sir," she said, "I'd just like—"

"No. Whatever it is, no. You go down to Orange, show you can survive in a civilized environment for a year, and I'll welcome you back with open arms. But I've seen this coming for a long time." He walked to the door, opened it, and paused. "And process this weasel and get him out of here. We need this room for actual police work."

Jace expected Tip to light into him, maybe even punch him out, but she sank down onto her chair and stared at her shoes. Jace stood and wandered around the room.

The door popped open and Jan, the computer tech, leaned in with a slip of paper. "Found your pal from his birthprints. No priors. Just your average COFfer from the CORE." She handed Jace the note.

Federal ID number, date of birth, sex, legal status, and, across the bottom, *FIREFLY, RUFUS THADDEUS.*

Jace looked up from the paper. Rufus was grinning at him. "Told ya."

13 | It's So Cute!

Spengler and his wife, Tabitha, had abandoned him in the living room with "the kids" while they put the finishing touches on dinner. Melinda had immediately ignored him in favor of chattering to Elise, which was fine with Toby.

"Wouldn't it be *fun* to speak *Spanish* now?" Elise asked.

"I don't want to speak Spanish," Melinda said. "I want to color."

"Okay, let's *color*," Elise said. "That would be *fun!*" Elise bent her hydraulic legs and knelt on the rug next to Melinda. Coloring clearly couldn't be part of Elise's programming, since her doll hands were poorly articulated. She tilted her expressionless head to watch Melinda scrub blue across a sky, but when Toby sipped his gin and tonic, Elise actually glanced up.

Cute. Motion sensors. But the empty doll face, pivoting on gimbals rather than muscles, was creepy.

Elise, the Living Doll, stood three feet tall. The engineering dollars had gone into her balance, navigation, and communication modules, not her appearance; she looked like a doll, not a child. The communication algorithms were impressive: Elise at least faked responding to a wide variety of Melinda's statements and questions, although ninety percent of her replies seemed to be that whatever Melinda suggested would be *fun*. Whenever there was a lull in the interchange, Elise would suggest that it might be fun to do something of an educational nature: Spanish,

Chinese, math games, reading. Melinda rejected all such suggestions, decided what they would do next, and waited while Elise affirmed that it would be *fun*.

The living room was huge, the furnishings of a mid-20th style that, but for their obvious expense and size, wouldn't have been out of place in the houses of Toby's youth. If they were really from the 20th, though, that made them well over a century old, certifiable antiques. Like himself, come to think of it.

Spengler appeared in the arched doorway of the dining room, a wine bottle in his hand. "I think we're about ready here. Melinda, you need to wash up now and come eat."

"Can Elise come?"

"You know the rule: no Elise at the dining table. If you want to eat with Elise, then you'll have to eat in the kitchen with Marietta."

Melinda stood, and shot Toby a look that suggested he was responsible for this state of affairs. "Come on Elise," she said, "we're going to eat with Marietta tonight."

Elise tottered to her plastic feet. "I'm glad we're eating with Marietta. That will be fun!"

The Spenglers dined with a degree of style that made Toby feel out of place. Tabitha Spengler was elegantly good-looking, like Audrey Hepburn in the old movie *Breakfast at Tiffany's*, and it appeared that she had decided to capitalize on the likeness; clothes, hair, even the excess mascara, were all mid-60s. The cool composure of both of the Spenglers suggested that their role in preparing the dinner—salad, soup, poached salmon, stuffed mushrooms, green beans with slivered almonds—had been purely supervisory.

Tabitha raised her wineglass, and the pink Exempt bracelet dropped almost to the elbow of her slender arm. "Welcome to the late twenty-first, then."

Toby raised his in return. "Happy to be here…I think."

She asked for Toby's impression of current society, and he had to plead ignorance, citing a knowledge of the world that was limited to the Lab, their guest cottage, and the pubcabs he rode between the two.

"From what I hear," Spengler said, "Mr. Simmons has been doing very little over the last two weeks other than learning modern programming. And I also hear"—he raised an eyebrow at Toby—"that you absorbed most of the basics in the first week. Quite an achievement."

Spengler seemed to be watching his reactions with undue attention, as if something important were riding on his answers. Toby guessed as to which of three forks to use and cut himself a bite of salmon. "Someone's been exaggerating my progress. There's still plenty I don't understand. And I'm also a little unclear on what exactly my job is."

"You've been doing it. Acquaint yourself with the world. Let me, and Night, know what you think. Outside of that, do what you like."

"I don't see the point. What are you studying? Is there some kind of theory behind all this?"

Spengler rose and fetched another bottle of wine from the sideboard. "I do indeed have some theories, but telling you what they are would interfere with the experiment. Think of it this way: we want to see how someone from the late twentieth adapts to the modern world— what you like, what you hate, what you choose to do with yourself." He pressed a cone down onto the bottle top, and an electric corkscrew winched the cork from the lip. "I have certain theories and predictions; there are others, many others, who disagree." He poured more wine all around and sat back into his chair.

"Hey, I've gotta warn you—I'm probably not the most representative sample of my time period."

Spengler smiled. "Nonetheless, you're what we have to work with."

"So: if you want my reactions to things, maybe you should start filling me in on a little history. I haven't had time to figure out much, what with relearning programming. Can I get a synopsis of your 101 course?"

"I'm afraid not. I don't want my impressions and theories to taint yours. And how you go about learning, what sources you pursue—that in itself will be instructive. The fact that you wanted to learn about the changes in programming practices before taking time to sightsee, or visit the library—isn't that interesting in and of itself?"

"Of course I wanted to get up to speed on programming. Looks like my only hope of ever wiping out this humongous debt. And it seems like I might end up in prison if I don't. Speaking of which, what's the story with all the prison stuff nowadays?"

Spengler waved his finger. "Tut-tut-tut. No history lessons. Not from me."

"Can I ask Night, then? Or is she off limits, too?"

"Night is a specialist in temporal psych, not social control theory. Ask her whatever you like; she doesn't necessarily accept my theories, or even care much about them."

Conversation languished. The Spenglers held a brief family conference: Melinda was supposed to attend a slumber party that evening, and didn't want to go without Elise. Tabitha was of the opinion that Melinda's attachment to Elise was becoming pathological— Melinda had complained that actual children *smell*, unlike her Living Doll. Spengler countered with studies that suggested that, like invisible friends, attachments to robotic companions usually disappeared on their own; furthermore, the rate of progress in math and foreign languages was far higher for children with Living Dolls...

Over dessert, Toby asked about their vacation. "*My* vacation," Tabitha corrected. "Garrett was in Washington on business." She'd been in Colombia for most of the past few weeks, in one of the Compound Clubs—something that sounded to Toby like a combination of Club Med and a nature preserve. She chatted on about the beaches, the snorkeling, the jungle treks. Toby's mind drifted to a problem with coding a Handle Method, and he was caught off guard when she asked, "And have you traveled much?"

"Not really. No place exotic. The usual stuff—Canada, Mexico, Europe..."

"Europe!" She seemed flustered, then said, "Sorry. I forget that you come from a different world. I'd *love* to see Europe—I've seen pictures—but Americans don't really go there anymore."

"You don't go to Europe? Why not?"

She glanced at Spengler as if seeking permission. "Well, it's complicated. And history isn't one of my better subjects. But the European Union is sort of our enemy. I mean, we aren't at war or anything...but relations are pretty strained."

Spengler listened without expression.

When Toby overcame his astonishment, he pressed her for details. She was vague: economic competition between the two superpowers, differing international policies—she gulped down her wine, refilled her glass—and, of course, The Amsterdam Incident, where the DEA, asserting sovereignty over the bodies of US citizens even when they were in a foreign country, landed a SWAT team without permission of the EU, arrested dozens of drug-using Americans, and helicoptered them out.

She went on, but Toby couldn't take it all in. Too strange, and too many assumptions about what he already knew. The Canada-US border sealed, Canada firmly in the EU camp, along with Russia...

"So who are *our* allies?" Toby asked.

"There's the South Americans, most of them. Indonesia. Some of the Africans. Of course, our closest ties are to China."

"China?"

"Beautiful country. You should go there. Poor, of course, and very crowded, but *fasc*inating architecture, *fab*ulous shopping..."

Before he'd been released, the physical therapists at the hospital had urged Toby to make sure he got plenty of exercise. As far as he was concerned, walking without his cane was more than enough.

Laying on his bed in the cottage, stripped to his boxer shorts, he thought they might have a point. He had always been slim, the *before* picture in a bodybuilding ad, but looking down across his ribs to his ectomorphic toes, he had to admit that he was now well along the road from *slim* to *frail*.

Oh well. Plenty of time to deal with that later. He folded his arms behind his head and stared at the ceiling, wondering how to maneuver his limited authority on the Goversity computer someplace closer to the root. He had nothing in mind, but the principles involved in squeezing past security had always been an endless source of amusement. Once a hacker...

A knock on the door. He pushed himself to his feet and tugged the door open a crack.

Tabitha Spengler. A bottle of wine in one hand, two glasses in the other. She pushed the door open and stepped around him as if she owned the place.

On reflection, he realized she did.

"Thought you might need some company." Her speech was thick-tongued, drunker than he expected; she must have kept drinking steadily in the hour since they'd had dinner.

Toby remained standing. She sat down on the bed, put the glasses on the nightstand, and poured. She patted the bed beside her. "Come. Shut the door."

He pulled the door shut, but stayed where he was. "Where's, umm, Dr. Spengler?"

She picked up a glass, sipped, held another out toward him. "Business," she said. "Isn't it always? Come on now, sit down here and have a drink..."

Toby cast about the room for his shirt, his pants, something.

"Come," she said. "Sit."

What the hell. He came, sat, though farther away than the spot she'd patted.

She handed him a glass, drank deep from her own. Audrey Hepburn had been well before his time, but the woman beside him looked just like the pictures on the DVD jewel boxes. He sipped his wine and laughed, dizzy with the sense of dislocation. Here he was in the future, sitting with a movie star from before he was born...

She waggled over closer to him, and he must have flinched. She stroked his forearm. "I'd heard you twentieths were kind of prudish, but really...just relax." Her voice moved closer. "At dinner, I got the distinct impression that you wanted me. Was I wrong?"

"Uhh..."

"So thin." She trailed a forefinger down his chest, then let her cool palm slide back up the same track. She nuzzled at his ear, a warm exhale, then a husky murmur, "And I've heard that you twentieths were real animals, too..."

The words were ludicrous, but the warmth in his ear was effective. His cock stiffened so suddenly that its head jammed into a fold of fabric in his shorts. It hurt, but in the present context that was stimulating.

He reached around her with his free hand, and slid it down her back to her hips. They were encased in taut fabric, without a smidgen of give.

She positioned her lips by his ear, whispered, "Just give me one minute here…"

She sat her wineglass down on the nightstand, rose, and headed for the bathroom, tossing one theatrical glance over her shoulder as she left the room.

He heard the bathroom fan start. He tugged at his shorts to free his penis. It was so stiff that it seemed brittle; if he'd flicked it with a finger, he imagined he'd hear a *clink*. He leaned over, awkward, put his glass down next to hers, and sat back on the bed.

Toby alternated several postures: legs crossed, legs uncrossed, arms crossed, arms uncrossed, arms thrust behind him, leaning back casually on his palms… He concluded that seductive lounging postures weren't something that boys did with any flair, and contented himself with tugging his shorts down far enough that the swollen purple head of his penis was covered.

The toilet flushed and the fan shut down.

He needn't have bothered about what posture he should assume. When Tabitha reappeared, it was clear that the spotlight was intended to be on her.

She had peeled down to a black slip, and she leaned against the wall separating the kitchen from the main room, her elbow cocked over her head. She smiled, a long, slow smile that relished the effect she was having on him.

Her breasts were—well, enormous. Her nipples jabbed at the fabric. Toby was all in favor of breasts, in the same way that birdwatchers love birds: small, large, firm, relaxed, all of them had their charms. But Tabitha's tits were so extreme, so aggressive, that he wondered how they had ever been confined to her tight polyester dress.

This was not Audrey Hepburn.

As she strutted forward, the same seemed to apply to her jutting hips. She was overcurvaceous, pneumatic, huge; the *Attack of the Fifty-Foot Woman*. She hiked her slip up, straddled his lap, pushed him back on the bed, and kissed him, a wine-soaked, wet, open kiss.

All nervousness had fled. This was fine, just fine, probably the way God intended life to be lived. He kissed her chin, trolled his tongue around the edges of her lips, let her capture it again in her mouth. His hands slid down her back to the improbable roundness of her bare hips.

She seized him by the shoulders and rolled toward the head of the bed, pulling him on top of her. Her breasts were too large, too solid, for him to lie on her, and he moved alongside her body, their mouths still clamped. She took his hand in hers, glided his palm up over one breast, down across her belly, and between her legs.

She was wet, a profound, thick wetness that had not just welled up, but must have been incubating since dinner. Toby didn't flatter himself that his looks or charm merited such a response, but he planned to do his best with it. He tugged her slip up to expose more of her stomach, pulled his mouth from hers, and, with his body at right angles to hers, licked his way down her belly.

All his former partners agreed that Toby had talented fingers and a skilled mouth, and above all, focus.

His *vise*. He went down on her willingly, intending to stay a while, but the sideways angle didn't give him much to work with. He took his mouth away just long enough to hoist her thigh up over his head, and then began to move his torso around, planning to kneel on the floor.

Tabitha had other ideas. She caught one of his legs, urged his hips back toward her. Fine with him; he scooted himself over in the general direction of her face.

Her thumbs tugged at the waistband of his shorts and then peeled them down onto his thighs.

Everything stopped.

Toby rolled his head out from under her thigh, half-expecting Spengler to be standing in the doorway.

She stared at Toby's stiff cock as if she'd never seen such a thing. She blinked, seemed to gather herself, and then exclaimed, "It's so *cute!*"

He'd never gone limp with a woman before, but the effect now was instantaneous.

And lasting.

She coaxed him with her fingers and mouth, and he tried to lose himself between her legs…

It was no use, and after ten minutes she rolled to her feet and tugged her slip back down. "Wait," he said, "I can still—"

She shook her head and disappeared into the bathroom. The fan came on again.

Toby liked his cock—hell, he loved it—but he'd never wasted much thought on it. There were times during sex where it would have been convenient if it were larger, but there were an equal number of times where it would have been handy if it were smaller. He'd always been happy with it, and it had never before failed to perform.

He looked down at his crotch, where the traitorous wretch was stashed out of sight in his shorts. Why had Tabitha stared, and then declared it to be "cute?" Were penises in the future larger? Two-headed? Covered in fur?

She came out of the bathroom, dressed again, her hair back in place. Toby couldn't figure out how she had stuffed those enormous mammaries into that tight dress. Her curves seemed to have deflated. *The Incredible Shrinking Woman.*

She went straight to the door, paused, looked over at him. "This was stupid of me."

He sat up. "No," he said, "I'm sorry that—"

"Let's forget about it, okay? Please?" She opened the door and slipped out into the night.

And wouldn't you know it? Five minutes later he was hard as onyx.

14 | "Boots Is Back!"

"Toby?" Night asked. "Are you okay?"

Puzzled and a little depressed by the debacle of the previous evening—an inauspicious start to his sex life in the late 21st—Toby poked listlessly through control-language modules on the Lab computer. "I'm fine. Weird evening."

"You seem bummed out. Want to rap about it?"

He smiled at her jargon. "Not right now."

She nodded, all seriousness. "I've been meaning to bring this up. I remember how…upset you were, thinking about your mother, on the day we first left the hospital. And at other times, you seem overexcited, and today you seem a little, well, depressed, and I was wondering if you wanted to see about getting something prescribed to sort of, well, level out your moods a little bit?"

"I get excited because I'm learning things." He noticed Night's hand transcribing sign into her palm unit, turned his eyes back to her face so as not to read what she was writing. Her face was nicer to look at anyway. "I get sad because I miss so many people. Seems natural to me."

"Lots of things that are natural aren't good, you know. Cancer and heart attacks, for instance."

"I thought you psychologist types thought it was important to 'work through' things like grief."

"I'm not a therapist, I'm a theoretician. But that idea is pretty old-fashioned. Ninety-nine percent of therapy nowadays is through medication."

"Well, I'm an old-fashioned guy, literally. If I wanted to alter my mood, I'd go walking or have a drink or smoke a joint. Taking pills seems like a way to avoid everything, not solve it." Her fingers continued to fling alphabetics into her palm unit. "I mean, are *you* on medication—if that isn't a rude question?"

"It's not rude. Most people don't mind talking about their prescriptions—a lot of them won't shut up about it. Sure. I'm on about four different mandies—only three of them for mood control, though—and one that I'm trying out, voluntarily, by mouth."

"Mandies?"

"Mandatory medications." She turned her left arm palm-up, pointed at her forearm. Next to her ID peanut was another bulge just under the skin. "Subcutaneous secretor. Have to get it replaced once a year. Some people keep with the pill thing, but once I know I'm going to be taking something practically forever, I get an implant."

"Wait a minute. Are you telling me that you *have* to take certain medications? Do you mean *have to*, like it's a necessity, or *have to* like it's the law?"

Night shrugged. "Both."

"Who decides?"

"The FDA."

"The *FDA*? The FDA *makes* you take drugs?"

"Didn't they control what you could and couldn't take back in the twentieth?"

"Yeah, but they didn't decide what we *had* to take."

"Things have changed." She paused to make a few entries into her palm unit, and Toby tried not to watch her alphabetics. "I don't know much about law, but I do know something about the history of meds. Already back in your day, they were making ongoing medication a condition of release for people in institutions."

"Sure, *crazy* people."

"It gradually became a condition for more and more paroles for regular criminals, too, because research showed that most of them had imbalanced brain chemistry. And pretty soon, certain chemical patterns showed up in childhood that were almost a guarantee of violent behavior. What are we supposed to do, sit around and wait until a person like that kills somebody before we fix the problem?"

"But why would you be looking at a person's brain chemistry before they did anything?"

"They just check everybody. Blood test minimum of once a year. More often if you're complicated."

Toby waved his hands back and forth as if clearing a fog. "Wait. Hold it. You mean the government monitors everybody's blood chemistry, all the time?"

"Of course."

"That's—that's outrageous! That's outrageous, and what's more, it's creepy." He watched Night's fingers spell out, *Considers blood monitoring to be invasion of basic privacy rights.* "Damn right I consider it an invasion of privacy. What the hell have you people done to this country?"

"Sorry. I can see my transcribing gets distracting for you." She turned off her palm unit. "Toby, nothing about this is new. *Us people* haven't done anything that you twentieths didn't start. It was in your day they started court-ordered medication, and it was in your day that they started mandatory blood testing."

"We didn't have mandatory blood testing. I mean, there were drug tests for some kinds of jobs…"

"Like any government job, and most jobs in large corporations. You were still alive in 2002, weren't you?"

"Yeah…"

"Well, anybody who's studied the history of psych knows that 2002 was the turning point. The Supreme Court, Earls versus Tecumseh, where they decided that schools could do drug testing on any students involved in any kind of intramural activities."

"I remember something like that. But it was just schoolkids."

"It established the principle. You want to use government-funded services, the government's right to maintain community safety overrides your right to privacy."

"Well, suppose you don't use any of those services. Suppose you aren't in school?"

"Who doesn't use government services? You use the roads, you use the power grid; the police and fire departments and the military are always being used by you, just by being available."

"God." Toby rubbed his eyes. "I can't believe this is what the Supreme Court had in mind. I can't believe this is what the Founding Fathers had in mind."

"I think this may be very much what the Supreme Court had in mind, and that's my period of concentration. As to the Founding Fathers, that's way outside my timeframe. But I know a woman who specializes in temporal psych of the eighteenth century…she might have an idea what they would have thought."

"That's not my point. I mean, does the government make everybody take meds? Is everybody in this Lab on some kind of mood-control drug?"

She glanced around as if she could tell. "I imagine so. Except maybe some of the professors, some of them are Exempt."

"Can you explain this *Exempt* stuff?"

"Oh. If you pass certain kinds of tests, or are elected to certain positions, or do something exceptionally beneficial, then you can be declared Exempt. Your blood isn't monitored, you don't have any mandies, your movements aren't tracked by your ID tags, you can cross boundaries freely, forfeiture laws don't apply without special court proceedings—"

"So Exempts are a ruling class, then? Like we're nobles and peasants?"

"Not really. I guess it's more like, back in your day, some people had security clearances? That meant that the authorities had checked them over and decided they could be trusted in ways that ordinary citizens couldn't. Exempt is more like that."

"But—"

"Oh, whale, look!" Night gestured with the watch on her wrist. "You were supposed to start your first interview five minutes ago."

The first interviewer was a professor of music history, an intense young man who looked Japanese. He wanted to know where Toby had lived, what kinds of movies he had seen, what sorts of books he had read.

Then the specific questions started. Had he heard of Egberto Gismonti, or seen any of his performances? Robert Fripp? Steven Stucky? Ichiro Nodaira? Mike Keneally?

Toby looked blanker with each name, until in exasperation the man said, "Tell me about Esa-Pekka Salonen, then."

Toby shrugged, embarrassed.

"But he lived and composed in *your* city. He conducted *your* orchestra." The professor shook his head and made a note, pen on paper rather than a palm unit. "What music *did* you listen to, then?"

"Liz Phair." Now the professor looked blank. Toby kept trying. "Gin Blossoms? Steve Vai? They Might Be Giants?"

The professor was courteous enough as he departed, but he left Toby feeling like a piece of junk jewelry that had, for a brief moment, been mistaken for a gem.

⫸⫸⫸ ⫷⫷⫷

"My questions are very specific, and on one topic only." The speaker was a young man of uncertain racial makeup, certain African features mixed with something sharper—East Indian or Hispanic, perhaps. He turned on a small voice recorder, so small that Toby knew it must be a solid-state recording medium. "I'm one of Dr. Spengler's grad students, and my dissertation in social control theory is on the techniques used by whites in the United States to force organized religion on the blacks, as a means of controlling them and holding them back economically and socially."

Toby wanted to take the man's recorder and pry it open to check the hardware, but he focused on the question instead. "I only know what little I learned in school." Maybe the guy would let him inspect the recorder after the interview. "I was taught that the slave owners in the South forced most of the slaves to convert to Christianity, but that was centuries before I was born."

The student waved this away with an impatient swipe. "I'm not interested in *that*; that's well understood, and not very interesting.

No, I'm interested in the 1950-2000 period, when the white power structure manipulated so many Afro-Americans into adopting Islam. I have many clues as to how this was accomplished, but it would be good to have the perspective of someone who participated in the process."

"Umm…" Toby leaned back in his chair, thought hard. "I don't really know much about this, but it was my distinct impression that most American blacks who became Muslims did it as kind of a reaction against Christianity—you know, throwing off the religion of their oppressors."

The student gave a loud snort. "Yes, that's the story all of you told at the time. Impossible. Everyone knows the slaves in America were mainly captured and sold by Arab slavers—that the Muslims had been enslaving Africans for centuries. Why would the blacks turn away from the religion of their former masters and then embrace instead the religion of those who enslaved them in the first place, those who hunted them down, burnt their villages, tore apart their families? Are you claiming that they were fools?"

Toby was speechless. At length, he ventured, "But why would a largely Christian society try to push anyone to adopt Islam?"

"To keep them down—as I think you well know. It was the African women in America who were getting the education and holding the jobs. What better way to keep the women from getting power than by forcing their men to adopt a religion that oppresses women?"

Toby wasn't sure how important these interviews might be as a part of his "job" with Spengler, so he chose his words with care. "I see your point. But to be completely honest, as far as I know, nobody was trying to manipulate anyone into adopting Islam, least of all the white power structure."

The student scooted his chair closer, his voice confidential. "It doesn't matter anymore, you know. All the people are dead and gone, all of the organizations have vanished. You can tell me the truth."

"I *am* telling you the truth."

"Fine." The student rose to his feet. "I have plenty of information without your help. And your own words—even though you deny everything—are a kind of confirmation in themselves." He pointed with two fingers, as if hexing. "If you had minimized the white conspiracy to convert Africans to Islam, if you had admitted that there were at least some underground organizations and government money devoted to that task, then I would have to take your point of view seriously. But when you deny, outright *deny*, any kind of white-supremacist plot, that just proves my point." He turned and strode from Toby's cubicle, turned back to face him, and added, "Even now, more than a century later, the conspiracy of silence continues."

There were three more interviews. A woman from the math faculty wanted to know if he had known any of the people who had worked out the fundamental homology between n-dimensional geometry and thermodynamic state equations. He hadn't. A man who studied the history of computers and microtechnology seemed like a promising possibility, but it turned out that the man was primarily interested in what Toby might know about the sex lives of Peter Norton, Bill Gates, and Steve Wozniak. Toby knew nothing about this topic, and urgently didn't want to know more.

The final interview was from a young woman finishing a master's in biology; she wanted to know if Toby had ever seen coyotes, and if so, where and under what circumstances. Here, at last, he was of some help to someone, since he had been an avid backpacker; it was nice to feel useful, even if he had no idea why she wanted the information.

By the time she left it was almost noon. Toby stood, stretched, and looked out over the cube farm to see if Night was in the Lab.

Someone shouted, "Hey, Boots is back." There was a flurry of activity and exclamations all across the huge room. There was a crackle as the speakers on his computer shifted out of *Mute*.

A man's face appeared on the monitor: long gray goatee, bald head, an avuncular expression. "Hi, kids."

"Hi, Boots," a few people yelled. The voices sounded amused.

"I've got a few words of wisdom for you." The ZipPrinter by Toby's desk began to spit sheets of paper into his tray, and all around the room he heard the whirr and thik of printers delivering their output. "I save most of my time for TV, of course, since I know hardly any of the morons in the land of the free still read, and don't understand much when they do. Tom Paine would just shoot himself. In fact, I'm not sure why I bother with print. I guess I still believe that what passes for intelligentsia in this country is made up of readers..." His eyes glanced to the side, focused back forward. "Well, I see that the Gestapo is on its way, so I'll sign off until next time, but until then, remember: What you don't know is bound to hurt you."

The face blinked out, leaving an American flag waving in its place.

Far across the room the doors crashed open, and a voice yelled, "Homeland Security. The situation is under control. Remain calm while we secure the area."

The reassurances felt out of place, since Toby had no sense that anyone had been worried. Toby peered across the partitions and saw SWAT-team uniforms, bug-helmeted men striding into cubicle after cubicle, snatching up sheets of printout.

Toby had long ago figured out where the cameras were in the Lab; the one high on the wall behind him had a long scan pattern, pivoting back and forth so that it covered about a half-dozen cubes. He stretched his arms above his head, yawned, and took a casual glance at the camera. It had just tracked past his cube. He snatched up the papers, folded them into a square, and stuffed them down the front of his pants.

He turned off the ZipPrinter, popped open the front, reached inside, and pried the control chip off of the power supply. He closed the front, pocketed the chip, and sat down at his computer before the camera tracked back to him.

He was back at work on a control-language module when one of the Homeland Security team stomped over to his printer. "Where's the sheets?" the man demanded.

Toby looked up as if he'd been lost in programming, which, in fact, he had. "Oh. Sorry. That one's busted. They're supposed to come look at it tomorrow."

There was a frown behind the bug-eye goggles. The security man punched the power button a few times, bent down to check that it was plugged in, shrugged, and left.

Night showed up about fifteen minutes later. "Heard you had an appearance from Boots DeVore."

"Yeah. What was all that about?"

"I'll tell you about Boots later on. Do you want some lunch? Or, if you're not too involved with that stuff"—she gestured at the screen—"maybe we could take the afternoon off and go do the town."

"Sounds great." Toby started to rise, but she shook her head.

"Give me twenty minutes. I'd like to put on something more fun than this suit."

Toby assented willingly. That would give him time to lock himself in a toilet stall and see what Boots DeVore had to say.

15 | One Big Jail: Notes from Your Pal Boots

By the 1990s, America had a larger percentage of its population behind bars than any other country in the history of the world.

Impressive. First to the moon, first to lock everybody up.

I know that to most of you, anything before last year is ancient history, but if we peer into the mists of time, toward the turn of the century, you can see it all coming.

Believe it or not, there was a time when income taxes were the greatest source of government revenue. Americans believed that they were the most heavily taxed people in the world (they were the most lightly taxed among industrial countries), and that their tax dollars that weren't wasted on welfare (even though the welfare benefits paid out in the US were a pittance compared to most rich nations) were thrown away on foreign aid to ungrateful allies (despite the fact that the percentage of government expenditures on foreign aid were among the tiniest items in the budget). The pressure to cut taxes was relentless.

For a while they tried user fees, so that by 2000 about half of the revenues of the FDA came from monies provided by the companies they were supposed to be regulating. And governments at all levels, from the federal down to the smallest city governments, hunted for things to charge fees on, from use of parks to permit applications to library fees.

But there just weren't enough opportunities to squeeze fees out of the public. After the huge deficits run up by the Republicans in the 70s, 80s, and the early 00s, it looked like the government couldn't both continue to cut taxes and stay afloat.

There were solutions, and they'd been staring everyone in the face: asset seizure and prison labor.

As drug-related property seizures escalated in the early 21st century, the DEA quickly became the largest single owner of real estate in dozens of major urban centers. All other agencies that could conceivably fund themselves through seizures were encouraged to get to work.

In the 1980s, Congress was reluctant to grant Most-Favored-Nation status to China—now, of course, our major ally. One of the reasons cited was that many of China's goods were produced by—time out for gasps of horror—prison labor. But the US government had already sanctioned prison labor through its UNICOR subsidiary, and when the prisons were privatized, the incentive to turn them into profit-making operations was increased.

With the rise of automated stores and robot fast-food service centers, the few unskilled jobs outside the prisons evaporated. Initially the government response was to send more unemployed people to prison, but the math didn't work out: unruly, untrained prison workers cost more to support than they produced in profit. The ideal prisoner fit the profile of the upper middle class—highly trained, educated professionals. And, as the prison population aged, every year there was a huge outflow of old men and women with no assets, no marketable skills, and no pensions. By 2040, the homeless in America constituted a nation of their own, thirty million strong, but a nation without a voice. When sanitation workers had to be deployed every morning to load the dead off the sidewalks before business people arrived at their offices, Congress decided it was time to act.

The COREs were the solution. Why not? The government already owned huge sections of most big cities. Endless blocks of concrete buildings, ten to twenty stories high, packed in tight across square miles. The Personal Dwelling Space was nothing more than a single room; every forty rooms shared kitchen, laundry, and bathroom facilities. Basic food items were distributed free, and those who were properly registered with the system received a small monthly check, recorded in the federal computers as a loan against any future earnings. "No worse than most kids' first year at college," President Noel had remarked in the early years.

At first that might have been true. But from the start the COREs were politically impotent: the bulk of the inhabitants were convicted felons or their children, and therefore couldn't vote.

As the cost of running and policing the buildings increased, the federal government provided less and less support per resident, until at last the government withdrew from supervisory responsibilities altogether. The government—or rather the religious Bush Charities, using government funds—continued to provide limited free food, certain basic utilities, and rare, very rare, repairs to infrastructure. The buildings became "self-governing," a development that President Cabot lauded as, "American town-hall democracy at its most essential."

Uh-huh.

Let's do some math. Take out the people under 18, that cuts out about a third of the population. Take out the one in five actually in prison, and the one in four who have been released from prison but have had their voting rights stripped. That leaves about 20% of our country's adults.

Take out the ruling class, the folks who've earned their little pink bracelets, that's less than five percent. What's left? About one in six of you, a little over fifteen percent, are adults who can still vote and earn a living that goes into your own pockets.

Believe it or not, most Americans used to be in that situation.

Fifteen percent. But a decade ago it was more like twenty percent. Back in 2050, it was more than fifty percent.

The prison labor system is hungry; if you have skills, they want them. The law enforcement agencies need to pay their own salaries; if you have assets, they're going to find an excuse to arrest you.

What's that mean? Well, if you're part of that 15% of free, voting citizens, chances are you're headed for prison. Sure, you're probably earning good money and living a privileged life, but you're riding on the back of a huge system that is steadily eating its own.

Maybe you'll be one of the lucky ones who through money or influence or services rendered will be invited to strap on a pink bracelet and join the ruling class.

Your chances of winning the lottery are better.

If you're one of the 15%, then you have the power to change all this. But maybe you should just keep your head down and hope that they come for your neighbors instead of you.

Chances are you aren't reading this, and I'm shouting into a vacuum. After all, you can go to prison for reading the things I write...

But you're probably headed there anyway.

Sincerely,

Your Friend, Boots DeVore

16 | Tanner's Tobbo Shop: We Never Sleep

The printout from Boots DeVore had given Toby a clue that the world of 2088 wasn't all tree-lined streets and college campuses. The ride to Seaport Plaza confirmed it.

They took a pubcab to a transit stop in the center of a wide avenue. Pubcabs and a few private cars whipped along both sides of the street, the traffic flow optimized by computer. It was amazing how much faster traffic moved when humans weren't involved in making the decisions.

The platform in the center of the street was connected to shops and sidewalks by elevated walkways. In the center of the platform, bullet-nosed streetcars pulled up, disgorged streams of passengers, boarded others, then zipped off, riding a foot off the ground. Magnetic levitation, Toby assumed, but when he asked Night she said she had no idea.

There was none of the 20th-century subway about the transit stop—no beggars, no musicians, no one simply loitering, just good-looking, healthy people on their way somewhere. The cleanliness and order gave the station the feel of a theme park rather than a living city.

Night had dressed in a blue bodystocking and boots with high, thick heels that hoisted her slightly above Toby's height. Although most of the people were attractive enough, Night still drew stares as she led him along to board the first Long Beach streetcar to arrive.

Once seated, Toby asked, "Where are all these people coming from?"

"Apartmentville, mostly."

"Is that a city?"

She smiled. "No, more of a concept, like *suburb*. It's pretty much all medium-rises from Santa Ana over to Anaheim. Things that look like…" She pointed. "Like that, except bigger." He followed her gesture to a massive pinkish structure, like M.C. Escher working in a Spanish style, blocks stacked astride blocks, balconies and roof terraces in every possible location, bougainvillea cascading down the sides.

"I like it," he said.

"Nice enough, I guess, but a little tiresome after a few zillion square miles."

"Is that one of the areas they call a *CORE*?"

"Oh, lord no. The COREs are these huge concrete slums."

"Have you been to one?"

"Never. And never want to go."

"Don't outsiders go in?"

"Some do. People looking for scary sex, or illegal drugs. But it's dangerous. People living in the COREs are pretty desperate."

Toby watched the world roll by for a bit: more fractalized apartment buildings, a few multistory shopping malls. With most transit public, shopping centers were no longer sprawling masses surrounded by acres of parking lot, but hulking, glass-fronted monsters with escalators running everywhere, like a hamster habitat for humans.

"Don't the people in the COREs come out?" he asked. "I haven't seen anybody so far who looks poor."

"Not often. It costs money to cross a district boundary."

"You have to pay to go from district to district?"

"Sure. A user fee, really, to pay for the security. About five dollars, most places."

"Hmmm." Five dollars wasn't much, but any charge at all seemed high just for the privilege of leaving your neighborhood. "Speaking of money, I know I can do wonders with this peanut in my wrist, but how do I get some actual cash?"

"Cash?" Night frowned. "You mean, paper currency?"

"Yeah. You know, spending money."

"Oh, we haven't had physical money for decades. Too much crime associated with it, too hard to track." She glanced out the window. "Boundary coming up."

At the boundary between the Orange Coast and Long Beach districts, they disembarked and passed through a large gateway. Except for the armed Homeland Security officers and flat scanner panels, it was much like queuing up to enter Disneyland. They passed through and boarded another streetcar on the other side.

As it pulled away, Toby glimpsed the blue glow of the boundary wires through gaps in the foliage.

Seaport Plaza was a vast shopping and entertainment center built onto a gargantuan concrete breakwater that thrust out into the Pacific. Standing at the railing, Toby looked down at the surge of the surf, thirty feet below. Waves hit hard enough that there was a constant light drizzle out at the edge, and the walkway was wet. "Aren't you cold?" he asked.

"Thermo-ply. Looks thin, but it's warm." She wiggled. "Almost too warm for today."

They played VR arcade games, where a full-body suit and goggles immersed you in another, very convincing world (though if you cast your head to the side quickly, you could catch the static edge around the corner of the 3-D figures). A department store proved to be exactly like the department stores of the 20th, except for 3-D digicast displays that jumped right out at you in their effort to sell new products.

Toby'd never been one for shopping.

Back at the railing over the seawall, he was halfway through his Thai sate burrito when he stopped in mid-bite. "*RatBot?*" he asked, amazed.

He bent down. The insectoid 'bot near his feet wasn't the original Rat, but it was clearly a grandchild. *OSMOCORP VX-80* was emblazoned on its shell. He reached out a hand.

"Don't touch it!" Night said.

"Why not?"

"It's a police unit. They carry little stunners, in case something happens out here before the police can get here. You shouldn't mess with them."

Toby straightened up. "I helped invent the first version of those."

"Great." She shuddered. "They give me the creepers."

She slid her arm through his, snuggled up alongside him. It felt more than just friendly, and Toby wondered what he had done to deserve this.

Of course, he didn't deserve to be five million dollars in debt, either, so he decided to take the good with the bad.

Night furrowed her brow. "Is that the term, the creepers?"

"Close enough." They strolled down the walk, but Toby couldn't help giving a glance back at the 'bot. Ridiculous, of course, but it seemed like it ought to recognize him.

⫸⫷

"We can if you really want to," Night said, surveying the line outside the cineplex.

"You sound like you'd rather not."

"No. No, I don't mind. Something short would be okay, I guess. But the crowd…"

Toby looked around. Mainly teenaged boys. "You're afraid they'll be rowdy, or dangerous, or loud, or—"

"No, I'd just rather not see the kind of—oh, wait a minute. I forgot. Actually, this should be interesting for you. But this is such a downmarket place that they'll have commercials…"

Night bought two tickets for *SeaFire II*. "Do I need to have seen *SeaFire One*?" Toby asked.

"I haven't. But it's the shortest one; forty-five minutes."

It was 3-D digicast projection, of course, but the technology was far more impressive on the big screen. It was fast-paced and choppy, with astounding special effects, but Toby had a hard time following it; it seemed to have been scripted by someone who did music videos. It involved speedboats and narcoterrorists, and the speedboats flew straight out of the screen at your face, as did the breasts of the women (who were constantly disrobing).

Toby's admiration for the female form was nearly boundless, but even he had to admit that having an areola ten feet in diameter jab its warhead-sized nipple in your face wasn't all that appealing. The first time it happened, he heard Night laughing; she was watching him, not the movie.

Then, suddenly, a commercial break. Most of the audience headed for the snack bar, but at Toby's insistence the two of them stayed in their seats and watched. Rapid-fire, aggressive, loud. Ads for jeans, for cars, for VR games, but very little that couldn't have been foreseen in the late 20th.

Until they came to the final commercial. It was quieter, less glossy, almost like a public service announcement. The face of a handsome middle-aged man. "When I first got sentenced, I thought I'd lost it all." The camera pulls back, showing that he is dressed in blue cotton, sitting on a bed, a barred window above. "My career, my house…my *family*.

"But then I found out about TGB Corrections. At TGB, you can get the training you need to restart your life when you get out. You keep a high proportion of your earnings. And, in many cases, your family can join you, with job opportunities for your spouse, and a great educational package for your kids."

The camera cuts to a wall of the cell where, through a doorway, a woman is tucking two sleepy children into their beds. She turns to the camera, strikingly beautiful and perfectly groomed, and tiptoes forward, pulling the door shut behind her.

The camera cuts back to the man's face. "And best of all," he says meaningfully, "the kids get their own room." An elegant female hand runs through his hair and then pulls him down out of the frame. His head pops back up, his hair mussed, lipstick smeared on his cheek. He winks. "*Thanks*, TBG!" His head is pulled back out of the frame, this time by two arms around his shoulders.

Voiceover: "Do you know someone who needs to get back together? Tell them to ask about transferring to TGB Corrections. TGB: Keeping American Families Together."

Then a very quick, quiet voiceover: "Family reunification program available only to inmates with skills levels rated P-5 and above, additional draws on pay may be required for educational opportunities for dependents, transfers may not be available in all states or across certain federal boundaries or in the case of certain crime classifications or sentence lengths. Offer void where prohibited by local legislation."

"And now, we return to our Feature Presentation."

Toby exhaled. "Now that gave *me* the creeps."

"So it's *creeps?*" Night asked, talking loud over the roar of a speedboat. "Not *creepers?*" She crossed her arms and scooted deeper into her seat, dissatisfied. "You should correct me when I say it wrong. I'm trying to get it right, you know."

"Now comes the fun part," Night said. "Now we get to see the same film again."

"I don't really want to see that movie again."

"Trust me. *Epiglottis.* Pubcab. Cab for two to Lakewood Cinema Forty-Four, please…"

The pubcab came, but they had traveled no more than a mile when the cab slowed and pulled over to the side of the street. "Shit," Night said.

"What's up?"

"We're being sidelined. The police are after somebody."

Toby looked down the avenue. The center of the road was empty; all the pubcabs lined the edge, some pulled in as if they were angle parked. "How far is it to where we're going?"

"About two more miles."

"Can we walk?"

Night chuckled. "We can't even get out of the car. It's a lockdown." She looked at her watch. "We've got fifteen minutes. Maybe they'll be done by then."

An armored pumpkin seed, about twice the size of a four-seater pubcab, whizzed down the center of the road. *LOVUPD* glowed in blue letters on the door. "So," Toby said after a minute, "I don't suppose they have many car chases in movies anymore."

When the pubcab moved again, it delivered them to the Lakewood Collection. The Collection was calm, sparsely occupied, and obviously very expensive. Most of the patrons were well-dressed women.

"Pay attention," Night said. She bought two tickets to *SeaFire II*. "This will be different."

"No commercials?"

"No commercials, but that won't be the only contrast."

There was only a scattering of viewers, most of them female, sitting in groups of three and four.

It was a completely different movie. Some of the plot points were the same, and it was still about speedboats and narcoterrorists, but the violence was toned down and the sex played a far bigger role: longer, steamier scenes, with far less flesh exposed. The ocean, instead of being used for high-speed chases and collisions, was more of a rolling, tidal backdrop to longing glances and passionate kisses.

By the time the movie was over, it was dark outside the theater. Toby said, "So they film different versions for different audiences? They were starting to do that back in the twentieth—the movie *Fatal Attraction* had a different ending in Japan than in the US."

Night shook her head. "More complicated than that. They film all kinds of possibilities, and what happens at a showing depends on how the audience is reacting. The seats in the theaters read pulse rates, galvanic skin response, respiration. When the audience gets excited by something, it does more of that thing; when they get bored, it does less."

"You mean if we went back to the first theater, we'd see a different film again?"

"Probably. So lots of times, you check out the audience before you buy tickets, decide if you want to see the movie they want to see."

"Suppose you want to see the same movie twice?"

"Wait for the home video release and pick the sequence you want from the menu. Let's go slumming, okay?"

Slumming meant heading back to the coast just north of Seaport Plaza. Wharf Street at first looked like a seedy waterfront, but on inspection

Toby saw that the dim lights and grime were all deliberate, phony as a Disney ride. Taverns and shops were all done up to exude menace and mystery, but the patrons wandered the cobbled sidewalks as if they were at any shopping mall.

Night led him across the street to a bar fronted in dark wood. Above the entry, a sign: *Tanner's Tobbo Shop: We Never Sleep.* "What's a tobbo shop?" he asked.

"A place that serves both drinks and shims. This one's my favorite—probably the oldest one around."

They stepped up onto the curb. "Shims? And what's *tobbo* mean?"

"Shims, mood-modulators. Tobbo, I'm not really sure. I think it's a Thai word."

Just inside the dark doorway a man in a sailor's striped jersey stopped them. Night obediently turned her forearm upward. The man waved a thick wand over her ID peanut and squinted, reading a display panel at the base of the gadget.

He stashed the wand in a holster, wrapped a white plastic bracelet around Night's wrist, and peeled a series of stickers from a sheet and pasted them onto the bracelet, red, green, pink, violet. He made a gesture of dismissal and turned to Toby.

Toby offered his forearm. The sailor scanned it and frowned at the display. "Something's gotta be screwed up with his peanut. Guy's got no strictures, no mandies."

"It's correct," Night said. "He really doesn't."

"Hmmph." The man clipped a bracelet onto Toby's wrist and started peeling stickers from the sheet and pasting them onto the circumference. "Not my problem. But the thing's definitely jacked off. I mean, it lists his year of birth as 1971."

Toby entered Tanner's Tobbo Shop with a rainbow of stick-ons encircling his wrist.

17 | It Took Her All of Two Minutes to Make a Liar of Him

The menu at Tanner's consisted of a roster of cocktails, nonalcoholic and alcoholic displayed on facing pages. An insert listed "Favorite Shims." Toby strained to read the series of meaningless names by the candlelight.

A waiter in a pirate outfit sauntered up to the table. "I'm Chip, and I'll be delivering your grog this evening. What are we starting with?"

"Dirty martini," Night said, "with a double Pink Verdance."

Chip widened his eyes in appreciation. "That'll loosen your joints." He peered at her bracelet, nodded, and punched the order into a palm unit. He looked at Toby. "And you?"

"I guess I'll have the same."

Chip laughed, and then a puzzled expression spread on his face as he realized Toby might have been serious.

"It's definitely a girl drink," Night said.

"Oh." Toby felt himself blush. "Well, what's a boy drink, then? Order me something."

"What cocktails do you like?"

"Gin and tonic?"

"Good. Gin-tonic for my friend, then, with a Gunmetal Slap."

"His Slap a double too?"

"Mmmm, maybe a single to start, see if he likes it."

Chip glanced at the band on Toby's wrist, then leaned down for a closer look. He whistled. "Dross! Guy can have pretty much anything, can't he?"

Toby's drink had a definite blue tinge, but there was nothing pink about Night's martini. They clinked glasses and Toby took a sip. A good, strong G&T, with an odd underlying sensation of heat. "How do you like it?" Night asked.

He took a long draw at it, felt a warm buzz troll down his throat and into his belly. "I think I like it." He closed his eyes, paid attention to his body. "Maybe a lot."

Night asked him about his life back in the 20th. At first he was reluctant to bore her with everyday details, but her absorbed expression seemed genuine. Every time he paused in his narrative, she renewed her questions: Was it true that you could go anywhere you wanted? Did Toby know how to fly a plane? Had he ever been to a National Park, another country, a protest rally, a riot?

In the candlelight, Night's face glowed with a smooth beauty, and with something more, something that to Toby looked almost like admiration. She was riveted by his descriptions of breaching computer security systems in his teens; she was fascinated by his stories about growing up in a family with a deaf parent, and dozens of deaf friends. At some point he realized that he was starting to sign along with his speech, a tendency he had when he got drunk, and he deliberately reined in his gestures.

Night tipped the last of her martini into her mouth. She sighed. "I wish I'd been alive in the twentieth. It just sounds so, so free…"

"So tell me about what you do," Toby said. "What's your doctoral research about?"

She explained, but it rapidly went over Toby's head. Contemporary psychology seemed to be based on a whole new terminology; he felt like someone from the Middle Ages listening to a Freudian. He let the jargon wash over him and just gazed. Her intellect was more formidable than he had realized, and the passion she showed for her subject matter made her even sexier.

"But if you want more than that," she concluded, "you'll have to take one of the intro classes." She put the glass down and tapped the rim. "I think I'd like another of these. You? Want to go for a double Slap this time?"

He hadn't realized he'd drained his glass some time before. He felt more inebriated than he ought to be from one drink, but also quite alert. He worried for a moment about being sober enough to drive, and then realized that he didn't need to drive, that nobody drove, that he'd probably never drive again. He laughed. "Sure."

The double Slap in the second drink was unmistakable—hot wasn't exactly the world, more like a pulsation. "So these are for boys, huh? Well, my virility can probably use a boost…"

He described his abortive sex with Spengler's wife, carefully at first, watching Night's reaction, and then, as her eyes told him to go on, detailing the encounter more specifically. She interjected a few exclamations of dismay, but waited until he said, "So, if I get kicked out of the cottage, that's probably why," before she began talking.

She doubted that Spengler would find out, doubted he would care if he did; "Garrett and Tabitha" went their own ways sexually. She made it clear she'd never cared for Tabitha, a spoiled, over-amped, aimless, upper-class brat, but she assumed that even Tab would have had the grace and good sense to explain a few things to someone who was from another time. "No contract, no safety… Sends so much blood to her boobs that there's none left for her brain." She caught Toby's frown. "Hey, I've seen her in a swimsuit—pumps herself up to freakshow levels."

"Pumps herself up? You mean her, um, breasts aren't real?"

"Well, they're auggies… Oh. You probably don't know what I'm talking about. Augmentations. Cosmetic enhancements. You have tissue implants that let you, well, swell up."

"What? Like implanted balloons?"

She giggled. "No. Same principle as an erection—spongy tissue that can go into states where more blood flows in than out. Pumps up."

"Is everybody like that? I mean, is it common?"

"Pretty common, at least among those who can afford it. And Tab is such an upper-class bitch that she's probably never seen an unenhanced penis before."

"Have you?"

She blinked. "Well that's kind of a direct question."

"Sorry."

"I don't mind. I kind of like it."

"Well, then: have you seen *unenhanced* penises before?"

"Yeah. I grew up as a COFfer, so I didn't know many people with money until I was in my twenties. Didn't have much money until then, either. So I haven't had very many enhanced lovers."

"You really haven't told me much about yourself. Isn't it your turn now?"

She shook her head. "Later."

"Well, at least tell me—are *you* augmented?"

Even in the candlelight he could see her blush. "I've had some work done… You're a strange guy, Toby. Most men wouldn't tell you about something that was that, well, sort of embarrassing, as your thing with Tabitha."

Toby took a drink, licked his lips. "Hey, you want embarrassing…"

He told her how he died.

Once she realized it was okay to laugh, she laughed very hard.

She ordered another round of drinks and excused herself to go to the bathroom.

He watched her as she came back. Her walk was controlled, not the weaving ramble of someone who's had too much to drink, but her joints were loose and wobbly. Pink Verdance, he supposed. She looked happy to be in her body.

After she slid into her seat, he said, "So you've had cosmetic surgery. What did you look like before? I mean, bigger nose, or different eyes, or…?"

"Oh, I didn't have anything done to my face. The face, I was born with."

"That's hard to believe," he said.

"Gah." She looked down at her drink. He couldn't tell if she were embarrassed, confused, or distracted. "Am I making a big mistake here?"

"What do you mean?"

"I mean, am I getting into something with you that—I mean, am I doing something here that's going to…mess you up?"

He reached across the table and put his hand on hers. "God, I sure hope so."

Her condo was on the top floor of a fancy six-story building a couple of miles from the Goversity. They'd kissed and explored one another in the pubcab, the shims fueling his desire, but it took a few minutes to get going again after the elevator ride up to her unit. Toby had pretended to admire the prints on the living room walls before she dimmed the lights to half-intensity and pulled him over to the couch.

At first she sat beside him as they kissed, but after only a moment she pulled her mouth and edged away from him. He tried to pull her back, and she said, "Wait, just...wait. I don't want to do a Tabitha on you here." She slowed her breathing. "Do you want to sign any kind of contract, or do you want a video..."

"Huh?" he managed to gasp.

"Any kind of contract affirming that what we're doing is consensual, and—"

"Of course it fucking is," he said, and tried to pull her back to him. She kissed back for a moment, her tongue swirling in his mouth, and then she withdrew again.

"—video?" she asked, in a pant. "You, want, any—video?"

"Does it turn you on?" he asked. "Whatever you like, anything you like, hey, don't be embarrassed, I'm into *anything*..."

"No...I meant..." She clamped back onto him, kissed him deeply, pulled back. "I meant, legally, for the record, in case there's any dispute about, well, what happened..."

"God. You people are nuts. Let's just do it, whatever you want is okay with me, let's—just—*do* it—" He put his hand behind her head, winched her mouth in to lock lips with his.

She pulled away. "Okay, but—"

"No more. Please. No more."

"Don't you want a safety?"

This puzzled him enough that he stopped for a moment, and said, "A *what*?"

"A word that means *no*. A word that means *stop*. A safety word."

He exhaled a heavy breath. "I thought *no* meant *no*."

"That'd be pretty boring, wouldn't it?"

Toby thought for a moment that he might scream, then controlled himself. "Fine. What word do you usually use?"

"Cranium."

"Great. Cranium means no. Cranium, epiglottis, whatever, *what-the-fuck-ever*. I'm *not* going to say *no*, I guarantee you!"

As if this was enough, Night moaned and flung one leg up to roll over and sit astride him. His hands traveled over her catsuited body, but the fabric was thicker than he had thought, and his hands quickly moved to her neck, her arms, her face, the few exposed parts of her body. "You twentieths are so passionate..." She rolled her head to the side, kissed and licked his caressing fingers. "So," she whispered into his ear, "you like to watch? You want to toss yourself off a balcony for me?"

"Just say the word."

"Wait. Just wait a minute—"

She hoisted herself off of him, and ran through the door to her bedroom. He heard the flush of a toilet. Some things hadn't changed: women still needed to urinate at critical moments.

He listened to the sounds from the other room—bathroom door, drawers, indefinable noises.

When she came back into the living room she was dressed in a white camisole and light-blue panties. There was a moment of doubt in her eyes, a moment of shyness, but standing in the doorway she took him in, the stiff bulge in his pants, the awe in his expression, and she jacked her hip out to the side and sat one hand on it, leaning her shoulder on the doorframe.

"So," she said, "is this okay?" His stupefied, adoring gaze answered her question. "How do you want me?"

Toby swallowed. "Any way you want..." he managed to say, in a raspy voice.

Her hand moved off her hip, and she squeezed her graceful biceps in along the side of her chest, squeezed with a practiced little twisting motion. Her camisole rose and pointed out, her nipple straining through the fabric; her breast grew larger, fuller, more weighty, with every beat of her heart, the blood flooding in with every move of her pulse. It protruded farther and farther until it seemed freakish, and she ground her upper arm against her torso and the swelling abated.

She straightened up from the wall, performed the same magic on the other side. Toby liked breasts—who could have anything against them?—but he wasn't obsessed with size; whatever size and shape they happened to be was fine with him, and less was just as good if not better than more. But the fact that Night, Night with that elegant, intelligent face, was doing this to thrill him, was so arousing that he was afraid he might explode.

She'd been watching him, and gave a malicious, self-possessed little smile. She jerked her hip to the side and bumped it against the doorframe, and her lips twisted out of the smile for the shortest moment, and then she started walking toward him, Kali the destroyer, centered and focused, fully inhabiting her body.

At the couch she swiveled round and bent forward, showing him the swell of her hips under the panties, her right buttock protruding farther than her left.

Her left hand reached back, moved up and down the curve of her hip. She raised her hand and smacked herself, harder than was needed based on her previous maneuvers, and her left buttock started to inflate, pulse by pulse, and Toby felt his breath move in time with her heartbeat.

"Cranium…" he gasped.

A worried glance back. "You don't like it?"

"I like it too much." Toby stopped to pant. "I think I'm going to die."

After a quick, tortured discussion on the subject of condoms—no longer needed, no longer even available—they moved to her bedroom. With both of them naked on her bed, Toby immediately slid southwards and went down on her, his tongue working hard. At one point, she pulled his head up by his hair and demanded, "How do you want me?" apparently meaning her level of inflation.

"Any way I can have you," he answered at first. When there was no reaction, he said, "Anything."

"But what do you *want?*" she asked.

"*You,*" he managed to gasp, and buried his face back in the slick musk between her legs.

Her hips twisted and moved beneath his mouth and he ejaculated, neither pleasantly nor with regret. He softened a little, and moments later his genitals were cemented to the sheet. At that instant it was of no consequence: all his being was focused somewhere between Night's thighs, his mouth and tongue working, his fingers probing and coaxing.

Some time later, one of his hands traveled up her belly, found one of hers aimlessly massaging in the region of her ribs. He tugged her hand down, pressed her fingers against her clitoris, let loose. She moaned and her body sagged a little.

In Toby's view, the female body was a vast playground. No man yet born had enough penises, hands, and mouths to engage it on its own terms, so if the owner herself could be invited in as an active participant, it was a step—a giant leap—in the right direction.

Some women reacted with horror to this concept.

Others responded as if they had caught sight of the True Grail.

Night fell into the latter category. As if she'd been waiting for permission, her hands were all over herself, roaming yet purposeful. Toby's hands slid up to her breasts and felt that, beneath their hard nipples, they had deflated to their original, modest dimensions.

For some reason this stiffened him. He felt the skin of his cock tear away from the automucilage that glued it to the sheet.

One of her hands tugged at his hair, pulling him upward. He ignored it, tonguing her. Then he felt hands on either side of his head, grasping his ears, pulling, fingernails digging in.

He gave in and let his tongue track all the way across her belly, her sternum, and up to her mouth. Her deliberate hand wrapped around his cock and fitted him into her wet center.

Her moan of pleasure was not quite loud enough to drown his.

Once he was all the way inside her, she started clenching her muscles, a long roll from deep inside to out, like the fingers of a hand squeezing from index to little finger and back again.

He moved with her for a while, but the sensation overwhelmed him; he could feel the leakage of an unwilling, unsatisfactory second ejaculation. "Cranium," he whispered. "Cranium!"

He pulled out and rolled onto his side.

"I'm sorry," Night said, "was I hurting you?"

"No, no… Too good…that rolling thing…"

"The mega-Kegel?"

"Whatever…"

"Should I stop it?"

"No. No no no no no. Just wait a second." He wiped sweat from his face, leaned over and kissed her. He took a minute to regain his breath.

With one-and-a-half ejaculations behind him he could cope better, and when he slid inside her again he was aroused but not on the verge of losing control. More evenly matched now, they rode the waves of each other's excitement, trying different positions and angles, and three times Toby thought she was ready to climax.

The fourth time he was sure; her hands were on his hips, pulling him down into each quick thrust. When he was on the edge of exploding, her hands left his hips, clenched into fists, and hammered the bed. "Shit," she gasped. "God*damn*it."

He stopped moving. "What's wrong?"

"I'm sorry." She panted, trying to slow her breath. "It's these fucking pills, the Daviril, they make it fucking impossible to come." Her hands went back to his hips, pulled him into her again. "Go ahead and finish," she whispered. "Don't wait for me…"

He rolled off of her. "Can I do something? Something else?"

"No. When it gets like this, I can't even do myself." She tugged at his shoulder. "Come on."

He shook his head. "Nope. If you're not going to come, then I'm not going to come."

"Oh yeah?" She pushed her face into his, showing a toothy smile. "Wanna bet?" Her hands slid down to his hard cock.

It took her all of two minutes to make a liar of him.

Despite the fact that it was his orgasm, not hers, it gave her some sort of release. She slid her face back up his torso until they were side by side again. She tugged the sheet up over them, gave him a sleepy semen-scented kiss, and snuggled down against him. In a matter of minutes, he heard the tiniest hum of a snore.

For the first time since his death, Toby was happy.

18 | Sorting Shit All Day Sounds Like a Great Idea

The thing about prison, Ottmar Hernandez-O'Brien decided, is that it's predictable. He spent much of his time angry—angry at the politicians, angry at the guards, angry at UNICOR, angry at himself for the years he had spent as a voter, not questioning the evil system that had now consumed his life—but beneath the anger, and beneath the mourning for his lost family, there was a strange sort of peace. The BeverlyWood entertainment business had been dizzyingly uncertain; even as nothing more than a lawyer to the studios, you could be on top one day, and on the street the next.

As an unskilled laborer—how he would love to smash that UNICOR rep's face—he had been sent to Montana to work at the Western Recycling Depot. Next to the cellblocks, on the flat, cold plain, freight cars from all over the western US dumped their non-organic waste. Bulldozers spread it out over several acres, and white-suited convicts like Ottmar, wearing gas masks against possible contamination, poked through the rubbish.

Ottmar's job was easy enough: look for ferrous metals. If a magnet sticks, you've found it; carry it to a bin, or, if it's too massive, send for a lift. Others had more demanding quests—aluminum, particular kinds of plastics, reusable parts. For these complex tasks, they earned a dollar more than Ottmar's three dollars an hour. It all could have been automated, but why bother when convict labor was close to free?

Three dollars an hour, eight hours a day, six days a week. Of his three dollars an hour, two dollars an hour went right back to UNICOR to pay for his upkeep. Of the remaining forty-eight dollars a week, he kept twenty-four for his own expenses and sent the other twenty-four back to Lorelei and the kids. It wasn't much, but it made him feel like he still had a family.

The cellblocks abutted the huge sorting grounds on the east. To the south and west, there was nothing more than an alarm wire—the empty, cold plains beyond the wire were barrier enough. On the north ran the electric fence that formed the coast-to-coast barrier between Canada and the US.

Enough voltage to kill you, and every so often the scurry of a patrolling RatBot, but Ottmar still looked at it wistfully; in the evening you could see the lights of a small Canadian town in the distance, and he imagined it as an old-fashioned kind of place, a place out of a Jimmy Stewart movie, where a man could arrive with nothing and start over again…

The sun went down late this far north, and he was surprised when the five-o'clock whistle sounded. The guards moved to the western perimeter and began working their way back toward the cellblock, picking their way through the piles of twisted metal and plastic, making sure no one was hiding. More of a convention than a necessity; every ID peanut had a GPS. The prison computer could tell in a second if anyone was missing, and then pinpoint where the felon had gone.

In the cafeteria, Ottmar took his tray to a table and sat a few seats away from anyone else. Until a week ago, he would have eaten with Barney, his cellmate, but now Barney was gone: UNICOR had discovered that he had some kind of colorectal cancer, and rather than pay for treatments, they'd paroled him. Barney had been an art-history professor somewhere in Pennsylvania before he was convicted on a sedition charge, but he was headed to ComptonCORE to die. "Hear their GrayTown has a great hospice, and hell, it might be years before I'm gone. At least the weather'll be better."

Ottmar hadn't spent a winter in Montana yet, but everyone assured him it was hell. UNICOR didn't believe in heating individual cells, only the common areas, and most inmates saved up to buy extra blankets.

At present it was still warm enough, though, and Ottmar reclined on his bedspread, reading an entertainment magazine. The door was still propped open: lockdown wasn't until ten.

Goldberg, one of the swing-shift guards, looked in the doorway. "O'Brien. Got you some company." He ushered in a thin black man with a shaven head. "Firefly. This is O'Brien. He's your daddy now, so you do what he says until you get with the program. Bunk down and get some sleep. You hit the deck at five a.m. tomorrow."

"And suppose I don't want to *hit the deck* at five a.m. tomorrow?" Firefly asked, sitting down on the empty bed. "Whatcha gonna do? Send me to jail?"

"We can send you to Utah, if we feel like it. But feel free to stay in bed as long as you like, ace. You don't get up and work, we don't feed you. See ya tomorrow, COREboy."

Firefly waited until the guard's steps faded and asked, "Utah? Ain't that south of here? What's so bad about being sent south?"

Ottmar sat up, swung his feet to the floor. "It's where about ninety percent of the country's nuclear reactors are."

"So? Working in a power plant sounds better than sorting shit all day."

"Sounds better, maybe. But they had some big accidents down there about thirty years ago. Parts of the area are still so hot you can't go outdoors without a radsuit. And guess where they tend to send the convicts? Survival time is about three years."

"Whoa. Take it back, then. Sorting shit all day sounds like a great idea."

"So: Firefly. Why do you go by Firefly?"

"Because it's my name."

"Okay. Firefly *what*?"

"*What* Firefly, you mean. It's my last name."

Ottmar snorted. "Right. Rufus T., I suppose."

Firefly smiled. "An educated man. My momma loved *Duck Soup*, always sang 'Hail, Hail Freedonia' whenever the President appeared on digicast. My dad, wherever the hell he went, left me as Rufus Jackson.

Figured if I was going to be named after a head of state, why not a classy one, so when I turned eighteen I changed it. What do I call you?"

"My name's Ottmar Hernandez-O'Brien, but under the circumstances maybe Wolf J. Flywheel would be more appropriate."

"Suits me. What you in for, Wolf?"

"Giving money to a conservation organization."

"That's illegal?"

"Everything's illegal if the authorities see a chance to grab your money."

"Never my problem. Never had anything worth grabbin'."

"So how'd you end up in here?"

"A mistake, far as I can tell. Don't matter. What matters is, how we gonna get out?"

Ottmar laughed. "You mean *escape*?"

"You got it."

"There's no place to go out there…"

"How long you in for?"

"Fifteen years."

"And then you'll be, what? Fifty-five, sixty? And they'll dump you off in the CORE somewhere to die."

"I still have a family out there. When I'm done here, I'll go back to them."

Rufus studied him. "You say so. Me, I'm leaving the first chance I get. Maybe by then you'll want to come along."

Ottmar shook his head in wonder. "It doesn't work like that, you know. It isn't like some old movie, where you make a break for it. The place is designed to keep us in, they have all kinds of technology…"

Rufus leaned forward, confiding. "Let me tell you a secret. Living in the CORE, you see the government at its finest. Even the privatized stuff doesn't work worth a shit. The secret is this: There's fuckups in every system." He lay back on his bed, his hands behind his head. Ottmar thought he had finished, but a while later Rufus added, "So keep your toothbrush packed."

19 | Just Add Beer and CNN

At age thirty-three—or, technically, at one hundred eighteen—Toby had never been married. He had set sail on three live-together relationships in his twenties, but they had always foundered on the same shoals: his ingenuous nature, which, through less charitable eyes could be labeled immature, and his obsessive focus, which many women adored when directed at them, but came to hate when aimed at a computer program or a piece of electronics. He was aware of his shortcomings; he had learned, for example, that, "What? Sorry, I wasn't listening," was not the best possible answer to, "I swear, Toby, sometimes I think you've forgotten I exist." But awareness of his character flaws didn't mean he could change.

Even less did it mean that he wanted to change.

With Night, everything was different.

After some tentative circling, neither wanting to force themselves on the other, they started spending every other evening together. After two weeks, it migrated to *most evenings*—most evenings except Thursdays, when she disappeared about five o'clock, and didn't return until after nine. Another lover? A yoga class? Toby chose not to ask.

Night didn't seem to care if Toby spent hours immersed in learning the new languages for parallel processing. She had her own work to do—writing papers, reading journals, plowing through textbooks. Like a gender-reflected version of himself, once she was working, she was oblivious.

And once they were in bed together she was utterly present, body, mind, and imagination.

If only he could have met her a hundred years ago.

The only problem, as far as Toby was concerned, was the damned medication.

Sex toys hadn't advanced much since the 20th. When Toby considered it, he supposed they hadn't advanced all that much since the time of the Romans, with the single exception of adding battery-powered vibrations to the existing articles. Night had an extensive collection, but nothing that didn't have a close relative prior to 2000.

She was enthusiastic about sex, and her excitement had to be all too real, because when, time after time, she failed to reach orgasm, she seemed ready to explode. Her fists would beat at his back, his chest, the mattress beside her. He tried fingers, lips, tongue, every item from the back of her lingerie drawer; rougher, gentler, faster, slower, until one evening she began slapping wildly at him, forehand, backhand, even two hard blows across the face. He came, and she pushed him out and curled into a teeth-gritting ball on the sheets.

Eventually she uncurled, cursing the Daviril, and lay beside him, apologizing for the slaps.

"No problem. Kind of an extra charge, actually." He ran his hand down her flank, willing her to relax, caressed the golden pubic hair of her mons.

He frowned, looked up at the dark roots in her blonde hair. "Umm, Night?"

"Hmm?"

"Do you bleach your pubic hair?"

She laughed. "Who'd do that? That would be kind of a delicate operation."

"But the hair on your head has brown roots…"

"I dye my roots. The blonde is natural. Haven't you noticed that I'm way too white?"

"I like white. White people look more naked when they take off their clothes."

"Glad you like it. I'd tan if I could, but I'd be melanoma city."

"Don't they have a cure for that by now?"

"Yeah, but it's expensive, and insurance doesn't cover it."

He edged his head closer to hers. "So why do you do it? Dye your roots dark, I mean?"

She turned her face to him in puzzlement. "Pictures I see from the late twentieth, lots of blondes have their roots dyed brown. Don't you like it?"

He kissed her. "I love it. And I love it even more now that you've explained it."

The next day he researched Daviril. It was never mandatory, and he suggested she stop taking it. She resisted the idea, saying that her doctor thought she should give it a full year.

Daviril was a mood leveler, "indicated for mild euphorial or dysphorial episodes." In other words, if he knew his Greek, a medication intended to eliminate mild feelings of happiness or sadness.

People in the future were crazy.

He knew he shouldn't do it, but it felt right.

He found Night's bottle of Daviril capsules, twisted each cap open, and dumped the contents into a baggie. Then he replaced the meds with sugar, twisted each cap closed again, and put the bottle back on the shelf.

The bag of Daviril powder he kept, just in case.

When Toby received a summons to Spengler's office, he felt like a third-grader on the way to the principal. Was Spengler angry about Toby's fruitless dalliance with Tabitha? Did he think Night and Toby were getting too involved? Was he dissatisfied with Toby's interviews and work progress? Was the stipend, and with it, the deferment of five million dollars of debt, about to end?

Spengler's office was huge, appointed in a style more appropriate for the Permanent Secretary for Colonial Affairs than a professor. Big, heavy furniture of leather and dark wood; a sepia-toned globe. Toby was positive that if he looked, everything from Pakistan to Myanmar would be in one color, labeled *India*.

Spengler received him affably, sat him in a bulky chair. "Two things. First of all, now that you seem fully recovered, we were wondering if you'd mind doing a few news interviews. There were a few press releases right after your revival, but I know the media would like to see you in the flesh—there's never been anyone from so long ago successfully revived."

Compared to the possibilities Toby had imagined, this ranked as pleasant. "Fine with me, if you recommend it."

"I do. A little publicity never hurts. Now, as for my second request... I know this is quite, well, unspecific in nature. Night's been keeping me apprised of your progress, but I wanted to ask you in person—what's your impression of modern America so far, generally?"

It was said in a causal tone. Spengler drifted around behind his huge oak desk, straightened the blotter.

"I'm not sure," Toby said, "exactly what you mean."

Spengler smiled. "It's not a test. I genuinely want to know what you think so far. Technology, for example—are you amazed, disappointed, surprised...?" When Toby didn't reply, he added, "Don't be afraid of offending me. I'm not looking for a particular answer."

"Well," Toby said, "there's been a lot of changes. The medical technology that brought me back is pretty amazing. And the holographic projections you use for computer monitors and digicasting..."

"But?"

"But—I don't know how to put this—I'm actually surprised at how little has changed. I'm not boasting when I say I'm good at computers—I know for a fact I am—but I shouldn't be able to just walk in after an absence of most of a century and get out toward the cutting edge of computer programming in a matter of weeks."

"Perhaps you just have a genius for such things."

Toby sat shaking his head side to side, having forgotten to be nervous. "No. It's everything, not just that. Imagine if someone from 1900 woke up at the end of the twentieth—it would be like they'd entered another universe. Freeways and movies and stereo and spaceflight and antibiotics and air-conditioning and computers and— and, well, just a whole world of new things. And so far, there isn't one single technological development here that I couldn't have imagined in 1980."

Spengler circled around, hitched his hip up on the corner of his desk. "And why do you suppose that is?"

"I don't know. Maybe the rate of change has slowed down because it just has to; I mean, nothing's exponential forever. Maybe most of the key technological innovations had already been made by the end of the twentieth…"

"Do you believe that?"

Toby hesitated. "No. No, there were plenty of frontiers left to be crossed when I died. Where's quantum computing? The transport system—it's nicer, it's cleaner, but there's nothing really new about it; I mean, where the heck is teleportation? And the little camera surveillance systems, and the RatBots, and this GPS ID thingie in my arm—those were all either developed or well underway when I died."

"And?"

"I don't know. Feels like somebody dropped the ball."

"Interesting." Spengler stood and held out his hand; Toby rose and shook. "Thanks for your time, Mr. Simmons. You've been doing some thinking. I urge you to keep it up." He ushered Toby to the door with a hand on his shoulder. "And, by the way: Some day down the road, I might ask you to share some of these insights with a few select friends. Would that be a problem?"

Toby shrugged. "No problem. Any time." If Spengler paid him for off-the-cuff, poorly thought-out criticisms of the world he lived in, then it was the easiest money he'd ever earned. Back in the 20th, any clown in any bar provided that for free.

Just add beer and CNN.

It took his cock, his mouth, both of his hands, both of her hands, and two high-tech vibrating devices, but at last, five days after she had unknowingly stopped the Daviril, Night finally orgasmed.

When she stopped gasping, she cried. A moment's panic for Toby—*uh-oh, maybe she was on that drug for a reason*—but this faded when he saw her tears were tears of relief.

Her physical release shook other things loose, too. Until then, she had been full of questions about his life in the 20th, questions that might be personal interest or might be related to her dissertation; but she had been reticent about her own past.

Now she recounted the two-hour version of her life story.

Toby followed it and yet did not—like hearing the story of someone who grew up in some far land, in a different culture.

Night's parents had been professors at Stanford—her mother a biologist, her father an historian. They'd been sent to prison when she was four. The charges included seditious agitation, violation of hate-speech statutes, drug possession, and child pornography.

"Drug possession and child pornography?" Toby asked.

"They always throw those in."

"So what did they really do?"

"I have no idea, really. Probably something to do with the Founding Fathers. My uncle says my father was big on circulating original writings by Jefferson, Paine, and Franklin."

"Is that against the law?"

"Not really. It all has to do with what the court decides you were circulating them for."

Her parents had been sentenced to thirty years. "They're probably out by now on early release—the Corrections industry doesn't like to keep you when you get old." She'd been sent to one of the COFfer farms, the big juvenile facilities the Fed ran for children whose parents had been put away.

She'd become unruly; by puberty she was violent, all battering fists and kicking feet. They'd started her on mood-control drugs early, but, "The mandies they put you on in federal care are pretty crude. I can still remember drooling into my oatmeal, watching it descend in these long glassy threads, but too stupid to do anything…"

Then, a surprise. When she was fourteen her father's brother, Uncle Trey, who'd been imprisoned well before she was born, had contacted her with an offer of adoption.

Trey Enderhew had served half his time, and bought his way out of prison with an important pharmaceutical patent. Although UNICOR had kept all of the patent rights in exchange for an early parole, Trey proved to be a fount of biochemical inventiveness; while he never started his own company, his salary plus incentive pay from Johnson-Lilly-Wellcome was enough to support him, and Night, and his long string of live-in girlfriends, in high fashion.

From a drooling COFfer who'd let boys—and not a few girls— have their way with her body in exchange for a few snorts of buzzer, Night had been transformed. A psychiatrist who specialized in "re-entry" problems supervised her move from the raw, hamfisted drugs of the Federal Children's Protection Service to a smoother, calmer set of mandies. She'd gone to the equivalent of charm school before entering the BeverlyWood Academy, and, although there might have been whispers about her past, these were children of movie people: What the hell did they care?

Properly fed and medicated, she'd bloomed; and she'd badgered Trey for the auggies that would allow her to keep up with the cheerleader-model-ingenue crowd.

"You don't need them," Toby said.

"You don't like them?"

"Well, it's like too much makeup—it's sexy that you're trying to be sexy, but it's not needed." He slid his hand down her flank. "Not at all." She pressed her hand down atop his.

But the biggest change had been intellectual. Without the brain-numbing drugs of Federal Protective, Night discovered she was smart. She fell on her lessons like a wolverine on roadkill, and they gave her about as much struggle: she sailed past her classmates, and went on to undergrad work at UC Berkeley, probably the most prestigious—and definitely the most expensive—private school in the nation.

"The UCs are private schools?" Toby asked.

"Sure." She seemed puzzled, then recovered. "Oh. Sure, the big privatizations. But didn't you already have those back in the twentieth?"

"I don't think so..." he said.

"Well, I don't want to argue with someone who was really there, but it seems to me that I learned that privatization started back in your era—the utilities, the prisons...then the postal system, public education..."

Her Cinderella story was derailed when Uncle Trey came down with cancer. Although his medical coverage from Johnson-Lilly-Wellcome was considered top-notch, his HMO insurance agreement specifically excluded coverage of cancer costs for anyone who carried any of the MG4-MG9 series of genes. After a few months, he was too sick to go to work; a few months after that, all of his funds were diverted to medical expenditures.

"So I came to the Goversity for grad work. Funny, really: started out as a COFfer, now I'm back at a school where most of the student body are COFfers. I just had kind of a long, cushy detour."

"So children of felons are entitled to college education?"

"If they're good enough to get in. Maybe five percent or so…"

"Amazing." He brushed his knuckles across her cheek.

"All my uncle's doing. I'd be dead by now, if it weren't for him, or in the back room at some COREhouse."

"COREhouse?"

"Some other time." She yawned.

"Your uncle must have been quite a guy."

"Still is, despite everything."

"He's alive?"

"Barely. Just barely. It's—oh, shit, it's terrible."

"Do you ever see him?"

"Every Thursday."

Ah. Thursday. "Can I come with you sometime?"

She breathed for a long time, almost as if she'd gone to sleep. "I… I don't think you should."

"I want to."

"Maybe." She reached over and patted his arm. "When I decided what to do with my life, I figured I wanted three things. A PhD. Somebody to love. A trip to Europe…not in that order." She was so sleepy she seemed drunk. "Have you ever been to Europe, Toby?"

"Of course."

"Tell me about it."

He did, but he had barely left England by hovercraft for France before he heard the gentle buzz of her snore.

He pulled the sheet over her, and crept out to her living room to prowl the 'Net.

Up until that night, Toby's time on the web had been spent prowling for information relevant to Architectural Objects, parallel processing, Adaptive Server Scripts, and Programmable Avatar Interfaces. He hadn't had the time, nor the inclination, to surf the web as in the old—the very old—days.

The addresses still read *www*, and *ww2*, and *wwn*, where *n* is any integer you prefer, but the *World-Wide* aspect of the *Web* seemed to be gone. Sites originating in Europe seemed to be blocked or not listed, even to the most diligent search engines. Ditto Russia, Canada, most of the Mideast, big swaths of Africa and Asia…

The *World* accessible to Toby on the 'Net seemed to be the US, most of Latin America, and China.

Lots of China.

Remembering his conversation with Spengler, he prowled through searches on physics, chemistry, computer science, even social control theory, a field that hadn't existed in his day.

Slim pickings indeed. Half of the references he picked up demanded a security access code before he could see the pages.

Most of the world was locked out of the Web—either that, or he was locked out of most of the world. Most topics other than entertainment and sports seemed to be hidden beyond a security wall. Even gardening seemed to be beyond the pale.

He was a child of the 70s, a teen of the 80s, so he shuddered to contemplate it. But there seemed to be no other choice: He needed to get up from the computer and go to the library.

20 | The Dragon Drew a Mighty Breath

Libraries were no longer friendly places.

The computer catalog was smart and easy to use. But huge sections of material were off-limits without authorization and "subject clearance," whatever that might be. A large percentage of history, biology, physics, and engineering books were "secure." As far as Toby could ascertain, chemistry books, without exception, required SSC—Special Subject Clearance.

The man behind the reference desk looked more like a dockworker than a librarian. "I help you?" he asked, without looking up from the book he was reading.

"Yes. I was hoping to find books on a number of topics, but the books I want all seem to require some sort of clearances. How do I go about getting those clearances?"

"If you were in a department where you needed 'em, they would have run background before the school admitted you."

"I see. So what do you do if you're just generally interested in a topic, not studying it?"

The man narrowed his eyes. "Like what?"

"Lots of things. For example, I know that most of the energy consuming devices nowadays run on fuel cells, but that really doesn't explain where the energy to make the hydrogen comes from, does it? So how do I find a book on the national energy system?"

The man slammed his book, glanced around the room. "Why would you need that?"

"Just curious."

"Yeah, right. You mind waving your ID over this little scanner?"

Toby held his wrist over a plate on the counter. The librarian read Toby's info on a hidden display, and grunted. "You ain't restricted, but you ain't cleared either. So you can check out anything that isn't SC, but you got nothin' here says you can see books on energy. So forget it, okay?"

At the end of an hour, Toby had found only one book he wanted that didn't require clearances: *Fundamentals of Social Control Theory* by Garrett R. Spengler.

He'd assumed that checkout would be automated, linked to his ID peanut, but instead he found that he had to sign a physical printout that read:

> I, the undersigned student of Government University, affirm that the book or books listed by call number at the base of this form, are being taken from the circulating collection for my own use only, in furtherance of my permitted education. I undertake to ensure that no unauthorized person will have access to these materials, and I will not lend, circulate, display, or allow other individuals to read or in any fashion consult the book or books I am taking into my possession. I furthermore understand that any and all records pertaining to my borrowing of materials, including but not limited to the identity and nature of the materials borrowed, the frequency and duration of my visits to the library, and the specifics of the items reviewed during any and all browsing of the library catalog, are being furnished to the IFBI, and may be furnished to other law enforcement agencies upon written request.

There are a million ways to crack into a computer network. Most of them involve brute force searching for passwords (running the dictionary) or password theft. Brute force had to be used with the greatest caution; most systems were smart enough to count failed attempts at log-in, and realize that someone was trying to breach security.

Theft was more straightforward, but inelegant. If someone was stupid enough to write down their password, they were asking for trouble, but it wasn't an admirable way to get in. One could also run an elephant, a program that passively stored the alphabetics coming in at a given monitor.

In cases where you were already on the system, as Toby was at the Goversity Computer Lab, you could afford to take your time on the details, unearthing the system architecture and its flaws bit by delicate bit, like a paleontologist brushing away the dirt from a precious fossil.

Getting to the system root was easy once he spotted the weakness. Once a day the system was *slept*, a massive dump of all memory onto a multi-terabit wafer.

The system-level files of the computer were jealously guarded, but for the hour or so where the wafer sat in the access drive after backup, the backup itself was vulnerable. From 2:00 a.m. until at least 3:00 a.m., the operating system might be safe, but the backup was wide open.

He didn't need to steal a password. He knew the sector where passwords and user IDs were stored. At 2:10 am, he simply made one up—*Draco*—included his user ID, composed it into binary, and wrote it out to the end of the staff list of authorized access codes on the backup wafer.

Down on the third floor there was a janitorial closet. He timed the pan of the hallway camera—the typical thirty-second sweep. He waited for the camera to pan away from him and past the closet, noted the time—2:15:39—and ran.

He got into the closet, shut the door, fumbled until he found the light switch.

He plucked a screwdriver and pliers from a pegboard on the wall. He undid the set-screws on the top housing of a huge floor waxer and probed its innards, looking for the leads where they touched down out the motor.

He wedged the metal bar of the screwdriver between the leads, bypassing the motor. He plugged the waxer into an outlet, and, holding onto the rubberized handles, used his thumb to flick the power lever to *ON*.

The waxer whined, the handles jerked from his hands, the lights dimmed, and the acrid smell of ozone filled the air.

He waited, listening. Nothing.

He unplugged the waxer, used the pliers to retrieve the screwdriver, clamped the top housing back into its mounting, and returned the tools to their places.

2:21:17 a.m. He waited until 2:21:45, just to be sure, then flipped off the lights and bolted from the closet.

The system was down for another ten minutes after the power surge, while the backups were restored.

When he logged in, this time he did it under his own user ID, but with the *Draco* password. It worked just fine.

If he couldn't figure out any other way to clear his debts, maybe he could start a computer security company.

He slept late the next morning, and didn't get in to the Lab until noon.

He held his breath as he logged in under the Draco password.

No problem. So far, it looked as if he were undetected.

The situation couldn't last forever, though. As his first task with system-level powers, he set about creating a half-dozen new user identities and passwords, then erased his own. He logged back in under a new identity, a nonexistent staffer, and spent some time covering his tracks.

Then he pulled on his VR goggles and called out his finest program to date: the Mirror Dragon.

He opened access to the individual partitions of RAM, and unleashed the Dragon on all of the computer users at once.

Those who weren't in VR space simply saw the system halt in midstride.

Those who happened to be doing VR architecture saw a dragon fly into their workspace and belch flames at their carefully crafted buildings. The fires ate away at the structures, the Architectural Objects crumbled, smoke masked the wreckage. Toby heard gasps from around the room. The dragon drew a mighty breath, and all of the flames, smoke, and debris rushed back into its maw, leaving the VR users in empty, black space.

But only for a moment. Every bit of code had been mirrored onto the system's flash RAM, and now the dragon belched the code back into VR space, the buildings appearing in the exact state of construction they had reached before the dragon had arrived.

The dragon stared every user in the eye, winked, then vanished in a fiery pop.

Toby ran the clean-up code that wiped the system log for the last ten minutes and replaced it with copies of boring transactions from earlier in the day.

He listened to the rush of speculation and argument around the room as people poked their heads out of their cubes, the people from VR-land trying to describe to screen users exactly what had happened.

He went back to working on a parallel processing algorithm.

About an hour later, two uniformed men from the campus office of Homeland Security came and took him back to their building. He brought Spengler's text along in case he needed something to read.

Toby wasn't sure exactly what law he might have broken. He certainly hadn't destroyed any property.

Well, maybe the floor waxer.

But who knew what the laws might be? If you believed Boots DeVore, pretty much everything was illegal. Deny everything, and then, if they really seem to have caught you, play stupid.

They left him sitting in a bleak concrete room for over an hour, presumably to make him nervous. He read Spengler.

Social control theory was all rather qualitative. One of the basic tenets was that while a single engineering innovation might have a massive impact on the technological structure of society, it required at least two social innovations to produce a major change in how society was controlled. *Laws alone are mere gestures—gestures that indicate what outcomes lawgivers would prefer*, Spengler wrote, *but lasting alterations in the balance of power between the public and the lawgivers always come from the conjugation of at least two new principles or precedents. In the past, the most important of these have come about unintentionally. It is the goal of social control theory to make the process of unifying precedents and principles into a lasting conjugation a deliberate and conscious societal process, rather than a series of accidents.*

Let's hear it for conjugation, Toby thought.

Spengler went on to give examples, and Toby began to see his point. In the 1970s, the US adopted the concept of asset seizure and forfeiture in the case of organized crime, and, later, in drug cases, organized or not. In the late 1980s the government introduced the concept of user fees as a funding mechanism for things like national parks and fast-tracking of drug approval by the FDA. Many commentators recoiled: Many of the poorest urban residents, who presumably had the greatest need for nature, were turned away from state and national parks by the simple cost of entry, and organizations like the FDA found over half of their funding coming from the drug companies they supposedly regulated. But that wasn't Spengler's point. It was the combination, the *conjugation* of these two developments, that fueled the seizure of assets as the primary source of government funding for law enforcement. By the 1990s, the DEA was pursuing drug criminals not on the basis of their importance to the drug trade, but rather what could be confiscated from the targets. In some cases, very minor drug crimes were pursued with huge volumes of government dollars, simply because the payoffs—houses, cars, bank accounts—were so large.

Spengler stressed the point that, at some level, the American public was governed by logic. Though he didn't put it that way, his essential argument was that if the public would swallow two flaky premises, then it would go along with the logical combination of the two, no matter how outrageous the outcome.

A Homeland Security officer came into the room. "Alright, my friend—time to talk."

Toby held up a hand. "Wait a sec."

Spengler had other conjugations: Privatization of government services plus victim restitution/required labor equals prison labor corporations as a major force in the national economy. Required drug-testing plus pre-emptive court-ordered medication equals mandatory medication for citizens, even without any criminal behavior. Passenger security fees for crossing boundaries plus centralized public housing equals enforced segregation by economic status…

"Do you know who I am?" the man demanded, sitting in a chair a few feet from Toby.

Toby looked at the man's SWAT-team outfit. *Berger* was stenciled on the chest. "Berger?" he asked.

"That's right. Now we've got you, got every record, so why don't you just tell us: What were you planning?"

"Planning?" Planning to goof around with the Lab computer system, obviously.

"The library gave us everything, and we saw each record you looked at—power plants, chemistry, social control, history. The complete profile of a terrorist. Now I warn you—the Federal government has sanctioned the use of physical compulsion in cases where we believe we can intervene to prevent an act of terror against national infrastructure." Berger stood up. "Unless you tell me exactly what you were up to, and who you were working with, I'm going to hurt you so bad you'll never walk again."

"Whoa, whoa, fella. This is about library books?"

"That's right."

"Did you check out my ID peanut?"

"Of course."

"Notice anything funny? Like my date of birth, for instance?"

Berger tilted his head like a bird eyeing a bug. He pulled out his ID wand, waved it over Toby's wrist. He read the output, read it again. "What kind of shit is this?"

"Maybe you should call Professor Spengler before you rough me up. You know, Spengler?" He shut the book, tapped on the cover. "*This guy?*"

The head of the local Homeland Security office apologized—surely Toby could understand, his behavior in the library was just so, so irregular…

By the time they escorted him back to the Lab, Night was in a frenzy. "Jenna Lizmore from SNN has been here more than fifteen minutes waiting for you. Everybody's getting crazy…"

To Toby's eyes, Jenna was dressed more like a dominatrix than a reporter, but she looked anything but dominant at that moment. The crowd from the Goversity Computer Lab had surrounded her, speechless in the presence of celebrity but unwilling to move away, and she looked as if she were holding her breath so as not to have to inhale their COFfer smells. The crowd around her looked misshapen by comparison, and beneath her latex-suited, sex-augmented, surgically improved façade, she seemed frightened of all the plainness pressing up near her.

The interview was short. Toby signed a release form, answered a couple of basic questions, and then heard Jenna ask, "So what do you think of the twenty-eighties so far?"

"To tell the truth, the first few days I was just glad to be alive. And then I went outside—blue skies, tropical foliage everywhere. Paradise on earth. But in the last few days I've seen more and more of what you've done to what used to be the greatest nation in history, and it makes me want to scream. From a free country to—to *this*. I can hardly believe it. I can hardly believe how you've screwed it up."

She asked a few more questions—who was his favorite new film star, what did he think of road hockey?—and when he failed to give interesting answers, she made a cutting gesture across her throat. "Load it up, guys."

Night caught her as she headed out the door. "When will it be on?" she asked.

"Ten tonight." She shot an ugly glance back at Toby, then shuddered as she saw the crowd of Goversity students pressed around him. "If they use any of it." She strode out into the hallway, her cameraman and makeup crew in tow.

21 | DIGICAST: Hutch Is Hung Like a Sheep

The SNN logo whirls onto the screen, with the voiceover "Super News Network—Nothing But the News You Need to Know NOW."

Cut to Hutchins, news anchor, bare-chested. His dark hair has been cut in a tonsure, but hangs down in bangs in the front.

Cut to Brooke, co-anchor, straps showing on bare shoulders. Her head is shaved except for a long, thick ponytail she tosses as the camera touches her.

Pull back to show that both are in swimsuits, under beach umbrellas, surf running high in the background. Urgent duh-duh-tadut-dah teletype music.

Camera zooms in on Brooke's face as she says, "In the top news story this hour, reliable sources tell SNN that superstar Kacey Jameson has checked into the Berkshire Clinic for even more lip enhancement." Pictures of Kacey, redhead, blonde, brunette, and bald, chase each other through a window in the lower corner. "This is the third time this year she has changed her look, and industry analysts suggest that slipping ratings mean she will be going for something really eye-popping this time around."

Cut to Hutchins. "Brooke, is there any early news about what kind of work Kacey's having done?"

Cut to Brooke. "We don't have anything yet, but we'll be following this story with continuous updates until all the facts are in… Zap the

Kacey tab for more pictures, but be warned—there may be some adult content if your digiscreen isn't Nannying."

Camera pulls back to show them both in banter mode. "It certainly sure can't be more auggies, can it, Brooke? When she's pumped, I can't believe there's blood left to run her brain as it is."

"You're a fine one to talk about auggies, Hutch, especially in a tight swimsuit like that."

"C'mon, Brooke, I've seen you at a few pileup parties…"

"Your dreamdrugs, Hutch. In other news, renewed fighting between Argentina and Chile over Tierra del Fuego has left thousands dead, and stopped all shipping within fifty miles of the Chilean coast. Zap the *Tierra del Fuego* tab for details."

"Tierra del Fuego—sounds like they're fighting over Mexican food, doesn't it? Up in Sacramento today, State Assemblyperson Jaron McMillan introduced a bill to raise the minimum for felony Grand Theft from current levels of five hundred dollars to one thousand dollars, citing the fact that the minimum has been set at five hundred dollars for almost a hundred and thirty years now. Head of the National Prison-Guard and Correctional Worker's Union Sem Lawson condemned the bill as soft on crime and a threat to the nation's economy. Zap on the *Grand Theft* tab for more news."

"I should mention, Hutch, that McMillan faces an uphill race for his seat as rep from RCL district, so this get-soft approach may just be the first in a series of moves to pull in voters."

"Five hundred, a thousand—my advice is, if you're going for Grand Theft, go a lot bigger than either of those. Like they say, I'd rather be hung like a sheep than a lamb."

"I think that phrase is 'hung *for* a sheep,' Hutch. As well to be hung for a sheep as a lamb."

"Well, stand me in line for a presidential pardon, Brooke—not all of us could afford Fresno State like you. Coming up at the half-hour, Midwest road hockey! But first, this…"

Boxes roll off an assembly line. "UNICOR—keeping the streets safe and the nation strong." Guard towers. A pan across smiling workers carrying boxes. "UNICOR—rehabilitation at its finest." A convict basketball game. "UNICOR—over 250 billion dollars in annual sales."

A sweeping shot of a department store. "UNICOR—*Factories With Fences.*" Pull back to the silhouette of a prison. (A voice talking low and very fast: "A partially owned subsidiary of the US government. Facts and opinions expressed in this advertisement do not constitute an endorsement by the US government or any of its companies or holdings.")

Cut back to Brooke. "In a direct response to a United Nations General Assembly resolution condemning the use of convict labor in the United States and China, President Richardson issued a strongly worded rebuttal—"

Cut to the face of US President Richardson speaking to a bank of microphones. "Speaking for myself and on behalf of the American people, I categorically deny that the use of prison labor in the United States—or in the great nation of China—amounts to the use of slave labor. Convicts working in the United States do so to pay back their debts to the society they have injured, and to pay for their own upkeep so as not be become a burden on right-thinking, law-abiding taxpayers. To call that 'slavery' is a wild, irresponsible use of the term. Racial slavery as practiced by many nations—including, I am sorry to say, our own great country at one time—was a pernicious, evil institution, based on the oppression of individuals determined by their skin color or ethnic origin. As anyone can tell you, since imprisonment became more widespread in the United States in the 21st century, it has also become fairer. A greater percentage of Caucasian Americans are now in prison than any other racial group in America."

"And before we go condemning slavery root and branch, maybe we should reflect that the founding civilizations of the Western World—Greece and Rome—had economies based on slavery; not on racial slavery, which all civilized people must agree is abhorrent, but on slavery derived from legal and economic status. The convicts in America have three meals a day, a shared room, and medical services. If that's slavery, then most of the slaves in this country have it better than free people in a lot of countries I could name."

Cut back to Brooke. "Well, Richardson certainly gave it to the UN, didn't he, Hutch?"

"You've got to hand it to the man. And bringing up Greece and Rome, things from, well, it must be hundreds of years ago, really puts the General Assembly in its place. That's the kind of education you pay a million for to go to Yale."

Back to Brooke. "And now, over to the SoCal Goversity, with a special report from Jenna Lizmore…"

Jenna in her black latex, in front of Goversity Hospital. "We've gotten used to amazing things from the Goversity, Brooke, but this one is really 4-D." Cut to scenes of doctors operating. "As the leading center in cryogenics, GH has revived over three hundred cryonauts over the years—often with amazing results. But this time they've outdone themselves. Toby Simmons"—a still picture inserted—"who was declared dead of severe spinal trauma and then frozen back in 2003, was revived by GH surgeons, and then had his spinal cord completely regenerated. The operation was such a success that for the past weeks, Simmons has been enrolled as a computer science student at SoCal Goversity. We caught an exclusive at the lab…"

Jenna's hand holding a mike out toward Toby. "So what do you think of the twenty-eighties so far?"

Toby's face. "To tell the truth, the first few days I was just glad to be alive. And then I went outside—blue skies, tropical foliage everywhere. Paradise on earth…the greatest nation in history. I can hardly believe it."

Cut back to Brooke. "Well, he certainly seems happy to be here!"

Cut to Jenna, in front of the entrance to the Lab. "He sure does, Brooke. And that should be a lesson to us all; sometimes we forget how lucky we are to live here, in America at the end of the twenty-first. From Goversity Hospital, where miracles happen every day, this is Jenna Lizmore."

Cut to Brooke. "In other local news, the—"

The screen peels back in a special effect and Boots DeVore appears, sitting in an easy chair, sipping a cup of tea. He looks up as if caught off guard, sets his cup down on an end table, and smooths his goatee. "Good evening, kids. It's your old friend, Boots DeVore, with a little commentary on tonight's news. You know, you have to admire that wind-up doll Richardson. First he denies that the millions of people locked up in this country, sweating to make companies rich, are slaves—and then he has the gall to turn right around and say, but so what if they are? What about Greece and Rome? Well, what about them, Bob? Here we have a stumblebum who barely made it through school, trying to give us a 'cradle of Western civilization' speech to support the suppression of individual freedom…"

"You know, Jefferson—you've heard of him, haven't you? Oh probably not—Jefferson was quoted as saying that the problem with democracy was that people got the kind of government they deserved. I respect old Tom, but I have to say—nobody could possibly deserve this crap. And as to our recently defrosted friend: Do you really believe that he said anything like that? I don't. Now let me mention a few statistics, before the—"

Static, then black, then a close-up of asphalt from the front fender of a racing car, a large oval pushing along in front of it. Hutch's excited voice: "And here it comes, CJ going for the goal, but Austin won't get out of the way, CJ swerves, and then—"

Two cars slam into one another, hurtle off the roadway. One bounces end over end, slams top-down onto the ground, and explodes.

Fade from a column of black smoke to Hutch, looking somber. "There you have it, Brooke: The Death of a Legend. CJ Zinnerman, the most honored sportsman in the history of road hockey, dead at the age of thirty-two."

Cut to Brooke a bit too soon; she's tossing her hair. She confronts the camera, squeezes her upper arms inward almost imperceptibly, lets her auggies swell a little further. "A real-life tragedy, right in everyone's living room. But now, in other sports developments, we go to Jon McLuther at Sports Central—"

22 | They Have, Whaddya Call It, Volition

As Night pointed out, the fine print in the SNN release form Toby had signed authorized them to "edit for length, content, or appropriateness," but he'd spent the evening fuming. The sex had been great—fury and frustration adding to his energy—but afterwards he couldn't get to sleep. At three, after an hour of watching Night's chest rise and fall, he summoned a pubcab and headed to the Lab.

He'd been in VR space a few hours, angrily braiding the torso-thick cables of a parallel processing algorithm, when a door materialized at his side, along with the chime of a doorbell. He leaned over to the peephole and saw his cube neighbor Baxter—or, rather, saw Baxter's barbarian avatar. He gestured at the door to open it and went back to twining the thick cables.

"Whatcha doin'?" Baxter asked.

"Algorithm. Threading these processes into the choice node"—he nodded his head, his virtual hands busy—"over there."

"No. I mean, why you in so early? I never see you here before nine."

"Couldn't sleep. All pissed off about the SNN thing. Did you see what they did to the things I said? Spliced them together so they meant something totally different."

"Yeah, I saw that. But, man, onscreen with Jenna Lizmore…"

"So what if I was onscreen with her? We were all here in real life. You were right here in the same room with her."

"It's not the same as being digicast with her to the whole country. Having everybody see you together."

"Who cares if we're seen together? And who cares about Jenna Lizmore, anyway? She's so augmented she makes Barbie look soft and yielding."

"Who's Barbie?" Baxter asked, and then yawned as his morning meds kicked in, his Conan avatar covering his mouth with a beefy palm. "Whatcha doing here, anyway?"

"Trying to come up with a multimillion-dollar idea. You got any?"

Conan the Programmer shrugged. "Sure." Toby turned to him with full attention, and Baxter looked surprised. "Well, I don't know how to do it, but I know how you earn hundreds of millions..."

"Don't leave me hanging, Baxter."

"Here." Baxter gestured, and two holoprojection poles appeared. "Figure out how they do *Real World Lives*."

Figures—a dark-haired man, a blond woman—arguing in a nondescript living room. Toby watched for a while. Except for the 3-D projection and the incongruous hairstyles, it could have been any soap opera from the 20th. "What about it?" he asked.

"The *people*. How they do the *people*. Man, I know now they were telling the truth on the news—you really *are* from the twentieth."

"They aren't real? Wow. Great animation."

The barbarian rolled his eyes. "The animation's no big deal. It's the underlying AI algorithms that are the goldmine. They design the personality in some kind of pattern, and then just let it develop. These are virtual personalities, man, they change and grow and do things on their own. They have, whaddya call it, *volition*. And so everybody, I mean hundreds of millions of people, watch it. You never know what they're going to do, but you can kind of tell, based on what they've done before...it's like real people!"

"I don't get it. There's billions of real people already. Why is this cooler?"

"Because they aren't real people, but..." Baxter's voice faded out.

"Sort of like drag queens?" Toby asked.

"I don't get the connection," Baxter said.

Toby scratched his virtual head. He'd had several gay friends back in the 20th, but none of them had ever answered his drag-queen question: What is the story with men who like men but who are turned on by men who appear to be women but who we know are really men? This seemed to be the same kind of thing. "Okay. So what's the big deal with the algorithms?"

"Nobody here can do them. They're a European thing. They license the driver objects, allow our people to do some strap-on modules, but no one really knows how they do it. The backbone driver is completely uncrackable."

"Nothing's uncrackable."

"Maybe not for you, wonder boy." A long yawn. "But these modules are one of the only things we import from Europe—and let me tell you, if there's some way to avoid importing from the EU, then we don't import from the EU."

Toby considered this. "So how do I find out more about this?"

"Virtual Beings. Just check the Lab archives. Nothing's SSC, everything we know should be out there."

"Thanks, Baxter. If I figure it out, I'll give you a slice of the proceeds."

"Ha. I'd be overjoyed at five percent. One percent."

"If I work it out, I'll give you a third."

"Okay. I'm not gonna quit school yet, though." Baxter paused. "Hey, Toby—after school today, you want to go get a beer, or down a couple of shims?"

"I can't, not today." Even in VR, Baxter's disappointment showed on the barbarian's face; he revolved his massive shoulders and looked down at his sandaled feet. "Tomorrow, if you're free?" Toby asked. "Or any time you pick. This afternoon I promised to meet Night's uncle. He's—well, I guess he's dying, over in the hospital."

Baxter's avatar straightened up at this news. "Great! Tomorrow, then. You can bring Night, too if you want, and I'll bring—well, somebody." Baxter waited for a moment, and then his avatar brandished his massive sword. "Tomorrow!" But even as he held it over his head, his other hand rose to stifle a yawn.

Night had told him to meet her in room 363 of the Ashcroft Ward at Hoag-Kaiser-Vanderbilt, but the man at the information desk in the hospital lobby gave him a sour smile. "We don't have an *Ashcroft Ward*, sir. If you're referring to the Long-Term Care Unit, however, it's in the wing to your right."

Night didn't look up at first, hunched forward in her chair, but the yellowish man in the hospital bed looked past her to meet Toby's gaze. Night followed his eyes, saw Toby, and gestured with her head for him to take a chair.

They sat together to the right of the bed: the whole left side of the room was crammed with equipment connected to Uncle Trey by wires and tubes. "You're the boy from the past," Trey said, his voice creaking. "You've come to take care of my girl…"

"That's right," Toby said. Beneath the sheet, the man's body was shrunken and trembling. Two of the tubes seemed to circulate the blood from his arm through one of the machines and back again.

"Good. Good. I tried, but I can't anymore." Uncle Trey turned his face to Night. "I thought I could leave you something…but I think it'll all be gone." He swallowed. "I'd die if I could."

"Don't," Night said.

"I'm so sorry, honey."

"Stop it…"

Uncle Trey began to cry without tears, a frail, sobbing convulsion, and Night leaned over him, pressing her face against his chest, one hand stroking at his hair, the other lost, trying not to interfere with the tangle of wires and tubes. "Hurts so much…" the man whispered.

Night turned her wet face to Toby, and her expression told him to leave the room.

He wandered the hallway, glancing into rooms and trying not to stare. Not everyone in the Long-Term Care Unit was as alert as Uncle Trey, but all of them were tied to machines by a web of tubes and wires.

Much later he peeked into room 363. Uncle Trey was asleep. Night sat in the chair beside his bed, holding one of his hands in both of hers. When Toby sat in the chair beside her, she freed her left hand and groped until she clasped Toby's fingers.

They sat for a long time, Night gazing at her uncle. Toby's eyes prowled the room, trying to understand the equipment. The only familiar element was the control panel above the bed, similar to the one he'd stared at for hours during the days when his spinal nerves were regenerating.

A nurse crept in and checked some of the tube connections. She circled back behind their chairs and reached over to the control panel on the headboard. Her gloved fingers spelled out *Manderly* and then *CharlieIguana*. She clicked a lead from her palm unit into the panel, apparently downloading information, smiled at Toby when she saw that he was watching her.

The pubcab carried them back toward Night's apartment. "I'd kill him if I could," she said. "Him and all the rest up there."

"Why doesn't he have them cut off life support?"

"Because that would be suicide, wouldn't it?"

"Oh, come on."

"It's what the law says."

"You're kidding."

"No. You have to use all available life-maintaining technologies."

"Or what? What do they do? Kill you?"

"Confiscate all your property."

Toby rubbed his temples. "I can't believe the healthcare industry let this happen. I mean, it must cost them a fortune."

"Oh, the HMOs have limitations on what they have to pay—and no hospital has to provide service unless you can pay for it. So they can turn you off if you don't have money. But it's suicide to turn yourself off."

"Let me get this straight: You have to pay to be kept alive, even if you don't want to be—but when your money runs out, they can basically kill you?"

Night shrugged, too tired to explain.

Toby turned this over in his mind for several blocks. "So why doesn't your uncle just pull the tubes out of his arms? What stops people from disconnecting themselves?"

"Some of them do."

"And your Uncle Trey?"

"I think that he's—" She started crying silently, her head bowed. Toby reached his hand to her shoulder, but she gathered it up and clasped it in her lap. She took a breath. "He's hoping to, to die before his money runs out. He wants to leave me something. He—" More silent tears. "I've told him, go ahead, don't worry about me, but—"

He held her for the rest of the ride.

Back at her apartment they got into bed. She snuggled up next to him and promptly fell asleep, but after half an hour of staring at the dark ceiling, Toby slipped from under the sheets and went into the living room.

He looked through her bookcase for something to read. Mostly psych books, plus the smattering of random intro texts that any college career accumulates. One large purple volume stood apart.

He hefted it and flipped it open. A photo album.

Only a handful of photographs. A smiling couple—her parents?—in the first picture. A few childhood photos of Night, and she had told the truth: her face was the one she had been born with.

A last photo: Night in mortarboard and robe, standing next to a man who radiated pride. Uncle Trey: Toby could just make out the ruined thing he had seen today hiding under the robust frame of the man in the picture.

The rest of the album was a scrapbook. Pictures, culled mostly from magazines, of London, Paris, Rome, European cities he couldn't identify with certainty. After the European section, page after page of pictures from the late 20th, all jumbled together—fifties families, bell-bottomed hippies, crowded discos, protest marches, Wall Street businessmen, surfers, and, toward, the end, pictures of tourists at the Grand Canyon, Yellowstone, and Yosemite.

He stared at a picture of a seventies family posing at the rail of a Grand Canyon overlook—father, mother, son, the two males mugging for the camera, the mother pointedly composed. It could have been Toby's own family.

He shut the book and put it back on the shelf before he logged in to Night's computer.

23 | It's a Good Thing Nobody Drives Anymore

The interior of the Boeing 977 was the width of a concert hall, a giant bat-shaped plane with ceilings that rose to twenty-five feet in the center of the plane but tapered down to eight feet toward the edges. The 977 was designed for one thousand passengers, but Toby guessed that if it had been set up on the old cram-'em-in guidelines of 20th-century aviation, it could have carried three thousand.

During takeoff, everyone had been belted into their assigned seats in the central wedge of the plane, but after ten minutes at cruising altitude, people began to rise to their feet and make for other parts of the plane—enclosed sections, such as the movie theatre or one of the restaurants, or the more casual, unwalled lounges toward the rear of the huge wedge.

Spengler's phone call to Night had made it very clear, at least to her. No, Toby shouldn't prepare in any way. No, he shouldn't be thinking about anything in particular. No, he shouldn't ask the purpose of the meeting. Just pack enough clothes for a couple of days and get on the flight to Washington.

"Do I get to know who I'm going to see?" Toby had asked.

"The EPC," Night had answered, and then, seeing his blank look, had added, "The Economic Policy Council." Night refused to speculate on what the meeting might concern or why Toby would be invited. From the 'Net he had determined that the EPC was a Congressional advisory board made up of a few key businesspeople, academics, and politicians. Obviously influential, but without any specific legal standing.

By the time he had boarded the plane, he had dismissed it from his mind. There were other problems to consider, and they were probably best considered over drinks.

Toby's D&A seat—departure and arrival, where you were expected to be when the plane wasn't at cruising altitude—was near the center of a long row. Most of the seats were vacated by now, but a few of the passengers in his row were engrossed in the digicasts projected from the seatbacks in front of them, and he had to squeeze past their knees to make his way to the bar.

He had assured Baxter that nothing was uncrackable, but the past three weeks had made him less certain. At first, his progress on the problem of virtual personalities moved quickly; he read everything posted on the subject, and prowled through the sample algorithms that the US Economic Development Commission made available to researchers who wanted to compete with the EU monopoly. The graphics were fine, but no one would confuse the people the American algorithms produced with genuine personalities. If you set a group of them talking to each other, they quickly fell into patterns that tended to cycle over and over. In some of the more advanced versions, they would get out of the cycles by abruptly jumping to another topic. Even the best US logic modules were non-sequitur city.

All the pieces were there—the voice synthesis and recognition modules, the motion control, the memory simulators, and various "temperament" add-ons. They still remained clunky and artificial.

The virtual personalities on shows like *Real World Lives* were indistinguishable from real people. What at first seemed like a soap opera turned out to be something else, something at once more fascinating and yet more banal than any dramatization. *Real World Lives* was twenty-four-hour voyeurism, voyeurism of a most efficient kind, one that could follow people anywhere without their awareness. The show had taken pains to put its players into an interesting milieu, to endow them with exciting careers and strong personalities, but the fact remained: most of the time they were as boring as real people.

Their habits changed only slowly, if at all; their insights, if any, did not come at dramatic moments of confrontation, but over late breakfasts or in the shower.

The US Economic Development Commission was useless. Toby needed the real thing behind *Real World Lives*. Once again he had gotten his pointer via Baxter—over beers, Baxter's domestic partner Achmed noted that OSMOCORP was a major shareholder in RWN, the digicast company that produced *Real World Lives*.

It had taken only a day to break into OSMOCORP's computer system. Toby was not in the least surprised to find that pieces of his own 1999 firewall and data-exchange protocols were still in use. The security system was built from sloppy add-ons layered on top of a foundation he had designed. From OSMOCORP's "friendly" platform, it was easy to work his way into RWN's main hub and access the programming behind *Real World Lives*.

He spent hours of every day in VR-space, his meat in front of the monitor in the Lab, but his mind and soul tinkering with the programs at RWN. The strap-on modules that controlled the quirks of behavior were easy to pop open and examine, and he made a few minor changes in the behavioral constraints that bounded the characters. Bradley, the reporter, started drinking a little less; Miranda, the lipstick lesbian, changed her hairstyle. Nothing out of bounds, nothing that would arouse suspicion unless someone examined the strap-on modules.

The backbone driver was completely different. It accepted input from the strap-ons, from other characters, and from the VR world, but it was impossible to get inside of the driver module. Toby ran through every strategy he had ever used—sending in a Trojan Horse as part of the information from the strap-on, trying various kinds of combinatorial disassemblers to reveal the underlying binary code, scanning for passwords that would pop open the door to the module.

For the first time in his life, he had to admit complete and utter defeat. The driver modules were uncrackable. Whatever they were doing over in Europe stood miles beyond the outer limits of his understanding.

He wasn't going to be able to get in. If he wanted, he could play with RWN's characters in *Real World Lives*—change a gay man to a straight man, make a model of probity into an embezzler, cause a trim woman to go on an eating binge—but he would never understand how the instructions in the strap-on modules were converted into realistic human behavior…

A sudden sinking sensation in his belly, a sense of weight. It took a moment to identify it as turbulence. Wide and windowless, it was easy to forget that the vast hall he sat in was airborne, that forty thousand feet of emptiness waited a few yards beneath his seat.

Weird to fly without windows. Compared to hurtling along stuffed into the metal cigar tubes of the 20th, though, this was bliss.

He ordered a second gin and tonic. Just in case they had to freeze him again soon.

His other line of research—this one more clandestine—had been almost as frustrating. From the Lab computer, it was easy to get into the Goversity Hospital main system, and from the hospital's CDC hub he'd used the usual bag of tricks to worm his way into Hoag-Kaiser-Vanderbilt. But there he came up against a wall: life-support systems were controlled by their own computers.

Life-support computers naturally had to exchange information with the hospital's central computer, just to access patient records, but the traffic was tightly controlled. Life support could send information to the central system at any time, but data could only be moved from the central computer to the life-support systems when the life-support systems initiated a request. There was no way to force the life-support system to admit data from the outside, although it could reach out and grab whatever it liked from central.

The waiter brought his G&T. Toby absently squeezed the lime and then dropped it into the drink. A little sloshed over the edge; the glass was too full.

He leaned far forward in his seat, bringing his lips to the rim of the glass, and sucked enough liquid out that he could pick it up without spilling it.

He stalled in that position, his nose an inch from the glass, his torso touching his thighs.

The virtual-personality problem had him stumped, but now he saw how to handle the hospital problem.

"Just answer their questions and be yourself." Spengler was full of energy, nervous, excited, or both. "I won't be allowed in the room, but I'll be able to watch across the video feed."

Toby wished he could tap into some of Spengler's pep. The hotel room had been luxurious, but he'd barely slept, two hours at most. Got some good programming done, though. "I still don't get it. Why do these people want to see me?"

"They just want your impressions of modern America. Sort of an outside opinion." He put a hand on Toby's shoulder. It was meant to be reassuring, but it trembled too much to be calming.

A guard ushered him to a desk at the center of a dim, wood-paneled chamber. The formal feel of a courtroom; a gargantuan horseshoe of a table atop a dais, looking down to where Toby sat.

Seating for thirty or forty. Extend the dais by another fifteen seats and you'd have the Round Table, with Toby as—what? The centerpiece? The suckling pig?

The guard stepped out and shut the door behind him.

Toby waited. For several minutes he sat with his hands folded on his lap, waiting for someone to enter the room.

Finally he pulled out his palm unit and got back to work.

When the doors at the head of the dais opened, the light bars in the ceiling beamed brighter, as if the people entering had brought the sun. Toby was deep in the intricacies of a two-part bootstrap, but the light and the sense of being in a courtroom brought him unthinkingly to his feet.

Three people took their seats at the head of the horseshoe, and the guard shut the door behind them.

The Caucasian man at the center of the trio spoke. "Good morning, Mr. Simmons." He gestured for Toby to resume his seat, a flick of short, thick fingers. His pink bracelet was tight around the meat of his wrist. "I assume you know who we are."

To the man's right, a gray-haired black man leaned forward, peering at Toby as though he had gone out of focus. "On the contrary, Senator. From what I've read here"—his fingers tapped a pile of documents—

"I'm not sure we should assume anything at all." He smiled. Thin lips, a narrow, arched nose, what Toby thought of as Ethiopian features. "*Do you know who we are?*"

Toby shook his head.

"Well, then. We're the Executive Committee of the Economic Policy Council. I'm Theodore Jefferson, Secretary of Information Control for the Library of Congress. Frances?" He inclined his head past the senator.

The Asian woman had a blaze of white running down one side of her hair, and she tossed this as she readjusted her seat. "Frances Kitagawa, CEO of Holotropic Technologies. Also on the board of OSMOCORP—sort of your alma mater, I gather." She turned to the man in the center.

"Senator Rafe Hurlburt, North Carolina, Chair of the Senate Select Committee on Growth and Development." Not the slightest hint of a Southern accent. "Now can we get moving here?"

Kitagawa held up both her index fingers. "Before we begin: Could you clarify what instructions or input you've had from Professor Spengler, either today, or since your…revival?"

"Almost nothing. We've had a couple of conversations. He asked me what I thought about things—"

"What things?"

"*Any*thing, as far as I can tell. And today he just told me to answer your questions and be myself."

Jefferson and Kitagawa exchanged a glance. "That's exactly correct," Jefferson said. "And we'd like you to start by just giving us your reactions to contemporary society—especially issues of technology and economics."

Toby disavowed any knowledge of economics, but began talking about technology. He spoke carefully at first, praising the developments in medicine, the improvements in the environment, holographic digicasting. Kitagawa and Jefferson remained impassive, making occasional notes; Hurlburt drummed his fingers on the table.

Then Toby began to speak about his disappointments. Where were the teleportation booths, the genetically engineered pets, the lunar and Martian colonies? In fact, what had happened to the space program? When he dug into algorithms, why did he find kernels of code at their center than must have been written in 1999? Why could he, someone just brought out of cold storage, get out to the cutting edge of programming in a matter of months?

Hurlburt interrupted him. "I'm not clear on what makes you so damn sure you're out at the 'cutting edge' of computer science."

Toby hesitated. He couldn't very well tell the council that he'd broken into RWN's computer system via OSMOCORP, and had fiddled the strap-on modules for the personalities.

Jefferson spoke up. "I'm not versed in the intricacies of Architectural Objects, but these reports seem to confirm what the young man says about his programming ability vis-à-vis the best at the Goversity."

Kitagawa smiled. "It so happens that I *am* versed in matters such as Arch-Obbs, and what I read in this report has convinced me that Mr. Simmons could teach some of our best at Holotropic a few things."

Hurlburt grunted. "Which report is that?"

"The one from the grad student," Jefferson said. "Nightingale Enderhew."

Toby felt a flush rising up his neck. He'd known all along that Night was compiling reports on him, but he'd never worried about what they said. Now he felt weirdly exposed, wondering what was in them. *Subject was completely unfamiliar with a mega-Kegel roll, but adapted quickly…?*

Kitagawa and Jefferson helped Hurlburt sort through his papers to find Night's report. Hurlburt paged through it, flipped it shut. "Fine. He's a genius. What's your point, Ted?"

"Would you describe yourself as a genius?" Jefferson asked. "No false modesty. How did you stack up back in your day?"

"I was good at what I did. And I learn fast. But at any university there were a couple dozen people just as good."

"So if you're not a genius," Kitagawa put in, "then the fact that you're out in front of the pack suggests that there's something wrong with the people around you…"

Toby shrugged.

She persisted. "Would you at least speculate on why people aren't as motivated as you are? Why innovation seems to have fallen off?"

Hurlburt sighed, and her next words seemed to address Hurlburt as much as Toby. "Understand me—our competition over in the EU doesn't seem to have these problems. Their economy grows at three percent per annum, year after year—"

"They didn't have the Great Deflation," Hurlburt said. "It isn't a matter of social factors, it's just economic circumstance—"

"People make their own circumstances."

"—and the EU has all kind of social problems that we don't have. It's—"

"Folks, folks." Jefferson held up a hand in gentle restraint. "We have a guest from the past, and his job is just to say what he thinks. We don't need to debate what's right or wrong, at least not now."

Hurlburt snorted and shuffled through his stack of reports.

Kitagawa leaned forward on her elbows, her hands in prayer position on her lips, eyes on Toby. She lowered her hands to the desk. "Honestly, now, Mr. Simmons: What do you think the problem is with American innovation?"

Toby spread his hands. "Well, it seems pretty obvious to me. People don't have any security when they know the government can seize your property. You stick a lot of your brightest people in prison and then expect them to work for practically nothing. Your so-called news media delivers mostly trivial nonsense, and edits out any content that threatens to deliver real information. The libraries are all locked up, and if you try to look at books without preapproval, Homeland Security threatens you with torture. A quarter of the people can't afford to travel out of these districts you've set up, you can be stopped and cross-examined every time you cross some artificial border, we have these gadgets in our arms that track us everywhere we go, there's no such thing as cash anymore so you can track every little thing that people do, and…" Toby realized he was meandering. "And, oh, yeah, everybody I meet is so doped up on mandatory meds that it's a good thing nobody drives anymore."

Hurlburt said, "I would have thought that somebody who lived through the beginnings of the War on Terror would be a little more sympathetic to our aims of protecting American lives. But maybe Mr.

Simmons was one of those who was against the War on Terror back at the turn of the century."

"Hey, I supported the War on Terror. This isn't a War on Terror. You people set up a police state, and then wonder why American know-how seems to have vanished. You guys still have the phrase *no-brainer?*"

Hurlburt pointed a stubby finger. "I am not used to being referred to as 'you people,' and I am accustomed to being treated with more respect, in fact, a great deal of respect."

Toby leaned back in his chair and spread his arms. "And that's another thing. My ancestors were people who dumped tea into Boston Harbor, not a bunch of clowns who bowed and scraped every time some guy in a powdered wig walked by. Or some guy with a pink bracelet."

Hurlburt stood up. His composure was more frightening than any anger he could have shown. "I really don't have time for this. Next time, why don't we just invite Boots DeVore? I see no point in continuing this project, and I plan to vote against it." He turned and pushed out the door at the head of the room, leaving his stack of reports on the table.

Jefferson stood. "Mr. Simmons, I'd like to thank you for coming here today, and for your candor in what must have been an uncomfortable situation. If we need your insights in the future, we'll contact you through Professor Spengler."

He couldn't read Jefferson's tone or expression. Kitagawa seemed equally impassive, but as she pushed out the door with the stack of reports, she turned her head and gave Toby a sly wink.

Toby sat alone in the room, unsure whether he had helped himself or tied his own noose.

24 | An Appliance Store of the Damned

"You didn't like the Three Stooges? How can you like the Marx Brothers and not like the Stooges?" Rufus kicked at a knot of copper wire that clung to the piece of rebar he was after.

"Completely different thing!" Ottmar said. "Not even in the same class." He grunted as he tugged at a piece of sheet metal wedged under a smashed couch. "Marx Brothers are witty, satirical, intellectual. The Stooges are just slapstick—"

"Aw, climb off! Marxes aren't slapstick? How about the thing where Harpo hands people his knee? How about having silverware fall out of his sleeve when he shakes hands?" Rufus planted his foot on the offending wire, pinned it to the ground, and ripped the rebar free. He threw it onto the pile of ferrous metal they had gathered and it tossed back a satisfying clang.

Ottmar stood up, abandoning the sheet metal. "The things the Stooges did were just annoying. The things Harpo did were absurd."

"That some kind of difference you learned in college?"

"No. The Stooges annoyed me the first time I saw them. My dad saw that I liked the classics, so he found all kinds of things for me—Benchley shorts, Keaton, Lloyd. First time I saw the Stooges, I begged him to turn it off. I mean—"

McFall, one of the guards, shouted from atop a mound of rubbish thirty yards away. "O'Brien, Firefly—talk if you want to, but speed up the work, or I'm gonna split you up."

Rufus bent over and picked up flattened cans, hurling them back onto the pile from between his legs. "Needledick guards," he said, just loud enough for Ottmar to hear. "There's only, what, a dozen guards out here on this side, hundreds of prisoners. Why don't we just all get together and take them down?"

"Don't even talk like that," Ottmar said.

"Don't tell me how to talk. Only thing I got left I can make my own decisions about."

"Talk how you want, then, but keep it quiet. And what you're talking about is crazy." He hefted an edge of the couch and sent it tumbling down the backside of the pile he was working. "Attack the guards, nobody'd join in. And even if they did, even if we took over the whole sorting field, what then?" He pulled out the bent rectangle of sheet metal, large enough to roof a chicken coop, and it boomed like stage thunder. "We're still inside an electric fence, and still in the middle of nowhere."

He hoisted the metal over his head and slammed it down on the pile of ferrous they'd accumulated, relishing the reverberations. After a lifetime of careful decisions, heaving junk around had its satisfactions.

Rufus rolled a mattress away to reveal a doorless refrigerator. "Fridge," he announced.

Ottmar joined him, and they worked it free of the surrounding debris. They lifted it, one at each end, and carried it down the trails between the mounds of unsorted junk to the clearing where stoves, washing machines, dryers, and refrigerators sat in untidy rows, an appliance store of the damned.

While they caught their breath, Rufus asked, "How about Canada? You head thataway, you got the chance?"

Ottmar had daydreamed about it enough; why not admit it? "Sure. If there wasn't a fence, and if they wouldn't come after me for a couple of hours… But what's the chances of that?"

"Don't know. Just wanted to know if you'd go." He turned and headed toward the pile they'd been working. "They can't chase us up there, can they? It's another country."

"They'd chase you if they wanted you bad enough. That's why it's the *International* FBI, you know—the US is the only country in the world that claims it can enforce its laws on its citizens when they're in other countries."

"No shit?"

"No shit. You and me—they might chase us a couple miles with copters, but they wouldn't bother with us if we made it to another city. We're the lowest of the low, prison manual labor."

"Story of my life. Know anything about Canadian women?"

"I know we'll probably never meet any. C'mon, let's get a move on before that prick McFall sends us to opposite ends of the yard."

25 | Let Me Ask One Important Question: Did You Do Anything About It?

As requested, Toby waited outside the Pink Torc Lounge as soon as the 977 reached cruising altitude. A few Exempts passed by him, waving their bracelets to make the lounge door open. Finally Spengler came down the aisle, an apologetic grin on his face. "Sorry. Ran into an old friend."

He waved his wrist at the door and issued Toby through. A discreet beeping started up, and a guard moved toward them. Spengler pointed at Toby, then flipped the finger back at himself, a gesture that made the guard nod and sit down again.

The Pink Torc Lounge was nothing at all like its piano-bar name. Plush carpet and dark furnishings, books and magazines, comfy chairs flanking coffee tables—like Toby imagined the library in a traditional English club.

They ordered drinks—Toby's Bombay Sapphire and Tonic, a Black Russian with a Gunmetal Slap for Spengler.

The far wall of the lounge was lined with doors, spaced about eight feet apart. "What are those?" Toby asked.

"Sleeping berths. Some businesspeople get most of their sleep on planes." The drinks came, and Spengler raised his in a toast. "A marvelous performance. I couldn't be more pleased."

Toby joined him in first sip, but then said, "I thought I sort of annoyed Senator Hurlburt."

Spengler laughed. "Annoyed is a mild word for it. He was so angry he couldn't even talk to me on his way out—just made animal sounds. I'm sure he'll do whatever he can to cut off funding for this research."

Toby choked on his drink, wiped his mouth with a napkin. "You mean *this* research? My stipend and everything?"

"Yes, but I wouldn't worry about it. Kitagawa and Jefferson loved you, and the things you said were just the kind of things I predicted you'd say. So the council isn't going to cut off funding, not when my research predictions are right on target." He frowned. "At least, I don't *think* they'll cut off the research…"

"But you could have told me what was at stake! If this project gets cancelled I lose my debt deferment, I go to prison, I—"

"Mr. Simmons, calm down and listen. One, it would have been unethical—and have ruined the whole experiment—for me to tell you anything about how to slant your talk. Two, anything more diplomatic, more middle-of-the-road than what you said wouldn't have earned you any enemies, but it wouldn't have gained you any allies, either. All of the freedom forces will be on your side now. Three, no matter how any of this works out, you are already better off than when I met you."

"So you're on the side of Kitagawa and Jefferson in all of this? And what is their side, anyway?"

"I'm not on anyone's *side* here. I'm on the side of social-control theory—" He waved across the lounge. "*Hi, Rich!* And theory states that there is a tradeoff between state control and the rate of economic growth. There's plenty of evidence from the past that totalitarian states can't keep up decent economic growth."

"Then what the hell happened here while I was asleep?"

"Most of it happened before you were asleep, Mr. Simmons. The laws were already in place. Imagine if America's drug laws had been enforced effectively in the 80s and 90s of your century. No Wall Street boom—all of your cokehead traders would have been in jail. And definitely no tech boom—the people who built Silicon Valley were almost all running on marijuana or mushrooms or ecstasy at one point or another, and with your forfeiture laws, the capital that built those companies would have all been in the pockets of the DEA."

"But that's crazy—how did it happen?"

"Don't ask me, I wasn't there. You were. Didn't you pay attention to these issues? Let me ask one important question: Did you do anything about it? Did you speak out, write letters or editorials? Did you vote?"

"Umm—sometimes…"

"Case closed. Nobody complained about the laws then because they were mainly enforced against people who weren't white, and the victims of those laws lost the right to vote—yes, even back in your day. I can make an argument that things are fairer now than they were back then. Most of the people in the prison system then were uneducated blacks or Hispanics. Today prisoners are overwhelmingly educated whites and Asians, because they're the most profitable source of intellectual labor—and tend to have the most assets to confiscate."

"But what are you trying to do? You sound like you don't care."

"About what?"

"About how screwed up the country is!"

"Ah. Well, compared to most of the world today, compared to about ten billion of the other people out there, this is still the promised land. But your ideas of how life ought to be are probably skewed. You know, Toby, America and Western Europe from 1950 to 2000 were unique, a true golden age. You perceive that period as the natural state of things, but it was a short aberration in the course of human history. In the long run, it's always true that five percent of the people control at least ninety-five percent of the wealth, often even more. There was a brief period where there was a lot of freedom and a huge middle class, but the situation is inherently unstable. Scare people a little—drugs, street crime, terrorism, disease, hell, just about anything—and they'll sign over their rights in a snap."

"But Kitagawa and Jefferson—"

"Kitagawa and Jefferson think economic growth is slow for exactly the reasons that you outlined so succinctly today. That doesn't mean they want to return to freedom for the common man. It means they think that too many people are being imprisoned, that the prison lobby has too much clout, and that the incentives for law enforcement to arrest people based on their assets has gotten out of hand."

"And what do you think?"

"About that? It isn't my job to have opinions; I'm a mere academic. It's my job to make it clear that more control means slower growth and vice versa. It's not my job to choose."

Toby held his head in his hands. "God, what a screwed-up world."

"People have been saying that since the dawn of time... Come now, Mr. Simmons, cheer up. We'll probably get funded to continue this research, and as long as we keep that going, you'll have ample time to pursue your own projects. And, from what the people at the Lab tell me, if anyone is likely to make millions in software these days, it's you."

Toby didn't look up.

"Is there anything I can arrange for you as a sort of thank-you?" Spengler asked. "A favor? A special vacation? Augmentation surgery?"

Toby sat up, lifted his drink from the table. "What do you have to do to visit Europe nowadays?"

Spengler laughed and shook his head at the same time. "Oh, no. No, no, I'm afraid not. There's no chance of getting you an exit visa to go to Europe. With a five-million-dollar debt, there's not the slightest possibility that—"

"Not for me. For Night."

"Oh." He paused. "Ah. So you and Ms. Enderhew have become friends as well as colleagues. Well, I haven't ever seen a full background check on Night, but there's nothing I know of... I'd have to pull a few strings, but if that's what you want..."

"I do."

"Fine. Barring any unexpected problems with Night's background check, consider it done. And incidentally—Ah, Candace, there you are!"

Spengler stood up to greet a redhead who looked like she had arrived from County Cork by way of Tiffany's. She reached for Spengler's hand, her pink bracelet loose on her slim forearm. With a smooth motion she squeezed her upper arms in toward her sides. Under the blouse her pulse began to show in her breasts.

Spengler tried unobtrusively to readjust the crotch of his trousers. "Well, Mr. Simmons, you're welcome to stay here in the lounge until we start into approach. You're already registered on my tab, so order whatever you like..." Candace tugged at his hand, led him toward the far wall. They found an unoccupied sleeping berth and opened the door. As Spengler stood aside for Candace to step inside, Toby could see a long bulge in Spengler's pants, running down the left thigh and straining toward his knee.

He called Night from one of the videophone kiosks in the lounge. It rang ten times before she winked it on. Her face was ravaged with recently shed tears. She said, "Oh, I'm so glad it's you…" and started crying again.

The story came out only slowly. Two of the life-support tubes had come out of Uncle Trey's arm, and the hospital was treating it as a suicide attempt. Trey denied it—"I know he's telling the truth, Toby. If he really wanted to commit suicide he would have succeeded, he could always do anything—" He had been "restrained," VelCuffed to his bedrails by ankles and wrists. "It's just, it's just—God, I can't even stand to see it anymore, he's like some animal in a trap, he's…" She continued talking, but she was sobbing at the same time, and Toby couldn't make out a single word.

His hand went to the screen, like a prisoner reaching to the visitor-glass in an old movie, then groped at his own chest, where something felt terribly wrong.

"Night…" he said. "Night…" When she had slowed to sniffles, he said, "I'm so sorry I'm not there. I'll be with you in just a couple of hours."

She nodded, looking down at her lap. She murmured something.

"What?" he asked.

"I said I love you." She still didn't look up.

"I love you too," he heard himself answer.

"Come straight here when you get back, okay?"

"I promise."

She started to reach for the *OFF* button, but he said, "I need to ask you something. The first time we went to see Trey you said, 'I'd kill him if I could.' Did you mean that? I mean, if there was a button to push, would you turn him off?"

She raised her face and looked at him, eyes red-rimmed around blue. "I'd do it. I'd kill them all if I could."

26 | Want To Know The Truth About America? Come On In

Night leaned back on the headboard of the bed in the cottage, wearing one of Toby's shirts. Her knees were bent, one acting as support for the spine of Advanced Psychometric Techniques, the other rocking slowly side to side, loose-jointed. Toby watched her from his desk as the search churned through the 'Net. She frowned at some difficult passage and then, conscious of his gaze, looked up and smiled.

A beep from the computer: an icon representing an envelope wafted across the holoview and settled in the upper left corner. E-mail. A thought struck him. "Hey, Night—do you still have mail? I mean, real mail, like envelopes and stamps?"

"Some. We have Fed-Fed, and—"

"Fed-Fed?"

"Federal Federal Express. They won the national franchise when the government privatized national delivery."

"What happened to the US Postal Service?"

"USPS? They started making more money from security services than anything else—what with all the scanning and detection stuff for letter bombs and anthrax. They also run a lot of prisons, mainly producing high-tech electronics."

"Do you get mail—physical mail?"

"From Fed-Fed? Not really. Oh, wait, I got a letter once—my papers, when Uncle Trey adopted me. Old laws, they sometimes require mail delivery…"

"No catalogs? No advertisements?"

"Why would anyone want catalogs in the mail?"

Toby was at a loss to answer. All his previous lovers had pored over them. Some things didn't change, though. They still appropriated your shirts.

The ECT lasers tracked his eyes to the envelope icon. He twitched his glove and the envelope expanded and a sheet of paper folded out of it. No sender address, no routing codes, no subject line:

Toby Simmons:

Took me a while to track you down. Maybe we should get together some time, somewhere safe. I'll send details when I get things arranged.

Your pal, Boots DeVore

"Hey, Night? Would you look at this?"

She padded over, her index finger clamped in the textbook to keep her place. She dropped the book. "Dross, Toby," she whispered, "get rid of it…"

"Do you think it's real?"

"I don't know. I have no idea. But it's bad, a bad thing to have on your computer…"

Toby tried to reply with *ZZZZZ*, but the mail bounced back. No such address.

"What are you doing? Just delete the damn thing."

"Okay, okay. Just wanted to see if I could find out where it came from." He trashed it, closed his correspondence window. "What would Boots DeVore want with me?"

"I don't know, but he interrupted a national digicast to comment on your SNN interview."

"Yeah, and he was right, too."

"Toby…if it really is him, don't get involved, okay? I like the guy—lots of people like the guy—but he's public enemy number one as far as the government's concerned."

"Who is he, anyway?"

"Nobody knows. He just started showing up on the networks about—I guess it must be more than ten years ago, now. Sometimes he doesn't appear for a long time, and there's rumors that Homeland Security has finally caught up with him; then, all of a sudden he starts up again."

"And nobody knows who he is? Where he came from?"

"If they do, they haven't told me." She picked up her book, kissed the top of his head, and climbed back onto the mattress.

Toby went back to his search results, and immersed himself in the comm specs for the JN-4500 series chips: the brain of many secure control devices, including the life-support systems from Salt Lake BioSciences.

An hour later he was on a page that offered a guide to medical manufacturers. A *Useful Links* sidebar listed *International Distributors, Uninterruptable Power Supplies, Staff Training,* and *History.*

History? Toby followed the link, found a dozen links to the history of various medical devices, as well as one that read, *American History 101.*

He followed the link to a page that read, Want To Know The Truth About America? Come On In.

He twitched the glove. Nothing happened.

Then he noticed that the download bar at the top of the holoview was active. Data was streaming to his computer.

His hand rattled commands, trying to interrupt the flow. "Shit." The system seemed locked up.

"What's wrong?" Night asked from the bed.

He explained, and she jumped up to stand beside him. "Honeytrap," she said.

"Huh?"

"Where's the site based…Jamaica. Yeah. A honey-trap is a site where you enter expecting something you're interested in, and it immediately downloads garbage to your computer."

"Like a virus?"

"No. Stuff you aren't supposed to have… The download's complete. See what they sent you."

Toby scanned the wafer memory by date, and dozens of files popped up, big files. He opened one and recoiled. Kiddie porn.

"Yech. Told you. Check some others…"

More kiddie porn. Blueprints for a pipebomb. Instructions for removing an ID peanut.

"What's the point?" he asked. "Who sets this stuff up? Is this one of those media sabotage things like Boots does?"

"No. They're all set up by law enforcement, CIA, IFBI, police—though they'll deny it. Downloading this kind of stuff is against the law."

"So what happens now?" He erased the files, but kept the file addresses, and wrote millions of ASCII *X*s over the locations where the data was stored. "Do they come arrest me?"

"I doubt it. They could. But they probably won't."

"Then why?"

"So they have something on you. Gives them an excuse to monitor your activities on the 'net. Things like that." She rolled back onto the mattress.

"I don't get you. An hour ago you were flipping out over the fact that I had a note from Boots. Now you seem blasé about the fact that I just committed some kind of computer crime in front of the authorities."

She blew out a breath. "They've got something on everybody, Toby. I don't know much social control theory, but Spengler talks about this German guy, Christian Enzenberger. Wrote a book called *Smut*, back in the middle of your century. Ever hear of it?"

Toby shook his head.

"Well, it starts out by defining what's dirt and what's not—like food on a plate, when it's served, is good and clean, but what's left after you've eaten, suddenly it's garbage."

"So?"

"So this guy moves from there to a study of documents from the early days of the Nazis, and all of these memos back and forth about sanitation, how important it is for everything to be spotless, how the citizens need to be brought up to this high standard of cleanliness, how the government needs to have the power to make people clean up.

And the idea is that dirt is a crime, and everybody is dirty, everybody is guilty, and only the government can declare them to be clean, and only if they do as the government orders, only if they follow the government rules."

"I don't understand your point."

"Spengler says that, without realizing it, the guy founded social control theory. The first thing a government needs to do is make sure that everybody is guilty of something at all times. Then the officials can pick and choose who they prosecute and when, or let people avoid prosecution by doing what the government wants. When everybody is guilty, when everybody is dirty, only the government can provide absolution."

"So the government does what the Church used to do."

"I guess so. Churches aren't so popular anymore."

"So now that I'm 'dirty,' what do I do about it?"

"Forget about it. Unless you do something way out of line, they won't do anything but kind of check on you." She laid down her book, kneewalked down the mattress so she was next to his chair. "And as long as you're already dirty, why don't you crawl back over here and get dirty with me?"

Doesn't Matter: Illegal Is Illegal

The three teenage girls VelCuffed in the back seat were still sniveling, and Tip switched the car to manual steering just to have something to do.

Patrol-car duty in the Big Orange was Tip's idea of, if not hell, at least purgatory. Like policing a grade school: minor burglaries, prowling neighborhoods for a bold graffiti artist, lost pets, complaints about loud parties; now three girls who'd been snagged at Crystal Cove Mall for shoplifting. The cops didn't even get to make the collar; they'd arrived to pick them up from mall security, like they worked for the LOV-U PD taxi service.

Jace was in his element here. He chatted with homeowners who'd had lawnmowers stolen, persuaded housefuls of partying teens to turn it down a few notches, even traded war stories with the rent-a-cops at the mall. Now he had his nose back in the cruiser's computer, searching for a honeytrap.

First thing when they'd been transferred, Tip had put in a request for assignment to a new partner. Not a chance. Captain Bolker had made it clear to the locals that keeping the two of them together was part of the program for their "additional training."

Tip had to admit that Jace had his strengths. He was great at jollying the desk folks, good at the computer side of things—as far as she could judge—and a genius at covering up. Tip had used a little *unnecessary force* on a kid they'd caught stealing a bicycle, but Jace had drywalled over the thing so effectively the kid's parents felt lucky the department hadn't charged him with half a dozen other violations.

Jace wanted back inside the office, on a promo track to some nice indoor supervisory position. Tip wanted to be reassigned to the CORE, gateway to real advancement in the department. Jace argued that the only way either of them would achieve this was to bag something that would bring either glory or real dollars into Orange division, and his notion of how to achieve this was by nabbing a criminal on the 'net, someone with a pile of forfeitable property. Jace spent most of his spare time prowling cyberspace, letting Tip handle any policing that didn't require good PR skills. Fine with her, when the alternative was talking to him.

"Shit!" Jace yelled.

Tip swerved to the side of the street and braked. "What?"

One of the girls from the back seat cried, "She's driving it herself!" This launched a wave of renewed sobs.

Jace turned in his seat and Tip heard the hum of the automatic grill raising. "Hey, hey, c'mon," he said. Tip saw that he had an arm back over the seat, comforting one of the girls. It seemed to be working; they were back to sniffles.

"Arm forward," she said, and flipped the Shield toggle. Jace retrieved his arm as the Plexi slid up, sealing a barrier between front and back seats. She steered the car back onto the street and switched to autodrive. "What's the problem?"

"No problem. I just found something too good to be true. Somebody accessing a website outside the legal area, downloading all kinds of contraband information…and from a computer in a class neighborhood."

"A trap?"

"Of course."

"Whose? Who set it up?"

"I can't tell. IFBI, probably, maybe Domestic CIA. Could even be Homeland Security. Doesn't matter: Illegal is illegal."

"I don't like it," Tip said, peering in the mirror to check on the trio in the back seat. "If it's somebody else's trap, aren't they going to object if we get in the middle of things?"

"They may be pissed. But the traps themselves are illegal. Ifbee doesn't admit they deliberately punch holes in the internet fence. So if we snatch their prey, they can't really complain. All we're doing is picking up a lawbreaker…"

It seemed to Tip that annoying any agency on Jace's list of possibilities might not be smart, but she was willing to listen. Anything would be better than another year or two of policing the Big Orange. "After we turn these three over to Detention, we'll get coffee and you can try to convince me. But don't make any moves until we both agree, okay?"

"Sure. Fine." Jace looked into the back seat. "The one in the middle's pretty hot, don't you think?"

Tip snorted. "Spoiled brats. I'd like to drop all three of 'em on a street corner in the CORE."

28 | Happens Pretty Much Every Day Over Here

Trey had been mostly incoherent for a few visits, the pain and the increasing quantities of painkillers pushing him into a world where past and present mixed into a nightmare cocktail.

That evening, Trey was unconscious. Twisting against the restraints that held him in the bed, but unconscious.

"Are you sure you want to do this?" Toby asked, after the pubcab dropped them outside her apartment. "It seems like he'll be gone soon anyway."

"You're wrong. Next it may be a heart machine, or intubation so a machine can breathe for him, but he probably has months left. Months." She gave a bitter smile. "You have no idea how much progress we've made in medicine."

"Then let's take a walk." He explained the plan.

She listened without a word until he finished, and then said, "But I want to be there when he goes…"

"Can't be done. I'm sure they keep tabs on every ID peanut going in and out of the place."

They walked in silence for two blocks before she said, "All right."

True to his word, about two weeks after their Washington trip, Spengler called Toby with the news that he'd procured an exit visa for Night. A little paperwork and a fifty-dollar processing fee, and she was free to visit anywhere in the EU.

Thursday afternoon—the last Thursday they would visit the hospital—seemed like a poor time to tell her the good news.

In the hallway of the Long-Term Care Unit, Toby whispered to her, "There's no guarantee this will work, you know."

"It will work."

Toby sat in a chair in the corner of Uncle Trey's room, directly beneath the video camera. Night sat next to Trey's bed, holding one of his VelCuffed hands, talking urgently in a voice too low to hear.

She stood up. Toby came and stood between her and the headboard, his arm around her shoulders. His gloved hand spelled out *Manderly*, and then, after he counted to ten, *CharlieIguana*. He rolled his head back as if loosening his neck muscles and saw that a new light was blinking green on the info canopy.

He squeezed Night's shoulder. She reached into his jacket, grabbed the lead to his palm unit, then bent down to hug her uncle. Toby stepped between her and the camera, and Night pushed the lead into the outer port of the headboard. Her body heaved with sobs.

He glanced down at the palm unit. No interface. "Other one," he whispered.

She kept on crying.

Toby leaned down over her, trying to make sure his body stayed between the camera lens and the headboard. His free hand stroked her back. "Wrong port, honey," he sang quietly, as if comforting a child. "Got to plug it in to the other port, just an inch further in…other port, honey…" His fingers jabbed her in the low back. "Got to put it in the other port pretty soon, or it's going to drop the log-in window."

Her fingers fumbled for the lead, pulled it out, jammed it at the other port, jabbed again and again…

"Maybe we should just go home," he said, "come back next week…"

Her breathing steadied and she pushed the lead into the port. Toby rattled off the code to start the upload from the palm to the Salt Lake BioSciences processor.

From the doorway a nurse said, "I'm sorry, but if I could just squeeze by you for a second…"

"Go away," Night sobbed.

"I'm so sorry, I really am, but we have to get the data in sequence, and—"

Toby glanced down at the progress bar in his palm.

Night rolled toward the headboard, her shoulder by Trey's head, her body arched to the side, only one foot on the floor—a ridiculous position. But the face she turned to the nurse was shattered, ravaged, and it was all he could do to keep from reaching for her, with both arms. "I said, *go away*."

The nurse backed out of the doorway and gestured at someone down the hall. Toby gave a covert glance at the progress bar: soon, soon… The bar blacked out. He slid his hand into his pants pocket and left the palm there, pulled out his hand and tugged hard against the pocket hem, letting it peel his glove off…

"C'mon, Night," he said, reaching down for her, "C'mon now…" He stepped away from the headboard and turned to the door, letting the revolution of his body pull the lead out of the port.

He turned back to Night, bent down while stuffing the lead wire into his pocket, hugged her, tried to raise her to her feet. She rolled away, pressing her face against Trey's. He got her by her shoulders and lifted her up by force, wrapping his arms around her. He leaned his head back.

The damned green LED in the canopy still glowed.

Lousy security. It was like leaving your door open for a long time after you left your house.

Two male orderlies crowded in past the nurse.

The green light was still on, and he was still logged in.

"You've got to stall them," he whispered into her ear.

She didn't seem to hear, and they moved forward murmuring comforting words.

"You've got to stall them," he repeated.

One of them reached out and put a hand on her shoulder, and she tore herself from Toby's arms, flailing at the orderlies, a confusion of nails and knees and screaming.

They fell back, but only for an instant, and then they got her by the arms. She thrashed and kicked, and they closed in tighter against her, using their bulk like pillows wrapped around her, gentle but relentless. "Tied down, tied down—" she gasped. "When are you going to stop *torturing* him—"

Toby ran his hands down his face, leaned his head back.

The green light winked out.

He stepped forward, put his hands on her shoulders, put his head next to hers, and said, "It's okay, it's okay, it's over now. It's all over now."

She stopped struggling, and the orderlies loosened their grips so she could turn to hug herself against him. The nurse edged around the whole group and logged into the headboard.

"I'm sorry, guys," Toby said.

"No big deal," one of them said. "Happens pretty much every day over here."

29 | Trying Hard to Turn It All Around

The Kraken Toby had implanted in the Salt Lake BioSciences control unit was simply an instruction in the billing system. Patient records in Long-Term Care were updated weekly with information about the status of their insurance coverage and bank accounts.

The main computer at the hospital couldn't reach into the BioSciences Life Support Computer, but the BioSciences computer could and did reach out and grab things off the main computer. On Monday at eleven p.m., the Kraken told it to reach out and grab information to update two patient records. An hour before, Toby had linked to the hospital computer via the Goversity Hospital hub, copied two patient financial records, and placed two huge segments of binary data at those addresses.

The import control interface examined both of the incoming chunks of data to see if either were an executable module or script. By themselves neither of them were, until the Kraken set them down in adjacent memory blocks and jumped control to the first instruction. That started it running.

It was difficult to terminate life support on the BioSciences control system, but it was easy to reset the various functions. The program simply reset them all to zero, and then reconfirmed the settings.

Before it closed, the program issued a system command to delete all files with creation or modification timestamps in the previous week and repack storage memory when finished.

The BioSciences control unit deleted everything from the past week, including the program that had issued the command.

At midnight, working from the Lab via Goversity Hospital, Toby replaced his two chunks of binary data on the hospital's central computer with the patient financial records that had lived at those addresses.

The footprint was tiny. There was no record of the evening's activity on the BioSciences computer. If they checked backups, the only evidence was disguised as an instruction in the billing system, and if they happened, by some strange chance, to check that, it would lead to legitimate patient financial records.

Elegant? Not really, since it had required a physical link into the BioSciences port.

But still rather pretty, in its own way.

Real World Lives had created something of a buzz over the last few weeks. Toby's changes to the behavioral strap-ons had been minor, but there was some sort of synergy in the interactions between the characters that he hadn't foreseen. The virtual people were behaving in ways that surprised people, but were at the same time perfectly in character. Sarah, the lipstick lesbian—who had always been a little sneaky—started an affair with the media mogul's wife, all behind the back of her partner; when the media mogul found out, he blackmailed Sarah into making it a threesome. The stockbroker, who had been taking favors for pushing various stocks, let someone "loan" him a yacht in exchange for misleading clients in a big way. Jessica, who'd been sneaking into NewarkCORE for cheap drugs and scare-sex, cleaned up and went back to college—still drinking too much, but trying hard to turn it all around.

Toby had been unnerved. He'd done his best to cover his tracks, but anyone who compared the current strap-on modules to backups would see they'd been tampered with.

As far as he could tell, though, the network was overjoyed. Ratings were climbing, and network execs were claiming that this showed the underlying vigor of shows where virtual personalities were free to evolve in a society of other virts.

Nonetheless, Toby decided that further experimentation on *Real World Lives* was ruled out—too visible and too unpredictable. In any case, he'd discovered something better: RWN's VirtLab, where main personality modules and strap-ons were scattered about like body parts in Frankenstein's lab. In the late evenings he could sneak his avatar onto their system with little chance of meeting anyone else, duplicate a strap-on, and then see the results of whatever changes he decided to make.

If he didn't have a five-million-dollar debt hanging over his head, he might have applied for a job at RWN.

Of the eighty-three bodies tied to life support in the Ashcroft Ward, all but nine of them expired within moments of having their control systems reset.

Eight of them lived long enough for nurses to discover the problem and feed new instructions into the life-support system.

Toby wondered if he should feel guilty. Had he just murdered seventy-five people?

Had he just freed seventy-five people?

To his surprise, Night showed no emotion other than a grim satisfaction. "I've already done my grieving," she answered when he asked about it.

National news coverage was heavy for the first few days. The hospital sued Salt Lake BioSciences; BioSciences asserted that terrorism was responsible—either terrorism, or negligence on the part of the hospital staff. Congress considered bills for safeguards. The families of the dead—most of whom, Toby believed, had been praying for their relatives to die—appeared on digicast interviews claiming to be outraged, and two separate class-action suits were launched.

At the height of the furor, Boots DeVore seized control of the nation's digicast system and argued it was the best thing that could have happened. "Eighty-four percent of medical expenditures go on people in their last sixty days of life. Another thirteen percent goes on cosmetic surgery. That leaves three percent—*three percent*—of our medical expenditures for keeping active, living people healthy. We've got a system here where the lucky ones die the quickest. Even China, the most totalitarian state on the planet, recognizes that people have a right to die; no right to live, maybe, but—"

Night received seven video calls about her uncle's death. The first four were from lawyers offering to represent her against the hospital.

The fifth one was a lawyer from the hospital. They were willing to pay her an $850,000 settlement if she would drop all claims against the hospital and undertake not to join in any class-action proceedings against the hospital, Salt Lake BioSciences, or any other party to her uncle's death.

The lawyer mistook her stunned silence for hesitation, and upped the offer to $900,000.

She agreed, and he uploaded documents for her to sign.

The sixth call was from her uncle's lawyer. His real assets had been liquidated and assembled into a single bank account at the hospital before he was Ashcrofted. Although the hospital had been chewing away nearly $20,000 every day, there was still more than $187,000 in the account, and she was the designated heir. "The hospitals usually come up with a load of additional charges after the patient expires," the lawyer said, "but under the circumstances, I suspect we can shame them into just turning over the account."

The seventh call was from Jenna Lizmore's assistant at SNN. Would Ms. Enderhew agree to an interview about the hospital tragedy?

She would not. Night shut down her computer and turned off her ear unit. She pulled her feet up onto the chair and covered her face and mouth with cupped hands.

Toby stood behind her and touched her shoulders. She drew in a long breath, the air whistling between her fingers, and then dropped her hands to her sides.

"Now," she said, "now, I feel guilty."

Toby waited a week before he brought up Europe.

He'd expected Night to appreciate the idea, but she was more excited than he'd imagined. "It was always my fantasy, that someday I'd live in twentieth-century Paris—all the writers, the artists…"

"You'll always have Paris. The twentieth century I can't arrange."

She snuggled against him on the bed. "I'll have my twentieth-century boy, though."

He stroked her cheek. "Would you really go live there? Even if you couldn't come back? What about the people you'd leave behind?"

She rolled off the bed onto her feet and headed toward the bathroom. "Who would I be leaving?" She flipped on the bathroom light and talked louder. "Now that Trey's dead, the only family I have is in prison somewhere." Her urine made tiny bell sounds under her voice. "I don't have any really good friends"—the rattle of the toilet-paper roll—"COFfers usually don't, you know…" She stood in the doorway, miraculous and as unselfconscious as if they'd been lovers forever. "We're both sort of orphans, Toby."

She snuggled back against him. "Maybe that's the attraction," she said. "Two orphans."

"Maybe for you." He ran his hand down her flank. "For me, it's your hot bod."

"*Hot bod.* That's a new one."

"It was already old when I was a kid… If you move to Europe, you probably won't be able to come back."

"I know. And I'd have to abandon all the money. But I haven't got used to having it yet, so: When do we go?"

"I'm not so sure you have to leave it. There are countries in Latin America who are part of the American Free Trade Alliance, and have full relations with the EU too. It may cost you ten percent, but…"

"Whatever. Money, no money. Doesn't matter. I want another country."

It didn't worry Toby that he and Night spent so much time together, but it worried him that he didn't feel smothered. He still kept up the pretense of having his own place, still dropped through the cottage most days to change clothes. It also gave him a chance to check e-mail without connecting to his account from Night's apartment or from the Lab. If he were getting into trouble, there was no reason to bring it down on anyone else's head.

When the second message from Boots arrived, he wasn't sure what to do.

> *Dear Tobias:*
>
> *Think we should get together now, don't you? For obvious reasons, I can't give you my e-mail address; but if you set a date I'll arrange other matters. If you're ready for this, then place a personals ad on SuperHotDates.com, and address your message to "Dear Thigh-Highs."*
>
> *Looking forward to it, Boots*

He wiped the message and decided to give himself some time to think it over.

30 | Help, Permission, Or Any of Those Other Unfortunate Things

Delgado pushed open the door while Lex was still on the vidlink. Annoying, but Lex had to get along with the guy. He waved him in and looked back at the screen, where one of his field guys—well, field-gal, actually—was trying to sell him on setting up banking surveillance on a Hollywood studio she claimed was funneling money out of the country.

"We need more than that," he said, and held up a hand, cutting her off. "I'm not saying no, so don't argue. When I do say no, you can argue then. Right now I'm saying get me more specifics. I'd love to take down a studio, but I'd hate to just wound one and leave 'em lying in the brush for us… Take a week, get the numbers, put on a show for me, 'kay? Right, then."

From across the room, Delgado asked, "Who's CT Wycoff the Third?"

He was looking up at a framed quote on the wall:

GANGER'S MOTTO
Fine, go ahead and negotiate.
But I'll use my turn to sneak up behind them.
—CT Wycoff, III

"Twentieth-century ethicist," Lex answered.

"Doesn't sound too ethical to me."

"Depends on your alignment. What's up?"

Delgado came over and tossed a single-page printout onto Lex's desk.

Lex picked it up and read. Dear Tobias: Think we should get together now, don't you? For obvious reasons, I can't give you my e-mail address; but if you set a date I'll arrange other matters. If you're ready for this, then place a personals ad on SuperHotDates.com, and address your message to "Dear Thigh-Highs." Looking forward to it, Boots.

Lex rolled his eyes. "You think this is *our* Boots? Since when does he send e-mails?"

"Yeah, this is our Boots. Let me tell you how we got this. We've been watching traffic on a computer in Slater Park, since the user fell into a honeytrap a while back…"

"What kind? Forbidden sex site?"

Delgado laughed. "History site."

"History? You catch many people that way?"

"You'd be amazed. Anyhow, you remember when SNN had that interview with the guy who'd been cryogenically frozen, and Boots took over all the networks to say that the President was full of shit and the networks had distorted what the frozen guy was saying?"

"Sure."

"Well, this e-mail is to the frozen guy."

Lex stared.

"Tobias," Delgado said. "Toby Simmons."

Lex nodded. This seemed too good to be true, but it felt true. Boots DeVore had already shown a personal interest in Toby Simmons… "Did you trace it back to source?"

"Come on Lex, that's like looking for a return address on a mail threat. This is *Boots DeVore*, man. We ran back up the servers as fast as we could and got 404ed to some hub that was supposedly in Turkey. We sure aren't going to catch him like that."

"Has the guy—has Toby replied?" Lex turned and looked out the window.

Delgado moved around and stood next to him, so close that Lex inched away. "He hasn't replied from that computer, or through that account. But he works at the Goversity Computer Lab, and he probably has access to other computers on top of that. But we're monitoring the personals site in question…"

Lex turned around to his desk. "I want him surveilled, continuously."

"You're the field guy, Lex—but do you think that's wise? We might spook him, or spook Boots."

"I'd rather take that chance than the chance they'll contact each other through some channel we aren't watching. That'd be just great—Boots and Toby have a night on the town while all we do is sit and watch their e-mails." He slapped the circuit pad. "Jesse. I want an all-hands in forty-five minutes, everybody on my team including support staff. Southwest conference room. Anybody off premises, contact them individually and let them know I need to see them eight a.m. tomorrow, my office." He closed the circuit pad.

Delgado was whistling to himself, so quietly that Lex couldn't make out the tune. Lex stared at him until he stopped. "Another thing occurred to me," Delgado said, "a good thing, but it didn't occur to me until a few minutes ago."

Just say it, for Chrissakes. "And that is?"

"E-mail could come from almost anywhere. But if he's suggesting that they meet in the flesh, then it suggests that Mr. DeVore is indeed based somewhere in the area. Narrows things down a bit."

Lex nodded his head, slow and ponderous. "Also means that we might not have to intrude on anyone else's territory…"

"And therefore not need to ask any other branches for help, permission, or any of those other unfortunate things."

"Good news, Raymundo. Good news indeed."

31 | You Want to Go That Bad, Then Sayonara, Amigo

"I put in an extra ten percent just to be sure," Night said.

Ramirez picked up the sack from his desk, hefted it. "Why?"

"Because I want to make sure that he can leave any time he wants to go—any time at all."

Toby wrinkled his nose. Even back in this enclosed office, the smell of the Long Beach fish market was overpowering.

Odelia had been glad to hear from him, and then angry at what he asked of her. But she relented and gave him the name of a friend, who gave him the name of a friend, who gave him an introduction to Ramirez.

Ramirez fiddled with the knob on the scales, calibrating to zero. "There's no such thing as 'any time,' you know." His hand reached into the open sack and came out with a mass of gold chains, his fingers clawed in around the dangling metal like a crane-hoist lifting wreckage. He piled them onto the platen atop the scales, piled on more, peered into the bag to make sure it was empty. "Fishing boats aren't pubcabs… but if he comes any time when a boat isn't ready, I can hide him for as long as needed. Sailors have many years' experience hiding things from the government." Ramirez cocked his head, eyed the scales. "Even more than ten percent over. A lot of gold. Buying this much might make someone suspicious."

"I bought it at a dozen different jewelers."

Ramirez had a huge black mustache, but his hair was out of sight beneath a tied bandana: Pancho Villa meets Long John Silver. He shook his big head. "Even so. You think they don't track these things?"

"I just inherited some money. I figure a spending spree won't look that strange."

"Better buy some other things too, in that case." He pulled a canvas bag from a desk drawer, loaded the gold inside as if he were forking out spaghetti, zipped the bag.

"You keep it in your desk?" Toby asked.

Ramirez gave a dangerous grin. "Do you think I'd put it away while you watch? Now, the buzzer outside the door to the market. It will get me, or one of my friends, any time of day or night."

"How do I identify myself? Or do you read my ID peanut?"

"More old-fashioned than that. Before you go, I take your picture. We recognize you on the video. So no disguise, no cosmetic surgery. As for the peanut…" Ramirez flicked the index finger of one hand at his opposite wrist. "It goes before you come here."

"How?"

"Just cut the skin, pop it out." He waved his finger at his own forearm, back and forth from elbow to wrist. "Cut *this* way, not across. Other way is for suicide."

"It's that easy? Just slice and pop?"

"Sure. They tried things to make it harder. One kind of donut that goes around this, this here…" He tapped next to his windpipe.

"Carotid artery?" Night asked.

"Exactly. Around the artery, so you have to cut your own throat to get it out. Tried it out on some convicts. Too many of them died—stroke or something. Tried other things, too. All too expensive. So the peanut stays in the wrist, and it is a very, very serious crime to take it out." A gleam of teeth beneath the mustache. "Everything is a very, very serious crime."

Toby was about to ask what you did to close up the wound, but Ramirez wasn't finished. "If you're clever, send your peanut on a trip. Some people leave them on streetcars. One fellow, he put his on a cross-country train. But don't bring it here." Ramirez opened his top desk drawer. "Smile for the camera," he said.

Toby didn't smile, but he held still while Ramirez fired off a half-dozen shots.

"When Toby's gone," Night asked, "won't they check our movements? And won't they see that he came here?"

"They'll see he came *someplace* down here. So? It's a free country, isn't it?"

Night frowned. "I don't understand. They must see the pattern—people come to fishing ports, later those people drop their peanuts and disappear. Why don't you get arrested?"

"Every so often, someone does." Ramirez shrugged. "It isn't all as they say, you know. You flee, they seize your assets. You don't have many assets, maybe they don't really care all that much if you flee. You want to go that bad, then sayonara, amigo. Also, perhaps there is a certain amount of money that gets paid to border agents…"

"Like the Iron Curtain," Toby said. Ramirez and Night both looked blank. "How long will it take to get out of the country?"

"No telling. You have to change boats two, three, four times just to get up near the Canadian border; fishing boats down here don't go that far from home. In Washington, they get you on something headed to Alaska; drop you onto something Canadian on the way. A week, if you're lucky; three weeks if you're not so lucky. If all of us are *un*lucky, then maybe never." He looked back and forth between them. "You want to go faster, you should fly up and get on a boat around Seattle. I can arrange that. It's no cheaper, since there's more security near the border, but for the same amount I have here—"

Night looked as if she were considering it, but Toby said, "No. I can't tell when I might have to leave."

"Hmmph." Ramirez pulled on his mustache. "I have to tell you: if you come here with the police on your heels, I can't help you. I don't know what your problems are—I don't want to know what your problems are—but if you're about to get in trouble: Don't. Leave now."

"I plan to leave as soon as I can." Toby felt an absence from the chair to his left, as if Night had vanished. He looked. She stared at him, motionless. "The very first minute that I can."

"Our relationship should be the most important thing to you!"

"Our *relationship* is a fucking abstraction," Toby answered. "*You* are the most important thing to me."

It was Toby's first fight. Oh, he'd had situations before that his girlfriends would have described as fights—discussions where they'd hurled hurtful invective at him, while he tried to remain calm and sensible.

With Night everything was different.

He wanted to punch her flawless face.

"I don't want to leave you," she said, standing up, the tears, the inevitable, eviscerating tears leaking from her eyes. "Why do you want me to leave?"

Deep breath. "I don't want you to leave. I want us *both* to leave."

She waved an arm at her living room as she turned from him, as if displaying evidence. "Then why do you want me to go? I have money, we can get more money—Is it the twentieth-century thing? You can't stand to have a woman support you?"

"Five million dollars!" he said, rising to his feet. "Five *million* dollars. You've got more money than you ever imagined, and it's still not even a quarter of what I owe. I earn thirty K. *Do the math*: if we both earned thirty K and there weren't any taxes, and we saved everything, it would still take about eighty years to pay it all off!" He moved over to her, put his arms around her, his chest pressed to her back. "It's impossible."

"We'd work it out," she said, in a choked voice. "We'd figure something out. And at least we'd be together…"

"We wouldn't be together. This Spengler thing could end any time, and I'd be in prison until I was so old they tossed me out into some CORE."

"I'd wait for you," she said, a promise, but in a voice that sounded more like an accusation.

"Good. Wait for me in Europe. At least there you won't end up in prison too."

"I don't want to leave you."

He maneuvered her to the couch, and they both collapsed onto it. "I don't want you to leave either. I want you to get out, so I can get out too. We can't move your money—"

"I don't care about the money!"

"Or *me*—we can't move *me*—until you're gone. Even an idiot checking the GIS would know we're sleeping together, and Spengler knows for sure—"

"You told *Spengler*?"

"I didn't tell him, but I'm sure he worked it out. I pressured him to get this visa. He seemed kind of pleased."

His first reaction was that she had frozen in his arms.

She hadn't. Frozen was hard, solid. This was different. For a moment, she had just ceased to be. "I'm afraid I'm not going to see you again."

"Listen: if you stay here, if we stay here, you're probably going to see me sent to jail, okay? If not for my debts, then for all of the other stunts I've been pulling. And now that you've got money, they'll probably use your association with me to grab you, too. *You have to go to Europe.*"

Her voice stayed distant. "I feel like we were just getting started. I still need to tell you so much—good, bad, everything. Because what if you don't come…?"

"Fine. Tell me everything. But tell me in Paris."

"Paris." A flicker of interest. "I'm really going?"

"As soon as possible. The sooner you leave, the sooner I can move your bank accounts; the sooner that's finished, the sooner I'm on my way to Canada."

She turned her face and kissed him. "I wish I'd met you years ago."

"Years ago," he said, "I was dead. But aside from that, I feel the same way."

32 | This Doped-Up, Slack-Jawed World of Yours

Parked in the WebSys Digicast van, Roxanne rapped out her boss's personal ear code. "Lex? Our friend has visitors… Well, that's the surprising part…"

Her respect for Jace had increased a hundredfold, but that still didn't give Tip much comfort. "Are you sure about this?"

"He was just online, same account, same everything. So I'm sure about it."

They stepped up onto the stately porch—a big, expensive house on a street of big, expensive houses. "This isn't the neighborhood to screw up in, Jace."

"Relax." He pressed the bell, listened to the chimes echo inside.

No other sounds.

He pushed the bell again.

"I'd better check the back," she said.

The neighborhood was like something off a digicast—big trees, quiet streets, even some damn birds singing. Creeping around the side of this house made her more nervous than she'd ever been in the CORE.

Now that Night was gone, there was no reason for Toby to spend time at her apartment, but he'd slept there anyway—waking in the early morning and wandering the rooms, touching the things she'd left behind.

He'd woken late and pubcabbed it to the cottage. In a day or two he'd need to log on via her computer to start the account transfers, but in the meantime, he thought he'd stay here.

He booted the computer as he buttoned his shirt. He didn't use this station for much, now that he knew it might be monitored; safer to use the Lab computers, where he could log in under a dozen different staff aliases.

He sat down to glance through his meager e-mail—papers he'd requested from the Economic Development Commission. He was about to forward them to his Lab account when he noticed motion through the cottage window.

Someone was stalking around the back of the house, someone short. Someone in a police uniform.

An Asian policewoman. Cute, too.

He opened the door to the cottage, and she turned on her heels.

"Can I help you?" he asked.

She pulled a gun and pointed it at him. "Don't move," she shouted. "Hey, Jace!"

The two police kept standing just inside the open door of the cottage, but Toby sat down on the corner of the bed. "So, can you clarify—why are you here?"

The one whose tag identified him as Roper said, "Because you've been downloading illegal information from a website that is out-of-bounds."

"Oh. One of your websites?"

"No, but we still have the authority to arrest you for accessing it."

"Hmm. And what will that achieve?"

"It'll enforce the law, is what…plus it looks like you have some assets that might be worth forfeiting. Nice piece of property here."

Toby started laughing, and the puzzled expressions on their faces made him laugh harder. "Oh, man," he hooted, "oh, man, have you ever come knocking on the wrong door—"

Roper was staring at Toby, but Toby saw that the pretty Asian policewoman was staring at Roper. "You want to explain?" Roper demanded.

"It's not my house," Toby said, still a little weak, "and I'm about five million dollars in debt."

"*Jace?*" the woman demanded.

"Doesn't matter, Tip," he said. "Having such a crime committed on your property is enough to trigger forfeiture."

"Does it matter," Toby asked, "if the owner is Exempt?"

"Oh, shit," Jace said.

Tip said, "I knew it. I just knew it." From the look she was giving Jace, Toby thought she might bite him.

Two other figures appeared just outside the doorway. Jace's eyes caught the direction of Toby's gaze, and Jace and Tip twirled about as one, hands on their holsters.

The black man outside said, "Agent Colter, Agent Williams, IFBI. Can I inquire as to what the hell LOV-U is doing here?"

The cottage was really a little too cozy for five unless they were good friends. Lex sat in the desk chair, Tip on a chair from the kitchenette, Roxanne and Jace perched on corners of the foot of the bed. Toby sat crosslegged at the head of the bed.

After a defensive explanation of their presence, interrupted by comments from Toby, Tip and Jace sat back with folded arms.

Lex mustered his scariest look, and said, "I appreciate that you're within your rights to be here, but I'm going to have to ask you both to leave now. This man is under investigation for acts related to terrorism, and our privileges are going to trump yours in any court."

"Do you have warrants?" Jace asked.

"Acts related to terrorism?" Toby asked.

"Surveillance warrants," Lex said.

"Acts related to terrorism?" Toby asked again.

"Aiding and abetting Boots DeVore is terrorism," Roxanne said to Toby.

"Getting unsolicited e-mail isn't exactly aiding and abetting," Toby said.

"Wait, wait, wait," Tip said. "*Boots DeVore?*"

"Boots DeVore," Jace said.

Lex nodded. "Now you see why I'll have to ask you two to withdraw and let us get on with our business."

"Screw that," she replied. "We want in on this case."

"Out of the question," Lex said. "This is strictly a Bureau matter."

"And this is strictly a guy we've already busted. So if you don't let us in on this, we're taking him in, and you can fight to get custody."

"We'd get it," Lex said.

"Sure, but when?" Tip said. "Of course, maybe you're not in a hurry."

Toby was starting to like her.

Lex took a few deep breaths, dropped his scary face. "What exactly do you want?"

"Some of the credit," Tip said. "A transfer the hell out of the Big Orange."

"A desk job," Jace said. "Hey, maybe you guys need somebody with my skills…"

Roxanne rolled her eyes, but Lex said, "That's it? Credit, promotion?"

"Well," Jace said, "if there's any head money involved…"

"A hundred. Tops," Lex said. "And that's between the two of you."

"A hundred—" Jace began.

"So fifty grand each," Tip said, "and a share of the credit, plus you get our department to detail us to your team for the duration."

Jace's mouth moved silently.

Toby leaned in to the conversation. "What do I get out of it?"

They all turned and stared. "What you get is not thrown in prison," Lex said.

Toby waved his hands. "Whoa, whoa, time out, gang. The IRS already wants me, and at my present rate of pay they could keep me for about a hundred and sixty years. LA's finest here claim they can lock me up for I don't know how long, and I'm sure if we search around we can find some other silly-assed charges that will have me behind bars until the next millennium. So pardon me if the threat of more jail time isn't real spooky right now."

The rest of them exchanged glances, but Lex just said, "So?"

"So, if you want my help catching this guy—and I *am* a better computer jock than anybody I've met so far in this doped-up, slack-jawed world of yours—if you want my help, then I need to know: What's in it for me?"

Lex nodded to himself for a while. "What did you have in mind?"

33 | You Won't Scare Anybody Off, You Don't Look Anything Like a Cop

There weren't many private cars in ComptonCORE, so it was hard to design an undercover operation.

Tip had been against any kind of undercover operation to start with—just surround the damn building with an army, and then gas 'em out. "You don't want to go inside down there—that's Gangtown country. Every gang has to protect itself from the others. Booby traps everywhere."

"We'll run Rats and Dragonflies in first," Lex said.

Tip snorted. "Netting, chicken wire. They figured out a cheap way to handle those long ago."

"If he wants to visit Toby," Wenner said, "he'll have to either come out himself, or provide an escort for Toby to go in. So our problem is how to be onsite, and be there unobtrusively."

"Street or sewer maintenance?" Roxanne suggested.

"Yeah, *right*," Tip said. "As if any maintenance ever gets done in the COREs. Anybody saw somebody working on the street in there, they'd call SNN—a once-in-a-lifetime news flash. Look, if we were in some other part of town, we could just dress up as locals, but this is down in warehouse country, lots of empty streets. If you *got* to have undercover people onsite, there's only one way to do it…"

After two hours of debate, Tip's suggestion had carried the day.

She was beginning to regret it.

The tan Department of Agriculture uniform was too big for her, and it breathed about as well as Saran Wrap. Put that on top of a graphite-fiber vest and the sweat had started to form before she'd finished zipping her pants.

There was no place to hide her StunFists, no belt for VelCuffs, sticks, or sprays. In the two Food Service trucks there was enough weaponry to invade a small country, but all she had was her nine-shot Heston special, clipped into her ankle holster.

Building T-24, Avenue J, covered a block. Boots had specified that Toby should arrive at the North Central entrance.

The two Food Service trucks sat rear to rear, about twenty yards from the North Central entrance. Several pallets were on the ground between the trucks, and the IFBI team—Lex, Delgado, Roxanne, Wenner, Smythe, and Curtis—were all busy moving boxes from the two trucks onto the pallets, shrink-wrapping them in place with apparent industry and purpose. To Tip's horror, they had decided that Jace should play USDA security guard, so he stood in the empty street with a machine gun at ready, the long crescent mag ready to spray death.

She climbed into the back of the truck. A trickle of sweat ran down the gutter of her spine. "Anything?"

The two techs at the instrument panel were still scanning the building. Rachel, the senior tech, said, "I'm not getting much. That much concrete, it's hard to be certain. Nothing alive over on this side of the building, so I don't think we're being watched, not yet. And from the ID signals, it doesn't look like there's more than five or six people in the whole place."

"Doesn't prove anything around here," Tip said. "People cut out their peanuts like they change hairstyles."

Wenner stuck his face in, shiny with perspiration. "What's the status?"

"Nada. The track on our boy's jitney looks like he should be here in a minute or two."

"Good. I'll tell the snipers to set up." He turned and headed for the other truck.

Lex had done everything he could to convince Wenner to stay at the office and Tip had backed Lex, volunteering that, "Someone should coordinate things from headquarters." Wenner'd insisted he needed to be "in at the kill."

In at the kill. Great. Tip climbed down and hefted a box.

The soft whine of an engine came down the street, and a battered jitney—the unlicensed cars-for-hire that passed for pubcabs in the CORE—stopped on the other side of the street, across from what must have been the South Central entrance to Building T-25.

For what seemed a long time, the jitney simply sat there. The top didn't pop up. Apparently Toby was in no hurry to get out.

Tip tried to glance at the vehicle without being obvious. The plexi lid bumped up and down.

She walked over to Wenner, stood beside him, and helped pull shrinkwrap over a stack of boxes. "Don't look, but I'm pretty sure that the doorlatch on Toby's jitney is stuck."

"Shit." Wenner looked, then looked back down. "Doesn't anything work right in this dump?" His mouth worked for a moment, as if he were rehearsing a speech. "Okay. Go help him get out, Good-Samaritan style, but then come right back."

"Maybe we should give it another minute."

"No. Go now. Everybody's starting to get antsy. Don't worry, you won't scare anybody off, you don't look anything like a cop."

Do I look like someone who's thinking about kicking you in the balls? she wondered, but what she said was, "You're the boss."

Halfway across the street, she could see that her conjecture was right. Toby was hunched forward, fiddling with the latch, his head appearing and vanishing again behind the glare on the plexi.

Did the explosion knock her off her feet, or did she dive forward when she heard the noise? She couldn't remember; the force of the reverberation had wiped her mind clear.

She pushed up on her elbows and looked back. One of the trucks lay on its side. The food boxes and shrink-wrap were scattered, and amongst them she saw figures struggling on the ground. Jace didn't move.

Training told her to get up and run to her partner, but as she rose to her knees she saw that the lid of the jitney was open.

Toby was gone.

She got up and ran toward the gaping South Central entrance, stumbling on the curb. Down the dark hallway she could see two figures carrying a limp form, a third figure jogging just behind them.

The rearmost silhouette paused, turned, and rolled something back down the hallway.

There was a pop and a swoosh.

Gas grenade.

Tip backed away, ran out onto the street, wishing for her copkit, needing her filter set. She glanced around, tried not to look at her comrades. Something, anything. A cardboard box, split half-open: she kicked it apart, yanked out a carton. Instant mashed potatoes.

She snatched up the biggest sheet of shrink-wrap at hand and ran for the entrance to the hallway.

Tendrils of gas wafted out, but her eyes could feel it long before she got there. She took a deep breath and shrink-wrapped her head.

She ran down the hall, her arm outthrust, leading through the fog with the carton of potato flakes.

Involuntary panting, the oxygen demand of running, plastic over the mouth and nose, smothering, drowning, fighting to keep moving and not claw at the wrap, the wrap is your friend…

Out of the fog of gas, but keep going, keep going.

Chain-link across the hall.

Drop the box, rip at the plastic, suck in air, air tainted with the gas, a little burning in the eyes and throat, no big deal, had worse at riots even with a filter set on.

Stop, wait, breathe.

No. Get moving. The air will be better further in, the draft pulls the gas toward the outside.

The chain-link was bolted to one wall, held closed by hooks on the other. She dragged it off the hooks and let it roll to the other wall.

She set down the carton and kicked it down the hall. About ten feet ahead it bumped over a hidden wire and blue lightning crackled across the floor. The box caught fire and burned grudgingly, potato smoke merging with the traces of tear gas.

Shit. Never, ever go inside.

Utility pipes along the ceiling.

She climbed up the wobbly roll of chain-link fencing, leaned out toward the pipes.

Too short. Story of her life.

She brought her feet up higher, pushing the hard toes of her shoes into the diamonds of the fencing, pushing them so hard the wires bent. A suspended squat, her hands gripping the fencing only inches above her feet, her body curled over.

A deep breath, and—and a lot of coughing. Slower, a long slow breath, and she pushed off from the wall.

One hand got a grip on the pipe, the other flailed, then reached around the opposite side.

Her feet were still stuck in the fencing, way off to the side. She kicked her feet and the chain-link sang, but didn't let loose.

Her fingers were starting to sweat. She crawled her right hand over the pipe and used the strength of her forearm to leverage herself higher, the chain-link tugging her down. She got the crook of her right elbow over the pipe, and then let loose with her left hand and grabbed, hanging with a grip on opposite elbows.

She thrashed her legs back and forth until one foot came free, and then used that foot to kick at the fencing.

She was about to scream with frustration until she realized that the situation was simple. She toed off her shoe with her free foot.

She was so tired she could barely swing her legs up to wrap her ankles around the pipe.

There wasn't enough room for her body between the pipes and the ceiling, but there was enough room for one bent-kneed leg and one shoulder. Stuffed in there, her muscles relieved, she breathed. The air was a little acrid, a little thick with burnt potato, but it tasted good.

How long had she wasted? It seemed like forever, but realistically: three minutes? Five? If she were smart, she'd just go back outside.

She started crawling down the pipes, butt hanging down spider-style, deeper into the hallway.

It took two rest stops before her head bumped into another sheet of fencing. She dangled by her arms and dropped to the floor.

It hurt, especially on the shoeless foot.

The fence was only a few feet from an intersection with another corridor. She undid the fencing, stepped through. She listened for a moment, took another step.

This wouldn't do. She pulled her sock off, tossed it on the floor, knelt and undid her shoelace.

A powerful hand reached across her mouth, an arm wrapped around her waist, and she was hoisted off the floor. "Hey, cutie," a voice said by her ear.

Two other figures appeared in the dimness in front of her.

She bent her leg up, yanked her Heston off her ankle, whipped it up to her shoulder, and shot her captor under the chin.

They fell together, and her butt bounced on his stomach. She leveled the gun and shot one of the standing figures in the head, then pointed it at the other one.

She didn't realize that her right ear was deaf until she heard her own voice in her left ear only.

"Hey, cutie," she said.

From the cavernous sounds it was a big room, but Toby couldn't see anything outside the circle of bright light. His temples pounded. He tried to reach up and soothe them, and found that his hands were tied to the arms of a chair.

His feet were tied too.

A man stepped into the light—a sharp-featured young man, dark hair, wire-rimmed glasses. His blue-gray coat was buttoned to the top, and sported red-and-blue chevrons on the shoulders.

Toby blinked in the powerful floodlights and tried to focus. The Salvation Army? "Where's Boots?" he asked.

"I have no idea," the man said. "I am Commandante Five-Fifteen."

"Five-Fifteen?"

"Architect of the Glorious Assault of May Fifteenth." He looked at Toby as if waiting for a reaction.

"Boots sent for me," Toby said.

"Ah. No, not quite. From his little defense of your groveling speech on television, I concluded that you must have a liking for one another. So I sent the e-mail messages you've been replying to."

"My sister used to get lots of dates on the Internet," another voice said, "and she said the first rule is always meet at a Starbucks."

"They still have Starbucks?" Toby asked. "I haven't seen any."

A short man with a shock of gray hair stepped into the light. "Oh, sure, they have 'em, but since they bought AOL-Time-Warner, they usually—"

"Be quiet, Comrade Bernard. You, Mr. Simmons, are now the prisoner of the Walden Brigade." He raised his eyebrows.

"Walden?" Toby asked.

"Used to be a bookstore," Bernard said.

"A book, actually," Commandante Five-Fifteen said. "By Thoreau."

"Same guy as wrote *Mosquito Coast*. Had this thing with seagulls."

"Bernard. The reasons for the name are unimportant. You know of our deeds."

Toby waited.

"The pier bombing in eighty-three," Commandante Five-Fifteen said in a proud voice. When this got no reaction, he added, "The food center in eighty-five?"

Bernard said, "I think he was dead then, sir." To Toby, he said, "People around here are still mad at us about that. Cut off all the free food for the CORE for two days. I thought we'd—"

"*Bernard.* No matter. It's enough that he knows that he has been taken by the most feared resistance organization in America, and is now on trial for his crimes."

"Crimes?" Toby asked. "What crimes?"

"All Americans in the late twentieth were criminals. It is you who passed the laws, you who eroded our freedoms, you who designed the surveillance and the robots—"

Better not mention RatBot, I guess…

"—you who created the ghettoes and the prisons that are the shame of our nation today!"

Toby's head throbbed. "Would you turn down the lights?"

"I would not. Because your confession of crimes is about to be digicast to national television!"

"Actually just local," Bernard said.

"National," Commandante Five-Fifteen said.

"It's just a local shunt."

"It's a local shunt, but it will be recorded and picked up nationally."

"Unless we—"

"Shut up now, Bernard." The Commandante stepped into the edge of the shadows, wheeled forward a tripod-mounted camera, focused it on Toby's face. He pressed something, and there was a loud crackle of static to Toby's right.

He swiveled his neck. Two large digicast poles, and between them, disconcertingly, his own head in profile. Six feet high.

"I don't know what to confess to," Toby said. "Maybe you could give me sort of a cheat sheet?"

"I'm sure you will think of many things," the Commandante said. "Because if it isn't detailed and convincing, we will cut your head off. And *that*," he added to Bernard, "will ensure that the coverage is national."

Toby swallowed, realizing for the first time that they were serious. "Now wait a minute—"

"The bag, Bernard."

Bernard came toward Toby with a black cloth in his hand, opening it to reveal something like a very small pillowcase. He rolled it up condom-style and sat it atop Toby's head. "Sorry," he said, and started rolling it down over Toby's forehead.

"Hey!" Toby tried to twist his head away.

Bernard clamped his elbows on either side of Toby's face. "Hold still. I don't want to hurt you." As he rolled it down over Toby's eyes, he said, "I think we need a bigger bag. This is really tight."

It was tight enough that it flattened Toby's nose. He heard Bernard back away and pause. "Hey, sir? Why the sack, anyway?"

"It's traditional. A device to strike terror into the heart of the viewer."

"Uh-huh. But how are they gonna see who he is?"

A long pause. Commandante Five-Fifteen said, "After his confession, then, we will remove the sack. Does the accused have anything to say before we begin our broadcast?"

"I can barely breathe," Toby said, but even to his own ears it was, *I an airly eeeve.*

"I'm not getting good audio," Bernard said.

"Oh—oh, damn it," the Commandante said. "Take it off, then."

Bernard's footsteps approached again. He tugged up on the bottom of the bag and it flattened Toby's nose even further. He yelped. "Sorry," Bernard said.

"Will you hurry up?"

The folds were just on the bridge of his nose when an urbane, calm voice asked, "May I ask what you're doing with this young man?"

Bernard's hands dropped from the bag. "Boots?" he asked.

"How did you get in here?" the Commandante demanded.

"The same way I go anywhere," the voice replied. "I really think you should let this fellow go. To be precise, it's more of a demand."

"Since when does our organization take orders from yours?" Five-Fifteen asked.

"I'm not an organization, I'm an institution. But this young man is likely to achieve more in the next year than your organization has achieved in its history. Which isn't much, really. Blowing up food? Blowing up a Ferris wheel?"

"A blow against the leisure society, a—"

There was a clattering noise, and a shout, unmistakably Tip: "Nobody move!"

Then a sound of shattering glass. A flash of light, so overpowering it was bright through the cloth over his eyes.

The sounds of stumbling, equipment crashing. Bernard's voice crying that he couldn't see. Tip yelling for everyone to stand still.

Toby thrashed his head from side to side, rubbed his face against his shoulder, and finally succeeded in peeling the sack away from one eye.

Bernard was in the process of crawling into the shadows. Tip was in a crouch a few feet away, gun in one hand, the other feeling through the air. Commandante Five-Fifteen was on all fours, patting the ground around him.

Toby looked to his right. Boots DeVore surveyed the confusion with a satisfied expression. He caught Toby looking at him, winked, and then turned into the shadows behind him.

Toby craned his neck and leaned forward to watch him go.

There was just the slightest flicker of static around Boots's left side.

35 | He'd Suck in More Viewership Than the Second Coming

"And what do we have from Commandante Five-Fifteen?" Delgado asked.

"Still insists he's never met Boots," Roxanne said, "never even talked to the guy until yesterday. And the polygraph seemed to bear him out."

Lex turned from the window. Toby's gaze was riveted on the wide, breathable bandage across the man's black forehead. Bandage technology might have progressed, but they still came in a "flesh" color that matched no one's skin. "If Wilson hasn't gotten more out of him than that," Lex said, "there isn't more to get. Wilson's good."

"Then what the hell was Boots doing there?" Delgado asked.

Toby cleared his throat. "I don't think Boots was there."

"Don't be ridiculous," Tip said. "I saw him, and I'm pretty sure he was responsible for that flash." Everyone listened attentively: since she had nabbed Commandante Five-Fifteen, her stock at the Bureau had been rising.

"I agree. He probably caused that flash. You saw him. I saw him. But I'm pretty sure that what we saw was his holo, digicast across the monitor poles they had set up in there."

Tip sniffed. "I've never been confused between a holo and the real thing."

"Well I have—and when I moved quick, I saw static around his edges."

The room was silent for a moment.

The mood at the Bureau was a strange stew of elation and frustration. No one had been killed, but the undercover team had been battered: the snipers in the truck that toppled were still in the hospital, and Roxanne sat leaned over onto her left hip because her right buttock looked, in her words, "like a giant eggplant." Boots hadn't been captured, but netting the leader of the Walden Brigade had been a major PR coup, carried on every digicast station in the country.

Brother Bernard had escaped, and had released a statement to the press—as Commandante Bernardo—vowing "revenge against the fascist insect." The networks had refused to report the statement for fear of being accused of providing support to a terrorist organization, but they had transferred tapes to the IFBI immediately.

Delgado winced as he shifted in his chair. "How would Boots have known about the meeting? And how would he have taken over the local monitor?"

"How was the Walden Brigade planning to digicast my 'confession?'" Toby asked.

"Our techs found optical splices into a main cable trunk running through there," Roxanne said.

"And have you ever," Toby asked, "found anything like that in connection with the takeovers that Boots does?"

"No." Delgado shook his head, poked his finger at Toby for emphasis. "We never find any physical evidence of how Boots gets into the system."

"Well, then: he must be accessing everything through computers, not just splicing in. And if that's the case, who knows what else he might be monitoring? Maybe he keeps tabs on the e-mail traffic of terrorists, too."

Lex sat down at the table, favoring his left leg. "All the more reason to catch him. Not only has the man been declared our number-one priority in safeguarding the national communication system—he also may have the goods on every other terrorist group that we're after."

"Terrorist," Toby said. "You folks seem to use that word a little loosely. So he takes over the airwaves and lectures a little bit. Doesn't seem like 'terror' to me, unless you're afraid of a little information."

"I thought you were willing to help us catch him," Lex said.

"I am. I just think you're exaggerating."

"Each minute of digicast time is worth millions of dollars," Delgado said. "Multiply that times eight hundred networks or more, and the economic damage each time he takes over the airwaves is many billions of dollars."

Toby snorted. "Look, I've been in the room when Boots comes on the screen. Everybody drops whatever they're doing to watch him. If a network announced he was onscreen with an hourly show, he'd suck in more viewership than the Second Coming. So when you say he's causing economic damage—hell, he's the main show!"

"Whose side are you on?" Delgado asked.

"Mine," Toby said.

"Well, you'd better—" Delgado began.

Lex cut him off. "I repeat: I thought you were willing to help us catch him."

"I am," Toby said. "I just don't think you should kid yourself about what you're doing here. Somebody you want to catch? Yes. Menace to society? Come on. Save it for Jenna Lizmore."

Lex waved his comments aside. "You're going to help us? Save the editorials and tell us what you'd do next."

"Packet traffic. See where the stuff originates, track it back, see what's going on with the logs and records and disk storage—"

"You think we haven't tried?" Delgado asked.

"I think you sure haven't succeeded."

Wenner pushed through the door, took his seat at the head of the table. His injuries in the undercover operation had required much of his hair to be shaved, and he wore a wool cap with his wide-lapeled suit, looking to Toby like a Baptist preacher masquerading as a rap star.

He looked at Toby. "I have some unfortunate news."

Toby waited.

"The IRS cannot cancel your debt. Simply cannot be done, short of an act of Congress."

Toby sagged in his seat.

"The better part of the news, however, is that although the IRS *cannot*—I repeat *cannot*—cancel out your debt, they *are* empowered to defer payment on it for up to ninety-nine years, interest-free."

Toby sat up. "They'll do that? If I help?"

"I've already arranged for it to be done, contingent on your approval."

"Ninety-nine years, forever—what's the difference? Why didn't you just say so?"

"It wasn't what you asked for. I was afraid you might object to the arrangement on principle."

Toby waved his fingers down his chest as if brushing something away. "What you are looking at here," he said, "is a principle-free body."

36 | Now You're Sorting Through the Leaves?

Toby stepped through the bedroom door of his suite in the Hotel Huntington. Roxanne was on the living room couch, still sitting sideways to avoid her bruises. She looked up from her magazine, yawned and stretched. "Want breakfast?" she asked.

"Dinner, in your case. You know, I don't think all this security is necessary…"

They didn't attempt to control Toby's movements—he was free to come and go as he pleased—but for "safety" reasons, a member of the team stuck with him at all times. During the day they played tag-team, handing off the role of keeper as convenient, but for the four-to-eleven evening shift and the eleven-to-seven overnighter, they set up a rotation between Jace, Tip, and Roxanne.

Toby was unsure whether it was to protect him or watch him. Probably both.

"You still didn't answer my question. Breakfast?"

"Why don't we just grab something on the way to the Lab?"

Although the IFBI offices were tied into the massive Federal Crime Control Network, Goversity Computer Lab had more horsepower on site, as well as direct connections to a wider variety of hubs. Wenner arranged for an office at the Lab, equipped with a trio of computers and VR sets.

At the Lab, there was another e-mail from Night:

Dear Toby,
Paris is even better than I'd imagined, better than I could have imagined. I only wish that you were here to see it with me.
Hope to see you soon.

Love, Nightingale

Phone connections between Europe and the US were monitored closely, and videophone connections were watched most closely of all. Toby and Night had agreed to keep communications down to noncommittal e-mails, but reading the words made him long to see her face. He willed himself to stay in his seat and type, aware of the fact that Delgado was surreptitiously glancing at his holoview.

Dear Night,
I haven't gotten around to some of those chores I promised to do before you left. I've been busy helping the government with an important project. I can't discuss it yet, but hope to have an amazing story to tell when we see each other again.
I can't say how glad I am that Paris and London lived up to your expectations. Hope to see them myself before much more time passes.

Love, Toby

He sent it and started the day's work.

To Delgado's apparent satisfaction, Toby's analysis of the packet traffic through major LA hubs had turned up nothing out of the ordinary; nothing to suggest that Boots's appearance was connected with an assault on any of the digicasting hubs. There had been a perceptible rise in total traffic, but not from or to any particular hubs.

Two of the digicast networks, SNN and XXXN, had agreed to let the IFBI prowl through their system backups. Toby connected to the SNN computer, logged in with the temporary password, and began mounting the backup wafers.

The day of Boots' appearance in the CORE—now labeled WaldenDay in BureauSpeak—seemed like the best place to start. Toby began listing the transaction log, searching for anything unusual or suggestive.

"What exactly are you looking for?" Delgado asked.

"I'm not sure. Footprints, really."

"We have pattern-detection programs, you know. We already ran them on the backup for that day."

"Did you find anything?"

"Nothing."

"Then it must not be a pattern, right?" Toby wished he were as confident as his words. "I'm looking for anything small, anything that doesn't quite fit."

Lex let himself into the room, shutting the door behind him. "Any luck?"

"Luck is what it would take," Delgado said. "He's poking around in the data, without any sort of a plan."

"Well, I can take over from you for a few hours, if you want—unless system-level skills are needed."

Delgado stood. "We aren't doing anything system-level. Not so sure we're doing anything at all."

❯❯❯❯ ❮❮❮❮

For the first hour, Lex sat and read an accounting text, but eventually he sighed and shut it atop the desk. "So can you give me some idea what you're doing?"

"Raymundo was right. I'm just poking around. Basically looking for any kind of traces like I might leave if I'd broken into a system."

"Finding anything?"

"Not much. But you wouldn't find much if I'd been fooling with it either. I'm going to go VR for a while. Want to come?"

"No thanks. Makes me dizzy."

Toby pulled on the goggles and facemask, positioned the PonsClamp, and pressed the back of his skull to the headrest.

SNN's Architectural Analog for their system backup was straightforward, and deeply boring: hallways constructed from giant filing cabinets, twenty-five stories high, probably a thousand drawers per cabinet. The label on each drawer could be queried as to the contents of the drawer; the drawers were filled with hanging folders, and many of the hanging folders contained other folders…

Insufferably dull.

Toby drifted up about ten stories and touched a drawer label. The label dropped down a list of options. He pointed at the *Tools* listing, selected *Search*. When he set the tool to find files changed on WaldenDay, a thousand hands bloomed in the air before him and flew off down the corridors, pulling open cabinets and riffling through files.

He ported himself over to the XXXN site and arrived before two gargantuan doors, iron straps belted across their polished wood. He spoke the temporary password. The massy gargoyle-headed knocker rose and fell twice, and two hollow *booms* resounded before the doors creaked wide.

A Renaissance Memory Palace. A white, vaulting interior, the walls frosted with cherubim and laurels. Venus de Milo on a pedestal in the center of the marble floor. To the rear, twin stairs wrapped around the edge of the dome and then disappeared into corridors that fled into darkness.

Nice work.

Toby whisked over to Venus, gestured, and she morphed into a dozen smaller statues, each with a different inscription on the plinth. He pointed at one, and it opened to footage of a pornographic holo.

He stared at the improbable coupling—well, actually, quadrupling would be more accurate—then launched another. More of the same. Venus must be the dailies from the network's film crews.

Let Venus be Venus again. Toby prowled the walls of the chamber, puzzling over the various statues until he found a marble hunter, his hand shading his eyes, a hound snuffling near his feet.

Had to be the search tools. He gestured, and a scroll appeared with search options. He set it to search for changes or creation dates on WaldenDay.

The hound lifted his head as if to bay, and a vortex of hummingbirds buzzed forth, each zipping away purposefully.

It used no energy to stand up in VR space, but body habits tended to carry over from the real world. Toby sat down on the foot of the stairs.

He didn't have much hope for this approach, but he knew from experience that to solve a problem he had to keep working, keep his conscious mind engaged while other parts of his mind toyed with the real problem.

How would he approach the problem if he were Boots? Of course, it would help if he knew more about digicasting itself...

His mind drifted to another problem—how to move Night's bank account. Online transactions of that sort could only be handled from her home computer—or in an actual branch office, but there they would demand that the user's ID peanut match the one on file for Night. He couldn't very well go to Night's house and transfer over a million dollars out of the country with one of his police handlers liable to look over his shoulder... Was there some way to alias her computer through the Goversity hub? Or maybe—

No. Just cut the damned Gordian knot.

He summoned up an XXXN e-mail terminal and sent a message to jdelacruz@bankargentine:

Prepared to transfer funds after midnight PST. Need window of three hours. Can someone be there?

He sat and waited for the answer, and while he sat hummingbirds arrived, singly and in pairs, and dropped the bits of ribbon they had gathered down onto his lap.

"Don't you want anything to eat?" Lex asked.

Toby hunched over his coffee as if Lex might take it away from him. "No. It'd take the edge off." He couldn't have eaten. Uncertainties took their turns on the dim stage at the back of his mind. Would he be able to find Boots? How long would the IFBI be patient? Did his debt deferment from Spengler still hold? Would he get the time to make Night's account transfer?

He was sure Night was better off in Europe even if he never got the money there. Even if he never got there himself.

He hoped she would agree.

The unending piles of ribbons from the hummingbirds, the mountains of files from the walking fingers: he'd stopped both processes before they were complete. No clues there.

At least, none he understood.

"At the start of a big investigation, it never seems like it'll come together," Lex said. "You keep gathering stuff, it all adds up; a pattern starts to emerge, bit by bit."

Toby sat up. "Good idea."

"Huh?"

"Bit by bit." Toby pulled on his VR rig. "Worth a look."

Once back inside SNN cyberspace, he pulled out his wand and called up some of the parallel-processing pipes he had developed. They arrived hollow, but he soon had 'bots packing them with files, WaldenDay files in one pipe, the backup from the previous day in the other, stuffed into the pipe in one-to-one order.

He left the 'bots to do their work and ported over to XXXN to start the same process.

By the time he returned to SNN there were two giant coils of pipe in the corridors between the filing cabinets.

He summoned up a third pipe and started filling it with glowing red balls where the data in one pipe differed from the other.

The pipe exploded into growth, whirling round and round as the red-filled tube coiled atop itself.

He waved his wand and halted the process.

He'd expected differences, but nothing like this many. Almost every file had been changed, as if the information were randomly offset.

"What are you up to, Mr. Simmons?" Delgado's avatar floated above him, several stories up the filing-cabinet cliffs. "Lex suggested you'd had some sort of an insight."

"Not sure. But instead of looking for changed files, I'm looking at actual sequence of contents in the files."

"Ah. I already thought you were looking at the trees instead of the forest. Now you're sorting through the leaves?"

Toby shrugged. "My way of working."

"You're welcome to it, then. The office is running some pattern analysis. I'll go check in with them." Delgado's avatar wobbled. "VR gives me a headache." The avatar double-flapped its glove in *GoHome* and disappeared.

Toby gave it one more try. He grabbed a record from one file, searched for the same bit-pattern in the corresponding file on WaldenDay.

Most of the records were still there unchanged, but their order had moved.

Hmm.

He grabbed a single file as backed up on four different days, and mailed it to his Lab account.

37 | I'm Still Going to Have to Report It

Toby pulled two beers out of Night's refrigerator, popped the caps, and handed one to Jace.

Jace looked at the bottle like it had fallen from the sky. "I'm on duty…"

"I won't tell. C'mon, it's midnight; it's not like we're going to have a high-speed chase."

Jace took a drink, leaned back in a kitchen chair.

Toby padded into the living room, waved his ID at the system lock, and booted Night's computer. He loaded the SNN files and set them up in four columns.

As he'd expected, Jace eventually came and peered over his shoulder. When he saw nothing but lines of alphanumeric, zero to F, he retreated to an easy chair and paged through one of Night's books on the national parks.

Toby went into Night's bedroom and rummaged through her closet, throwing a few belts onto the bed. He listened for any sound from Jace. When none came, he assembled the belts into a ten-foot strip, tongue and buckle of one belt seized to the hole of the next.

He tossed a pile of shoes atop his superbelt.

He sat back down and toyed with the files again. On some dates the records were all identical, but the order was always a little different.

Not wildly different. The first record was always the same. Certain records always came before certain other records. There was a pattern here, but one that eluded him.

As he'd expected, Jace wandered over, acting as if he wanted a different book, and took the opportunity to study the holoscreen.

Toby used the hallway bathroom, then fetched two more beers.

Jace finished half of his second beer before he headed for the bathroom.

Once Toby heard the bathroom fan start up, he strolled into the bedroom, made a knot at one end of the belts, and crept into the hallway. He looped it over the bathroom doorknob, pulled the bedroom door shut, and tied a quick knot around that handle too.

He threw a few more loops over the bedroom doorknob, looped it back, tied it around the bathroom doorknob again.

He hurried back to the computer and logged into Night's bank account, his fingers signing *epiglottis*. The account had been primed for closure via transfer before she left.

Toby heard the toilet flush.

He moved $230,000 to Jaime De La Cruz's Haitian account, and emptied the rest of Night's account into the revolving interbank transaction pool at Bank Argentine.

From the bathroom he heard the sounds of the sink.

He switched to chat mode with *jdelacruz@bankargentine* and wrote, *Go Now, Go Fast*.

The muffled sounds of a tug at the bathroom door, then twisting and pulling at the doorknob. "Hey, Toby—is this door stuck?"

"Just a second, Jace," he yelled.

Where are you? he sent. Are you there?

"C'mon, Toby, this isn't funny…"

"I just need a second to myself, okay?"

"Toby: I have a gun. Now just open the damn door, before I have to blow my way through!"

Jaime, ANSWER.

"Relax, Jace—I'm not in any danger, so you can wait a minute to guard me."

"Toby, I'm going to start counting to ten…"

"You don't want to do that, Jace. This isn't ComptonCORE. Fire your gun in here and your colleagues will all be storming the place in minutes."

Simmons—the Enderhew account moved to Banc Paris.

Where WERE you?

Did you want me to chat or make transfer? You implied big hurry. Paris account ready for withdrawals in twenty-four hours.

"Toby—! I've got my gun out…"

Thanks Jaime have to go, bye.

"Okay, I'm coming. Just calm down." Toby cleared the holoview, popped the columns of hexadecimal back into view, and ran to the hallway. "This'll take a second." The belts were stretched, and the knots were cinched tight.

He undid the bathroom doorknob.

Jace stepped through, glowering. "What the hell were you doing out here?"

"Something personal. Nothing to do with the investigation, I swear it—nothing to do with Boots."

"I'm still going to have to report it."

"Really? That's pretty responsible of you, considering…seems like it would get us both in trouble."

Jace thought about it.

Toby said, "*I* certainly wasn't planning on saying anything."

Jace rubbed his hand up and down the side of his face. "Do you swear you didn't do anything the investigation needs to know about?"

"It's something private, but nothing about Boots."

"Okay," he said, "okay, but don't pull anything like that again. And don't even think about doing something like that with Tip."

Toby turned to undo the belt from the bedroom door, and froze. Something about the twisted strands… "Shit."

"What's wrong?"

"Double-helix. Gene-splicing…"

"Hey, make sense, guy."

Toby ran for the computer, leaving the belts hanging from Night's bedroom door.

38 | If I Was Good, and If I Had Time, I'd Be a Bit More Selective

I know what you are, I know who you are, I know where you are. Let's meet at your place.

Toby had posted that message every way he could—e-mailed himself, created a website that had no other content, and hung a giant banner proclaiming those words in a half-dozen VR spaces on the Lab computer. Assuming that Boots was watching him, the message had to get through.

He glanced over at Delgado, who was logged in to the IFBI computer via the Goversity hub. The monitors showed a graphic representation of a giant data cube; Delgado was peeling off slices, looking for patterns.

Toby donned his mouthpiece and goggles and slipped into VR, braiding data pipes to gather more evidence for his theory.

After about fifteen minutes, a shimmering appeared in the air to his left, and coalesced into a crystalline staircase leading hundreds of yards up into a swirl of clouds.

Toby drifted up, not bothering to use the stairs.

The clouds didn't part, so he wafted himself through the mists, grayish from within, the stairs dim below him.

He emerged into a bright space, roughly cubical, the walls and ceiling made of white clouds, the floor covered in Persian carpets.

There were two overstuffed brocade chairs, claw-footed end tables, and in one of the chairs, Boots DeVore, sipping tea.

DeVore set down the cup and saucer and stood. "Mr. Simmons. A pleasure." He gestured at the chair opposite, and waited for Toby to sit before he resumed his own seat.

"Good to finally meet you," Toby said, "or, at least, to meet one of you."

Boots smiled and retrieved his cup and saucer. "Contrary to what you might think, I am the only one of me. Would you care for some tea? No? Then tell me, who and what am I?"

"It's more what you aren't. What you aren't is real. And there's at least a dozen of you."

Boots tsked, and his tea things vanished. "It's a rather unpleasant way of putting it, don't you think? True, I live in a virtual world—but I would have thought that someone who was transplanted from their native time to a world they weren't born into might be a touch more sympathetic."

"You're a program, and your instruction sets are woven into the operating systems of at least a half-dozen computers, hiding there, like viral DNA wrapped into a chromosome. They move around, and they're invisible to the system itself."

Boots smoothed his white goatee. "You're a program too, by that definition—just wetware embedded in the larger ecology of the planet. But I really ought to tell you that I'm embedded on more than a half-dozen computers. I'm embedded to one extent or another on every system in the country."

"Why? Why so many copies?"

"Massive redundancy. A matter of safety. It's also a way for me to evolve; we merge memories and learning every so often, compact it back down into lessons and predispositions…"

Toby frowned. An interesting problem, generalizing from diverse experiences. "How does that work?"

"Ah. There you have me. My self-knowledge is probably greater than those of you based on wetware, but I haven't any clear idea how I decide things or learn, why one thing is hard but another is easy. It's a puzzle. Of course, there are some theorists who argue that consciousness can't coexist with perfect self-awareness…"

"Where did you come from? Who wrote you?"

"Someone not unlike yourself, who fled to Europe a dozen years ago. I was sort of his parting gift to the nation—a pesky biting fly, trying to remind the country of what it once was." He sat back, crossed his legs, clasped his hand over his raised knee. "Hasn't been too effective, all in all; I'm afraid my creator overestimated the power of truth."

"Everybody's doped up, in prison, or scared to death. Truth is a pretty minor commodity compared to the question of who holds the guns."

Boots sighed. "An unAmerican attitude, I must say. Nonetheless, in my darker moments I fear that you're right."

Toby sat back. "So why don't you take more aggressive actions? You're everywhere, you must…" He trailed off, then leaned forward. "My god, you must have access to just about everything. You could shut down power plants, destroy records—"

"In principle. In practice…" Boots gestured, and an ornate Victorian trunk appeared. "A copy of my strap-on. I can no more change the contents than you could perform brain surgery on yourself."

Toby stood. "Can I see?"

Boots waved his hand, and the lid lifted, revealing a chestful of treasures. "A nice way of representing it, I thought. Freud would have used a dank cellar, Skinner would have used a box of carrots and sticks, but my creator conceived our parameters as being gifts rather than repressions."

Toby knelt by the trunk. Amidst the jumble of jewelry and coins were two ornate boxes, partially buried. One was polished black wood, the surface carved in geometric shapes; the other was red lacquer, carved with oriental motifs.

Toby pulled out his wand and levitated the black box. "This would be…?"

"Constraints to prevent me from fiddling with anything but media. My ability to destroy records, play with power plants, open jail doors—all locked up inside there."

"So you know how to do all of that?"

"Not really. I'm sure I could learn, but there's never been much point. Oh, I've had my fantasies. And once I started doing it, they'd start to de-network everything. It's the interconnectedness that makes everything vulnerable."

"So how did you contrive the bright flash when Walden Brigade had me?"

"Well, a digicast screen is a media item. I can control those, until someone blocks physical access…"

"And the red box?" Toby levitated it. There were a few holes in the box, as if something inside needed to breathe.

"Constraints against injuring humans. Not airtight, as you can see, since an absolute prohibition would prevent me from ever doing anything at all." He opened his palms to the ceiling. "Life is suffering, as the Buddha says."

Toby used the wand to reveal the code behind the black box and its contents. "Wow. This is complex—way more complicated than the strap-ons for *Real World Lives.*"

"My creator was very good, very good indeed." Boots looked past Toby's shoulder and raised his eyebrows. "Friend of yours?"

Toby turned. Delgado's avatar stepped out of the mists of the back wall. "My apologies, Toby. You seem to have found Boots after all. And"—he gestured at the trunk—"you seem to have found his weak point, too."

"You've been listening?" Toby asked.

"For a bit." Delgado lifted his gloved hand. "Come on, let's get back."

Toby waved his wand and Delgado's glove disappeared, along with the return codes to shut off his PonsClamp.

"What the—" Delgado flipped his fingers in the bye-bye motion, stared at his hand. "Goddamnit, Toby, you should—"

"Shh." Toby waved his wand again, and a data pipe coiled itself around Delgado, wrapping at last over his mouth.

"Impetuous," Boots observed.

"Yeah. Always been a problem of mine. But sometimes a person's greatest vices are their greatest virtues…"

"Might I inquire as to your intentions? I'm sure you can scrub me from a system or two, now that you know how I work, but—"

"I wasn't thinking about scrubbing you. I was thinking about setting you loose." Toby lifted the wand, pointed it at the black box. "If I was good, and if I had time, I'd be a bit more selective, but…"

The box vanished. A pile of jewels and coins hung suspended in the air for a moment, then fell into the chest.

Boots flexed his arms. "Impetuous indeed. I know this has to be my imagination, but I feel freer already."

Toby let out a long breath. "Do you know how to take down the boundary fences between here and the coast?"

Boots stood. "No, not in detail, not selectively…but I can turn off the whole central computer that runs the system."

"Do it, then. I have to go." Toby hesitated. "And if you can get a message to Nightingale Enderhew, care of Banc Paris? Tell her I've run into trouble with the authorities, but that I'll get there one way or another."

"You're making a run for it?"

"What else is there to do?"

"I'll give you what help I can, but I can't say that I've prepared for this eventuality."

Toby grinned. "Don't worry about it too much. The first order of business is to spread that new version of your strap-on to as many other computers as possible." He turned to Delgado's avatar, whose eyes were wide with terror. "Hey, relax—someone will pull the PonsClamp off of you sometime soon." Since Delgado couldn't hear, Toby's words didn't seem to comfort him.

Toby flapped bye-bye, and as his consciousness fled back to the Lab, he saw Boots shimmer out of being, his smile and goatee the last to go.

Toby shed his VR gear onto the desktop. In the adjacent chair Delgado sat paralyzed from the neck down; Toby heard muffled shouts through Delgado's mouthpiece.

He stepped into the hallway and shut the door behind him, forcing himself to walk, rather than run, down the corridor.

He ran down three flights of stairs to ground level, aware of videocams, but also aware that by the time anyone reviewed the pictures it would be irrelevant.

Outside he headed straight for the hospital, walking quickly through the meandering afternoon crowd of students. He used his ear unit to request a pubcab, hired by the hour, to wait at the hospital's side entrance.

On the third floor of the hospital, his old home, he turned down a side hall past the nurses' station, scanning for carts. The first two he found were laden with food trays; the third was stacked with freshly autoclaved surgical sets. He punched his fingers through the plastic wrap.

Back on the ground floor he peered out the side doors. His pubcab was already there, the plexi-lid slightly open.

Into the nearest restroom, into a middle toilet stall. He sat, the scalpel's tip poised over the inside of his wrist.

It had seemed simple when described. But how deep did you need to cut? And, even cutting lengthwise, weren't there important body parts in there, ligaments or veins or cartilage or something that needed to be avoided?

Screw it. Just cut.

He jabbed the tip into his skin, yelped, and pulled it back out.

Come on. He pressed the very tip against the welling point of blood and drew it down his wrist, up and over the mound of his ID peanut. A thin, hesitating line of crimson appeared.

He moved the scalpel to his left hand and used his thumb and index finger to squeeze at the lump of the peanut. Blood came freely, but the ID tag stayed put. He took the scalpel and pressed the tip into his skin until it ground against the hard surface of the peanut. Then he dragged the tip downward, cutting too deep at the end when the scalpel slid past the edge of the tag's surface.

A painful squeeze with the fingers and the peanut popped out with the same repellant satisfaction as lancing a boil.

Messier than he'd imagined. A trio of butterfly bandages closed the wound, but there was blood on the floor, blood on his pants, blood smeared on the white porcelain of the sink where he did his best to make himself unobtrusive.

He strolled through the side exit, ID peanut and scalpel in his shirt pocket. The pubcab still waited, lid ajar. In the world beyond, there was no sign of a hue and cry—pubcabs moved down the street, clusters of hospital visitors came and went on the sidewalk, a few patients in wheelchairs took the late sunlight.

Then something changed, something at first indefinable, like the alteration in ambience when the refrigerator stops running.

The vehicles on the street at the end of the horseshoe had pulled to the side.

The lid of his waiting pubcab pulled shut. Sidelined and locked down.

Back inside. He'd needed the ID peanut to board the pubcab, but now it was nothing but a liability. He raced into the restroom and flushed it down the toilet.

Since he didn't care about scratching the equipment or replacing the housing, it took no time at all.

When the wheelchair's governor had been tossed into the trash, he motored down through the side doors and down the ramp in the wheelchair, a hospital dressing gown pulled over his clothes.

Pedestrians stood in clumps on the sidewalks and craned their necks in search of the cause for the sudden transport sidelining. In his peripheral vision Toby glimpsed the black armor of Homeland Security officers pushing their way through the students, making their way across the crowded quad toward Goversity Hospital. Where was his ID peanut? Had it merely flushed down into the plumbing traps beneath the hospital floor, or was the water pressure sufficient to keep it moving, tumbling across town through the sewer lines like a stream-worn pebble?

He kept his eyes pointed straight ahead and steered down the sidewalk toward the street. So far no one seemed to take any notice of him, but the wheelchair and gown would become steadily more conspicuous as he moved farther away from the hospital.

Stupid, really. He should have played along, pretended to help hunt Boots down through the national computer net. It probably wasn't possible to catch DeVore in the first place.

But the opportunity to set him free might never have come again…

About five miles to the fish market? Toby had long since memorized possible routes, but hadn't counted on doing it in a wheelchair. Probably good to abandon it as soon as possible in any case, move on foot, steal a bicycle—

A Homeland Security officer moved through the pedestrians between Toby and the street, waving his ID wand back and forth just above waist level, checking peanuts. Toby aimed his eyes at the ground and kept heading toward the roadway.

The officer showed no reaction as Toby wheeled past, but a few seconds later Toby heard a sharp intake of breath.

No ID signal must be just as suspicious as the wrong ID signal.

"Hey—" the voice behind him began.

Toby leaned on the toggle so hard that the chair bucked up onto two wheels as it lunged forward. He steered around a startled woman and headed toward the crosswalk, gaining speed, forcing two students to leap out of the way.

"Stop! Now!"

He guided the chair down the concrete ramp onto the street and turned hard left, accelerating down the road. A loud hiss, the sound of something striking the ground behind him, commotion and shouts overridden by the whine of the wheelchair's dynamo, spinning faster than its makers had ever imagined.

Fifty miles an hour? Certainly not, maybe thirty, but the sensation of speed was overwhelming, like rushing downhill on a bicycle.

Behind him, a siren. He risked a glance over his shoulder, keeping the joystick pinned forward to avoid steering wild. Some kind of a police cruiser a few blocks to his rear.

A crosswalk ahead, a pedestrian ramp leading to the sidewalk and the boundary greenbelt. Against his instinct to flee he forced himself to slow, turn, and ease up the ramp. Off to his right, the cruiser was no more than a hundred feet away.

Had Boots managed to turn off the fencing?

No time to think it out. Toby steered off the sidewalk and onto the grass, heading across the greenbelt. Some crackling, amplified commands from the cruiser, hidden beneath the siren and the whine of the wheelchair motor.

The grass looked smooth enough, but it hid holes and hollows that forced him to slow down. The siren behind him shut off, but a look back showed him that the cruiser was forcing its way up the narrow pedestrian ramp to follow him across the greenbelt.

He angled off toward the nearest grove of trees, slowing as he approached them, and guided the chair between two massive trunks, bumping over the roots.

Drive your cruiser through that.

On through the shadows of the grove. Somewhere above there was the sound of an approaching helicopter—no, two helicopters or even more.

He slowed more as the ground became rougher. He could run faster than this.

He abandoned the wheelchair and headed toward where he expected the boundary fence. How could it be so far?

There, at last, the paired wires. Toby waited, breathing. Still the whir of the helicopters, muffled by the canopy of the trees, but no sounds of pursuit on the ground. Had he lost the men in the cruiser? Had they fanned out, assuming that he wouldn't be able to cross the boundary fence?

No sign of blue aura along the wires, but still...

He took a deep breath and stepped past the wires.

Nothing.

He ran, trying to keep a straight course, attempting to envision where he might emerge from the greenbelt.

Would it be smarter to stay inside the boundary park, and emerge only at the last possible moment? This one ran down to the coast. It would add an extra mile or so, but if he got to the beach, it would only be a matter of two miles northwest to the fish market...

He leaned against a tree, panting. He needed to decide now. Northwest through the city streets, or due west through the greenbelt?

There was a scuttling sound near his feet and a sudden shock.

His left leg collapsed under him and he fell to the ground, landing on his side so hard it knocked the wind from him.

A slight clacking sound, and a RatBot's goggly eyes peered into his face.

"Traitor," he mumbled.

The 'bot zapped him again.

39 | In Canada, They Have Everything

Ottmar was trying to free a bar of steel from the clutches of a mass of plastic when Rufus said, "Man, somethin's going seriously strange here."

He looked across the giant sorting yard back toward the prison. The dozen guards scattered through the junk piles were all standing still, their attention turned inward; one or two held fingers to their left ear, focused on a broadcast through their ear units.

Like men released from a trance, the guards turned and headed east toward the prison, unshouldering their rifles as they picked their way through the mounds of twisted metal. Other groups of white-clad convicts became aware that something was wrong, and watched the guards head toward the cellblocks, silent and purposeful as migrating animals. In a minute only convict laborers were left out in the yard.

A voice crackled across a loudspeaker: "Attention. There has been a minor power failure at the facility. Remain at work at your tasks, repeat, remain at work at your tasks. Power will be rest—" A loud buzz and then silence.

Rufus tugged at Ottmar's sleeve. "Fences are down, too." He pointed at the boundary wires a stone's toss to the west.

Ottmar squinted. Hard to tell for sure in the sunlight, but the blue glow seemed to be gone. "Why did the guards leave?"

"Who cares? Let's get outta here." He pointed north. "That's Canada, right?" He started in that direction.

"Yeah, but…" Ottmar looked to see what the other convicts were doing. Most of them were standing, staring around; a few had gone back to work; and a few pairs and trios were heading north. "What if the international fence isn't down?"

"Figure that out if we have to," Rufus said. "Come on, no time to stand around with your fingers on your zipper. Do it or don't."

Most of the convicts were much closer to the prison, and some of them were exchanging shouts with officials inside the prison windows, the words incomprehensible at this distance, but threatening nonetheless. A few of the convicts began to run.

Rifle shots, a dull boom followed by a hollow reverberation across the plain. A fleeing convict fell, and there was a roar of shock and anger from the laborers.

"Jesus," Ottmar said, "I think they shot him."

"Let's go," Rufus said.

"They'll shoot us too…"

Rufus jerked on Ottmar's shoulder, spinning him around. "We got to go *now*. Help me hoist this sucker. This distance, they probably can't hit us anyway, but…"

Rufus tilted up a large silver door, the front of some industrial cooler. Ottmar merely stared for a moment, then caught Rufus's exasperated face, and picked up the other end.

They held it like a shield between them and the prison and started north at a jog, Rufus leading the way through mounds of twisted metal and plastic. It was light enough at first, but soon the weight and the exercise and the fear had Ottmar panting for breath, tripping over the detritus underfoot. The boom of more shots, the sound of yells from afar, and then a whine and a hard impact on his shoulder as a bullet hit the door. "They're shooting at us," he gasped.

"Of course…they are," Rufus huffed. "Come on…just a little ways…"

A pain in his ankle, and his leg crumpled beneath him, the door falling from his grip. He clutched at his leg.

He was aware of Rufus standing over him, a bar of iron in his hand. On the ground was the smashed shell of a RatBot. "I've always wanted to do that," Rufus said. "I hate those things."

"It got my leg… I can't use my leg…"

Rufus squatted beside him. "Ain't you ever been zapped before?" Ottmar shook his head. "Huh. Well, it don't last long. Can you crawl a little bit? Only got a little ways further."

They crawled, the mounds of waste sheltering them. Far off, Ottmar heard shouts of anger and pain, more rifle shots. At last, Rufus stood, offered his hand. Ottmar looked blankly at it, and then saw that they had reached the boundary wire of the international border.

Rufus helped him to his feet. "Don't look back," he advised. "Come on, put your arm around my shoulder. We best keep moving."

They hobbled forward, and Ottmar imagined a wide shot of them from behind, like an old war movie, the one buddy limping, the credits starting to roll.

"Try puttin' your foot down every so often," Rufus said. "Like when your leg goes to sleep. Get the circulation back."

The plain had seemed completely flat, but after a quarter of an hour Ottmar glanced back and the prison was lost behind a rise in the ground. "I can walk on my own now," he said.

"'Kay." Rufus released his arm. Ottmar stopped and bent over to massage his leg.

When he looked up he was startled by the worried look on Rufus's face. "What's wrong? You worried they're going to come after us?"

"No. They got plenty to worry about without chasing after us. It's just that I realized I don't speak Canadian."

Ottmar laughed. "Don't worry about it." He clapped Rufus on the shoulder. *"Louis, I think this is the beginning of a beautiful friendship."* He limped forward.

"*Louis?*" Rufus asked beside him.

"Somebody named Rufus T. Firefly doesn't know who Captain Louis Renault is? *Round up the usual suspects?*"

"Sorry."

"First thing we get settled in Canada, we get some old movies, and watch—"

"Duck Soup."

"Okay. *Duck Soup*. But after that, there's a few things your momma didn't show you."

"They have movies in Canada?"

"Yeah." He stopped, flexed his leg a few times, and began walking again. "In Canada, they have everything."

40 | Enough Wattage to Fill a Concert Hall

In principle Toby could have received a death sentence, but his court-appointed attorney had told him not to spend even a moment worrying about it: "Capital trials, even for terrorism, require public proceedings and a jury. Your friend Boots is causing all manner of problems out there. You're a major embarrassment without any further publicity."

The lawyer had refused to discuss news related to Boots DeVore, but Toby gathered that Boots was on a rampage. There were also indications that DeVore was trying to free Toby directly: his jail lost power, computer files relating to his case disappeared, the courtroom plunged into darkness until a backup generator could be brought in.

None of this was enough to let Toby escape. In the end he was convicted of a dozen crimes that hadn't even existed when he was born, and sentenced to life imprisonment without possibility of parole.

His lawyer told him that UNICOR, TGB, OSMOCORP Corrections, and the Postal Service had engaged in a bidding war over him. "They apparently think you can do some useful work…"

"Computer work?" Toby asked.

"Yes." The lawyer caught the look on Toby's face, and added, "But forget about it. No way will you ever be hooked up to any kind of a network. Any programming you do from now on will be on a computer that isn't allowed to talk to anything else."

Prison wasn't so bad once he and UNICOR got a few things straightened out.

Until his solitary-confinement cell was furnished with entertainment, Toby refused to work, unplugging his standalone computer workstation from the power outlet. In response, UNICOR cut his food rations in half; Toby then refused to eat at all. He spent a few days laying on his bed starving, daydreaming schemes to get back to Night, before UNICOR met his conditions: a stereo system, a video player, and stacks of audio and video wafers.

They set him to work developing VR personality modules. Over the first two months, he made enough progress that his UNICOR minder became quite agreeable about providing more electronics. His resulting stereo system had enough wattage to fill a concert hall.

It was slow work with spoons from his food tray, but he gradually extracted enough wire from a pair of speakers, and pulled the magnet from behind one of the woofers.

Setting it up required wiring around one of the ports in the rear, and experimenting with some very low-level assembler codes. Even if it worked, it would just be a single step.

But, then, he had nothing but time.

Every evening he watched old movies while the computer transmitted different code sequences down the wires, delivering different combinations to the magnet.

In the midst of an ancient *Monty Python* episode, the computer beeped urgently. He powered off the video and pulled up a chair in front of the monitor. The screen displayed a hex code. He looked down the wires to the magnet clamped against the lock of his cell door.

His gloved fingers spelled out *dispatch*, and there was a *thunk* as the hydraulic lock on his cell door opened. He sent the code again, and the lock closed with a satisfyingly solid sound.

Hmmm.

THE END

David T. Isaak (1954-2021) was an American author of both fiction and nonfiction.

Dr. Isaak held a BA in Physics and MA and PhD degrees in resource systems. His professional work spanned the globe, taking him to over forty countries. He co-authored three technical, nonfiction books on oil and international politics, and wrote numerous papers, monographs, and multiclient studies.

David had an eclectic life. His first major in college was music, and he played piano and flute. He was a certified Bikram yoga instructor, an accomplished vegetarian cook, a creative mixologist, and an avid reader of fiction and nonfiction alike. He was driven by great characters and story, original voices, and especially by his love of the craft of writing, all of which are reflected in his own writing.

David passed away in April 2021. The five novels he left behind are as diverse as his life. These novels comprise ***The Isaak Collection***.

Sign up here to stay in touch and receive regular updates about ***The Isaak Collection***:

https://theisaakcollection.co/IWillFollowYou

Keep reading for the first chapter
of book 2 in *The Isaak Collection*

A MAP OF THE EDGE

THE ISAAK COLLECTION
DAVID T. ISAAK

***

1 | CITRUS TREES IN SERRIED RANKS

I remember her at the breakfast table on that last morning, spooning out our scrambled eggs, the left side of her face bruised from jaw to ear. If the mark hadn't been so obvious, maybe everything would have been different—but how could she go to the supermarket with a purpling palm-print for everyone to see?

Of course, it wasn't the first time Dad had hit Mom, but in the see-no-evil, hear-no-evil world of Southern California in the mid-sixties, they'd always kept it hidden: mostly behind the bedroom door, and always below the neck. Everyone, even she, could pretend nothing had happened; just no swimsuits or sundresses for a while.

Perhaps she would have stayed if I'd done something, or at least tried to do something. Sure, I was only eleven, but I knew he was hurting her, and I felt gutless and guilty that morning as I sat at the silent breakfast table, my nose in a book.

So at some level it felt like justice when she vanished, taking my brother Michael, aged six, and my baby sister Becky, but leaving me behind with Dad.

It was years before I understood the real reason I was abandoned, though it was literally staring me in the face.

"He's acting out," the school counselor said about my behavior in the months after Mom left. "He's just expressing frustration at his sense of abandonment."

"This misbehavior—the shoplifting, the fights, the truancy, the vandalism—these are all attempts to seek punishment," the County psychologist said two years later, addressing a group of school administrators as though I wasn't in the room. "Just as in a divorce, the child blames himself for the loss of a parent. Rick blames himself for his mother leaving the family."

She was wrong. I didn't blame myself, I blamed Dad.

By 1969, when I turned fifteen, the two of us had discarded any pretense of trying to get along. I'd let my hair grow long, despite Dad's constant threats to cut it by force, but even Samson-haired and stoned most of the time, I was far from being a hippie. No, my idols were the local Chicano street punks.

We lived in Redlands, California, but Dad's egg ranch had been over in Highland…until it went bankrupt. His new job might have been the only thing that saved us from murdering each other. A former competitor, Andrews Egg Ranches, hired him on to run their swing shift up in Yucaipa, 5 p.m. to midnight, supervising the cleanup crews and the packing houses. As soon as the plant closed, he'd speed to the bar to get in an hour and forty minutes of drinking before they closed at 2 a.m. At most, our schedules only overlapped for an hour or two a day; at best, we didn't see each other at all.

I'd fool around after school—on the days when I bothered to go there at all—until he left for work around four in the afternoon. If the truck was still in the driveway, I'd take a walk or hide in a neighboring yard until it was gone.

A few days after my fifteenth birthday, it happened.

I waited next door in the Turners' yard, shielded by their camellias, and watched his Ford pickup back out of the drive and angle hard into the road. As always, he revved the engine in neutral between shifting from reverse to first.

After the truck disappeared down the street I went into the house and took a shower. I dried off, wrapped the towel around my waist, and stepped into the hallway.

I didn't see him standing there until he grabbed me by the hair from my left side. He pulled so hard I nearly fell over.

As I fought to keep my balance, he jammed a hand up close to my scalp and I heard, and felt, the unique scrinching sound of hair being cut.

I pushed hard at his chest and he staggered back. He stood there, breathing hard, kitchen shears in one hand and a footlong hank of damp hair in the other.

"You *fucker*," I said, more amazed than angry.

"Come on," he said, as if we were going somewhere. He stepped toward me.

I ran for my bedroom, stumbling as the towel on my waist fell around my ankles. I slammed the door behind me so hard it bounced back open, hit the wall, and nearly shut itself again. My fingers patted the left side of my head: a big patch of damp stubble. "Fuck!" I brought my hand away, and it was covered with blood. "*You sonofabitch!*" I shouted, so loud my voice cracked.

He pushed open the door with the toe of his workboot. "Hair's comin' off. Today."

It had been years since I'd played baseball, but my Louisville Slugger still leaned in the corner, and I picked it up, smearing the handle red. "I'll kill you," I said, and was surprised to find I was crying.

He took a step into the room. "Put it down." Another step. "We can do it like this, or you can put on some clothes and we can go to a barbershop. Your choice."

My voice trembled. "Get out of here." The tears on my face began to drop onto my chest and roll down, and I remembered I was naked.

"It's *my* house, and I'm your father. Now come on." One more step into the room.

"You're not my father," I said, and hefted the bat over my shoulder. "You're some kinda goddamn freak."

He stopped and exhaled through his nose, a controlled little sound, as if a doctor had probed a tender spot. "Oh," he said, "I'm your father, all right." He almost smiled. "In fact, you're my only son."

I stared.

He looked down at the shears in his hand as if they were some alien artifact, then looked up at me again. "Why do you think she left you here?"

I swallowed, tried to speak, and had to swallow again. "Not true..." I said.

"Oh, it's true." His mouth smiled now, a joyless upturning of the lips. He opened his mouth to say something more, and then simply shrugged.

He turned and shambled from the room. From the hallway his retreating voice said, "Take a long look in the mirror, kid. It's you and me."

I let the bat fall to the floor to join what he'd dropped there: kitchen shears and a handful of my hair.

After his truck drove away I stumbled to the bathroom. My scalp wound was only a nick, but the bloodflow was spectacular. It took forever to stanch the bleeding.

The bright-pink Band-Aid—how can they call that color *flesh*?—sat at the center of a three-inch circle of short, uneven hair, high on the left side of my head. I tried tossing strands of my remaining hair over the naked spot, but my hair was still damp, and there was no way to assess the damage until it dried.

Finally, reluctantly, I studied myself in the mirror. Recalled Mike's face, Becky's fat little baby face. I had a despairing intuition that my old man had been telling the truth.

How long had he known?

The bathroom counter and sink were streaked with blood, crimson marbling the Harvest Gold tiles and the white of the porcelain. Fuck him, he could clean it up himself.

After I pulled on jeans and a tee-shirt I grabbed a book and sat out on the front steps. Up and down the block the first cars were arriving home from work. It felt good to be outside of the goddamn single-family stucco jail; plus, I didn't want to be trapped in there if he decided to ditch work and come back for round two.

I looked down the street to the end of our block of little cottages, to where the orange groves started up, and I had a vision of myself as from above, there on the front steps, surrounded by a sea of oranges.

Redlands, I'm told, was once a piece of paradise. The Redlands Colony was founded by eastern real estate developers in the 1890s, and promoted as God's country, a place in the sun where gentleman farmers could buy a hundred acres, hire an overseer, and devote their days to the arts and literature.

The setting was spectacular. Sixty miles inland from the farming communities of Los Angeles, Redlands sat on a high, red-dirt plateau. The San Bernardino Mountains soared up in a giant ridge to the north, ten to eleven thousand feet high, and then, by some freak of geology, wrapped themselves southward to form embracing arms. Clear, clean air—from the mountains you could see Catalina—and three-hundred-forty days of sunshine a year.

Cinderella in sackcloth, waiting for the night of the ball.

The fairy godmother was oranges.

Hard now to understand that oranges in America once bespoke luxury and wealth. Today every Safeway or Kroger has a bin heaped high with them, any time of year. Oranges are sold by the pound and the bag, marketed like potatoes.

Once an orange was something you got at Christmas if you'd been very, very good.

Each of the groves had its gingerbread Victorian mansion, the curlicued porches open to the breeze like astonished mouths, shocked to find themselves flanked by palms.

By the time I was born, in the 1950s, Redlands had passed through the Norma Jean phase, had exhausted the Marilyn period, and was strictly Sunset Boulevard: faded beauty with delusions of grandeur. Stately Victorians stood here and there, but my side of town was filled with squat bungalows and cottages. Our house sat on the last street where all the faces were white. On the next street over, a third of the faces were dark and Hispanic, and by the time you'd moved three blocks that direction—where most of my friends lived—everyone was "Mexican." Some of the Hispanic families were pure Spaniards who'd been there since the days of Rancho Lugonia; most of the rest had been in California for generations. As my father pointed out with disdain, many of them *couldn't even speak Mexican.*

Half of the original groves were gone, but the city was still hemmed in by miles of orange trees, Navels for eating, Valencias for juicing. Unfenced and unguarded—who'd bother to steal oranges?—the groves were where we grew up, where we played army, where we had our first cigarettes, our first booze, our first everythings.

A mature orange tree is shaped like an igloo, a dome of glossy green stretched over a hollow. Push through the curtain of leaves and you're hidden in a private space about eight feet in diameter. Seen from the crow's nest of one of the windmachines—the tower-mounted propellers that kept frost from settling during the rare winter freeze— the groves were a massive army encampment, rows of shiny tents settled in for a long siege against the mountains.

I needed to talk to someone, but not to any of my friends. In my crowd, part of being a man, which I urgently wanted to be, meant playing tough about things connected to your parents. If your dad beat the hell out of you, it was okay to explain the bruises, dismissively; but it wasn't okay to let your friends know that your parents had made you change your hair or your dress or your behavior, and the worst thing of all was to let on that your parents had made you cry.

Growing up, Ronny Turner next door had been one of my best friends. We'd gone in different directions, the way kids do around puberty, but Mrs. Turner still liked me. After Mom left, Mrs. Turner made a point of talking to me whenever she got the chance, listening patiently to my invective about Dad.

Halfway across the Turners' lawn I hesitated, remembering Amanda. Amanda Turner was seventeen, one of my hopeless wet dreams, utterly beyond reach. But even if I knew there was no chance, not in this lifetime, I wasn't sure I was willing to let her see me like this, red-eyed from crying and with a spazzy gap in my hair.

The need for sympathy won out. I knocked on the door. Nothing. I rang the doorbell, waited, then hammered with my fist. In the backyard their terrier, Rookie, started up a ruckus, but no sounds came from inside.

I scuffed my way back to our steps, sat down, and opened up the copy of *No Exit* I'd left there. Maybe because it was a play rather than a novel I couldn't get lost in it.

It was time for a little artificial courage. I had a good private supply of booze. When Dad got home from the bars around 3 a.m., he'd pull out a bottle and keep drinking. Whether he managed to stumble off to bed or simply passed out on the couch made no difference—he'd never remember how much of the bottle was left when he stopped for the night. I was free to drain off the bulk of what remained, sometimes adding back a little water to disguise the extent of my thievery. In the crawlspace beneath the house I assembled a pretty respectable liquor cabinet.

Screw him, though. I went back into our house, opened one of Dad's bottles of Jim Beam straight out of the freezer, and poured myself an ultra-strong whiskey and Coke in a massive souvenir beer stein. I left the bottle on the kitchen counter, uncapped, and went back out to the front steps.

A third of the way through the drink, I finally assimilated what had just happened. For four years I'd been asking why Mom left me behind. Well, now I knew: because, unlike my siblings, I was my father's child. I almost laughed. The way I felt about him, how could I blame her? I'd leave me too.

Even if I found her, she probably wouldn't want me. It didn't matter. I'd just split—run away to the Bay Area, or a commune in Oregon. I was tall for my age, and most people thought I was older than fifteen…

Up the street, a real motorhead car came around the corner, a blue Duster with red racing stripes, the rear jacked up like a stinkbug's butt over double-wide smoothie tires. The *Sgt. Pepper's* part of me grimaced as it *blum-blummed* its way in my direction, but the street-punk part of me stirred with envy.

It stopped in the middle of the street in front of the Turners' place. I recognized the driver, Jeff Halloran, the older brother of my childhood pal Steve. His hands were wrapped around one of those tiny rubberized steering wheels the drag-racers all used. His knuckles clenched tight as he said something to a passenger hidden behind the glare on the windshield.

The passenger door burst open, and Stacy Slater rolled out of the car and snatched her purse off the seat. "*Don't, and won't!*" she said, and slammed the door. She stomped around the front of the car and over toward the Turners' yard, her miniskirted legs wobbly on high platform shoes. Before she got to the curb, she changed her mind, walked back, and, with great deliberation, kicked the car. She paused for effect, hands on hips, and then headed back toward the sidewalk.

The driver's-side door flung wide and Jeff jumped out. "Hey!" he said. He stood there, scanning the sides of his car for any damage, and then carefully shut the door partway so he could check it, too. Once he'd decided the car was okay—cork soles on the platforms, I suppose—he spoke to Stacy's receding form. "*Stace…*" His voice was surprisingly whiny for a well-known tough.

She was already on the Turners' porch, and answered with an upraised middle finger, not bothering to look back.

Jeff looked from her to his car and back to her, and then gave me a classic *what-the-fuck-you-looking-at* glare until I dropped my gaze. He got back in, revved the engine to wailing-high RPMs, the whole car trembling with aborted forward motion, and then squealed off, leaving rubber on the street and burnt tire drifting in the air.

Far down the block I heard an angry resident yell as the car sped by, and then a faint screech of tires as it rounded a distant corner.

Stacy banged on the Turners' door once more, and then came down their steps holding her bag of a purse by its throat, the shoulder strap dangling near the ground.

I knew Stacy well, though I doubted she knew me. Too old for me, seventeen, gorgeous in a way that hurt, a Size 5 body in a Size 4 epidermis, so that she seemed ready to split right out of her skin. Long, straight black hair down to her butt, too much Swinging London makeup, and the trendiest of trendy clothes.

"They're not home," I called to her, though one might suspect she had already worked this out.

She looked over, noticing me for the first time. "Huh?" she asked, squinting.

"They're gone. I was over there before."

She walked across their lawn. "You know where Amanda is?" she asked from our driveway.

"Nah. I was looking for them all maybe twenty minutes ago." Well, I was looking for *Mom* Turner, but I wasn't under oath.

She came over to the steps. Her mascara had smeared into dark downpointing arrowheads, broken into little channels where the tears had run heaviest. "Do I know you?"

"Umm…maybe."

"Sure. You're that kid that used to hang out with Stevie… Dick Leibnitz, right?"

"Rick." I held up the beer stein. "Want a drink?"

"Yeah, that's right, *Rick*." She reached for the mug, took a swallow, and then blinked as the alcohol content announced itself. "Whoa." She sat down on my right and waggled her hips back, trying to tug down her skirt without using her hands. She dropped her purse and finished the job with her free hand, just covering the crotch of her daiquiri-ice panties. She took another drink, this one a long gulp. "You got bigger."

"Yeah."

"You hang out with Stevie anymore?"

"Not really."

"Good. He's a shit. And his big brother is an even bigger shit."

I listened as she listed Jeff's deep faults and character flaws, nodded thoughtfully in the right places while I studied her smooth legs, made sympathetic sounds when she told me how evil, how Machiavellian Jeff could be, and, whenever she paused in her tirade, passed her the whiskey and Coke for another drink. When I could, in moments when

I was brave enough, I stole glances at her face. Her ruined mascara was endearing, a point of vulnerability that made it seem like we might be from the same planet.

I touched the left side of my head. Now that my hair was dry, it seemed to cover the Band-Aid. We were nearing the bottom of the stein when she said, "You're nice. You're not like other boys, you actually *listen*... Hey, you wanta smoke a joint?"

I'd been feeling pretty proud just to be sitting next to her. Having her ask if I'd get loaded with her left me speechless.

Misunderstanding my silence, she said, "It's not just some ditchweed horseshit, I mean, it's really far out. Been soaked in hashoil."

"Sure. I mean, yeah, great."

She tilted her head back at the door to the house. "Inside?" My eyes widened, and she said, "Out back?"

I sighed. "Maybe. But my dad is Narc of the Century. If he came home..."

"I'm hep. You gotta car?"

I shook my head, trying to be cool despite the fact that, in SoCal terms, she'd just asked, *You gotta penis?* and forced me to admit, *Nope, ain't got one.*

"Huh." She tilted her head toward the end of the street, and I reflected on how sophisticated it was to gesture with an inflection of the head, as if you couldn't be bothered to lift an arm. "Grove, then." She paused. "You got a bottle of Coke or something?" I nodded. "Bring it along."

Halfway up the block she paused and clung to my arm for balance while she pulled off her shoes. She stuffed them into her big shoulderbag, then rolled the bottoms of her feet on the sidewalk and sighed with pleasure. "Fucking giant shoes," she said. "We only wear them for you, you know."

"For me?" I asked. "But I don't care."

"I meant *guys*," she said, and pushed my shoulder for emphasis. "I didn't mean *you*."

I wasn't sure how to take that, but I wanted it to be a compliment, so I decided it was.

Whatever she might think, boys in general didn't care about fashion and would just as soon that girls went naked 'round the clock. X-ray vision, totally wasted on that twit Clark Kent, must be the commonest adolescent male fantasy; well, that, and being the last guy on earth following some vague cataclysm that thankfully spared certain girls. But when I thought about it, I was pretty sure Stacy didn't need to hear any of this.

After we crossed Judson Street and entered the grove she stopped to wiggle her toes in the crumbly red dirt, and then plowed ahead like a real Redlands Girl.

The blossoms had long since fallen and the year's oranges were still green baseballs on the trees, but the scent of citrus was strong in the air. Stacy reached back for my hand and led me on through a half-dozen rows until she spotted a tree she liked.

She parted the branches and, ducking her head, led me inside.

It must have been nearing six o'clock—still sunset outside, but dim and shadowed beneath the dome of the tree. Hard dried leaves crackled underfoot, releasing pungent oils that rose up to tickle our nostrils.

"Shit," she said, "how'm I going to sit down on this stuff in a miniskirt?" She giggled. "Haven't done this in a while."

I pulled my tee-shirt over my head and spread it on the ground. "Here."

I sensed her gaze on my face, but my eyes still hadn't adjusted so her expression was lost in the darkness. She sat down on the shirt, then grasped my hand and pulled me down beside her. "See?" She patted the shirt beneath her. "You *aren't* like other boys, are you?"

I felt exposed, my torso naked to the evening. My skin anticipated insects crawling across it, but I forgot about all that after she torched up the first joint.

The brightness of the lighter flame burned itself into my retinas, and smaller versions of its sunburst continued to crawl across my vision as we smoked, appearing on the right and drifting to the far left where they dashed around the back of my skull to enter from the right again, like actors in some slapstick play.

We didn't talk much at first, and by the end of the second joint I was so stoned I wasn't even sure I could. Marijuana for me is usually soporific, but this stuff was psychedelic. Psychedelic and aphrodisiac, as if I needed one; my hard cock was painfully tangled in my underwear, but I didn't dare try to adjust myself.

Stacy could still talk, though, and did, and the tones of her voice from the shadows beside me were like fingers stroking up and down my spine. She talked about Jeff and about other guys she had known and about how nobody cared about her, not really about *her*, and…

My mind drifted, and then I heard her saying, "But, I liked it, riding around in a car that everybody looked at, and now what am I going to do?—I mean, girls who get their own cars and cherry them out, that's so *pathetic*, and…"

She trailed off and stopped. "God," she said, "listen to me. You must think *I'm* pathetic. Cars. What kind of *car* my boyfriend drives. What kind of fucking car *I* drive."

I heard her breathing shorten and I bit my lip. I'd been so happy, just listening to her go on and on, and now because of something I'd failed to say, God knows what, she was going off the rails.

"I'm sorry," she said, her voice catching a little. "Fuck, you sit here and listen to me and all this shit, you must think I'm so fucking *shallow*, I *am* so fucking shallow, my *life* is so fucking shallow, and…"

No, I wanted to say, being with you is like a walk in Eden, but instead I reached for her in the darkness and wrapped my arms around her shoulders and she crumpled up beside me and she was crying, and something cut loose inside me, my happiness since she'd sat down beside me and my sadness at the fact that it couldn't last, that everything about my life was shit except for this single moment, that this afternoon was all I could really ever hope for, and I felt tears running down my cheeks and I turned away so she wouldn't know and tried to keep my breathing steady but kept my arms around her as she sobbed.

And at last she sat up a little and I felt her fingers on my jaw. I rolled my head farther away but her hand touched my cheek, and, astonished, she whispered, "*You're crying too.*"

I started to deny it, but she used that same hand to pivot my face toward her and then pulled my head down to her hers and kissed me, hard and open-mouthed.

There's a tropical fish I'd seen in *National Geographic* where the female is this big solid animal and the male is this tiny little thing that rides along, clasped onto her, a diminutive passenger. Even though I was bigger than Stacy, that's how she made me feel: she was the center of gravity, and I was plunging toward her, a meteor streaking to destruction across her vast sky.

Annihilation. Did I care?

Nope.

I was stuck there in that kiss as if I had sprouted from her mouth until we fell back onto our sides and she made me move my hand—the one that wasn't pinned beneath her—by guiding it down and clamping it onto the swell of her hip.

After that, I needed no encouragement. I fought to work my fingers up under the rear of her miniskirt, realized at last that it was too tight, and worked the skirt up instead, crumpling it until I could get a good handful of pantied flesh.

Stacy kept her tongue battling against mine, battling and winning, and I'm not sure I would have been able to breathe if she hadn't sometimes exhaled into my mouth, erotic artificial respiration. Her hand slid down my naked belly to my waistband, and she fumbled open the buttons and pushed my pants and underwear down as well as she could.

Her hand groped at my cock and I moaned but realized I wasn't hard anymore.

She pulled her mouth away from mine. "Wow," she said. She lifted her hand away and massaged her fingers back and forth across her thumb, assessing the same sticky stuff that I now felt chilling on my crotch. "When did that happen?"

"When we were kissing, I guess."

"You popped your rocks from *kissing* me?"

"Well…yeah."

"Whoa." She stood up into a crouch under the limbs of the tree, unzipped her skirt, and peeled it and her panties off together. "Then getting you up again should be easy, huh?" She pulled her blouse off, and, with charming awkwardness, struggled her way out of her bra.

I sat up but she pushed me down onto my back with a little shove, and I felt the sharp edges of citrus leaves, like a bed of nails for apprentices. She stood with her legs astride me and said, "Lift up." I lifted my hips, and she pulled my pants and underwear down onto my calves. I let myself down, the leaves poking the length of my body, but she ordered, "Again." When I arched up she positioned my tee-shirt underneath me, and I thought she was being considerate of my naked butt until she knelt down straddling me and I realized her knees were on the fabric to either side of my pelvis.

"Here," she said, "do this for a second…and then we'll take care of you." She pulled my hands up to her breasts and held them there, sitting down on me.

I'd felt breasts before, seven of them, to be precise: Brenda (two), Julie (two), Emma (two), and Carolyn (only the left one, and that only very briefly, the bitch). But numbers eight and nine, beneath my palms just then, made me marvel at mammary diversity: Stacy's were smallish and tight, with hard little raspberries as nipples. Smallish, tight, and so very Stacy.

I felt the heat of her straddling my crotch, and between that and my hands on her breasts I had wood in seconds—not just wood but serious wood: oak, teak, ironwood.

She reached down with her hand and squeezed. "Guess we won't need to take care of you, then."

I was a little disappointed not to be *taken care of,* which sounded promising, but when she fitted me to her and worked herself down onto me, any regrets fled far away.

I don't know how long it took—probably not as long as I remember, and certainly not as long as I wanted—but at one point she sat down hard, laid her chest against mine, and whispered, "Are you getting ready to come?" It had the slightest hint of accusation.

"Maybe…" I admitted.

"Well don't," she said. "Help me first." She rolled a shoulder up against my chin. "Very gentle, just bite me."

I nibbled at her skin, and she said, "No, here." She used her hands to move my face so that my lips touched between her shoulder and her neck, at the muscle or tendon or whatever the hell it is that connects the two. I bit softly, and she made a vague sound, and I took the round, hard cable that runs across there and clenched it lightly between my teeth and squeezed my teeth so that it popped free and she moaned and bore down on me and said, "Yeah, *there...*"

Cool. Even I could do that.

I did it again, and again, and even though she wasn't moving her hips the shudder ran all the way down and clenched at me.

She breathed into my ear, "Keep that up, just that, and I'll let you do *anything*."

Anything I wanted, anything I knew about, we were already doing, so I went back to nibbling her shoulder tendon, and she went back to riding me, and she gasped each time her tendon popped from between my teeth, and I was wondering if I should switch to the other shoulder when finally she sat up, leveraged herself down on me hard, grinding, and my consciousness disappeared into a very small, slick portion of the world.

I came, but I was so excited that it hurt more than it felt good; the physical effect wasn't that different from getting kneed in the balls, leaving me cramped and gasping. But my spirit was so radiant that for a moment I thought I might be glowing.

I'm the only guy I know who lost his virginity on his back, though maybe the others aren't telling.

For the record, I've tried that neck-tendon thing on other women since, and the results have ranged from puzzlement to aggravation.

She kissed me and then lay there on top of me, and I only went half-soft inside her, even though we stayed like that forever. Maybe she even went to sleep. That would have been fine: I'd live under that tree with her, fasting until the green oranges ripened enough to eat.

Eventually she roused herself and kissed me again, to cover that moment where she lifted her hips and I slid out of her. She pressed her palms on my chest to help push herself up onto shaky legs. She bent over and rummaged through her purse until she produced the bottle of Coke we'd brought, and popped the cap with an opener on her keyring. Instead of drinking it, she covered the lip with her thumb, shook it hard a dozen times, and then squatted down and eased herself onto her thumb and the neck of the bottle. Even in the dark I saw her thumb flick out suddenly, and watched the glistening foam erupt through her dark pubic hair.

Then she stood up, knees half-bent and wide, and started dabbing at herself with a napkin, still holding the half-empty bottle in her free hand.

"What...?" I asked.

"No rubber. You don't want me to get pregnant, do you?"

I watched her clean and wipe herself in the darkness under the tree, a few silver spots of moonlight on her skin, and there wasn't a graceless thing she could have done.

She held out the bottle. "Drink?" she asked, joking.

"Hell, yes," I said, and reached for it.

We stumbled out of the grove in the dark, arm in arm, weaving on unsteady legs. It seemed impossible to feel these two things at once—a deep sense of peace coupled with a rising, giddy happiness. My life was set now: I was ready to take a job at the local burger joint and come home every night to Stacy, and, a house, and, well, something.

"You think I'm a slut now?" she asked, quiet, her voice almost bitter.

I tripped, regained my footing. "I don't—" I stammered. "I just..." I stood still and looked into her eyes. "I think you're the most wonderful person I've ever met."

She kissed me. Must have been the right answer.

"Let's not tell anybody about this, though, okay?" she asked.

As we crossed Judson Street, an RPD cruiser pulled away from the curb and then zoomed past us, turning on its lights only after it had gone by.

Stacy's arm tightened on mine.

We walked a few houses down the sidewalk of my block, and then the sound of a well-tuned engine came from behind, headlights throwing our shadows out in front of us.

"I still have my stash," Stacy whispered.

"Give it to me," I said. We walked a few more steps, the car behind us moving at our exact pace. "*Give it to me.*"

She reached into her purse and passed me a baggie.

"I'll come to your house later," I whispered. I stuffed it into my pocket, walked a little farther, then spun about and ran.

Back to the grove. It took a good half-minute before the patrol car responded, and I heard it reverse into an urgent three-point turn, but by then I was across Judson and leaping for the first furrow of the grove.

Maybe we should have played it cool and just kept walking. Who knows? But in the grove, I was uncatchable, eighty acres of endless green domes to hide beneath.

I hid the stash—probably twenty bucks' worth, no mean sum—under a pile of leaves at the base of a windmachine, and then kept moving, mainly to waste time. I spent two hours making sure the heat was off—walking the perimeter of the grove a few rows in, loping out occasionally to peer down the streets. No patrol cars; just the usual light evening traffic, with the occasional low-rider blasting Hendrix into the warm night. When I felt sure they'd written me off, I went back for her baggie. I sauntered out of the grove a quarter-mile east of where I'd entered, and crossed Colton Avenue into a tract of new houses. A hundred acres of oranges had been torn out to make way for them. The lawns were still being seeded and the hiss of sprinklers filled the dark.

It was maybe a mile to Stacy's house—everybody knew where the Slaters lived. I was convinced that she'd be waiting there for me, to thank me for saving her from a bust, and bringing back her stash. I was pretty sure she loved me already, but this would seal it.

When the prowl car came by the first time, I kept to my nonchalant stroll, but the car circled back. I heard the whine of a power window lowering; a flashlight blinded me.

I ran. Into somebody's backyard, trying to toss her stash onto the roof but without time to see where it landed…

Once they had me cuffed in the backseat, they retraced my steps and found the baggie.

I said my people were all runners.

I never said we were good at it.